Praise for Amanda Sun's *Ink*:

"The descriptions of life in Japan…create a strong sense of place, and set an exotic backdrop for this intriguing series opener by a debut author."
—*Booklist*

"The unique setting and observing how Katie learns to live in…foreign surroundings…make this story special."
—*VOYA*

"An enjoyable peek at a world very different from America, yet inhabited by people whose hearts are utterly familiar."
—*Publishers Weekly*

"A harrowing and suspenseful tale set against the gorgeous backdrop of modern Japan. Romance and danger ooze like ink off the page, each stroke the work of a master storyteller."
—Julie Kagawa, *New York Times* bestselling author of The Iron Fey series

"With smart, well-drawn characters, cool mythology, and a fast-paced plot that keeps you on your toes, *Ink* is a modern day fairytale that reminds us: Sometimes you need to get a little lost in order to find your true self."
—Amber Benson of TV's *Buffy the Vampire Slayer* and author of the Calliope Reaper-Jones novels

"Amanda Sun's *Ink* is a captivating story of love, passion, and the choices people make to keep themselves safe. The vivid portrayal of Japan kept me completely intrigued and immersed. A beautiful story!"
—Jodi Meadows, author of *Incarnate* and *Asunder*

"An imag ve and totally unique debut. Japanese gods, mysterious magics, beautiful *Ink* is a fresh brushstroke."
 thor of The Vicious Deep trilogy

ild selection

Indie Next Pick

A Chapters Indigo Top Teen Pick for 2013

A Bookish Young Adult Book for Summer 2013

A *USA TODAY* Young Adult Book for Summer 2013

Books by Amanda Sun

The Paper Gods series (in reading order):

SHADOW (e-novella)
INK
RAIN
STORM

Storm

ltsfn   10/28/15

AMANDA SUN

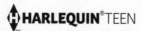

If you purchased this book without a cover you should be aware
that this book is stolen property. It was reported as "unsold and
destroyed" to the publisher, and neither the author nor the
publisher has received any payment for this "stripped book."

Recycling programs
for this product may
not exist in your area.

ISBN-13: 978-0-373-21174-6

Storm

Copyright © 2015 by Amanda Sun

All rights reserved. Except for use in any review, the reproduction or utilization of
this work in whole or in part in any form by any electronic, mechanical or other
means, now known or hereinafter invented, including xerography, photocopying and
recording, or in any information storage or retrieval system, is forbidden without the
written permission of the publisher, Harlequin Enterprises Limited, 225 Duncan Mill
Road, Don Mills, Ontario M3B 3K9, Canada.

This is a work of fiction. Names, characters, places and incidents are either the
product of the author's imagination or are used fictitiously, and any resemblance to
actual persons, living or dead, business establishments, events or locales is entirely
coincidental.

This edition published by arrangement with Harlequin Books S.A.

For questions and comments about the quality of this book, please contact us
at CustomerService@Harlequin.com.

® and TM are trademarks of Harlequin Enterprises Limited or its corporate affiliates.
Trademarks indicated with ® are registered in the United States Patent and
Trademark Office, the Canadian Intellectual Property Office and in other countries.

Printed in U.S.A.

For Kevin

1

Ways to Put a Kami to Sleep Forever
1. Leave Japan
2. Die

I tapped my pencil against the paper propped on my knees. Ten minutes, and I only had two ideas, the latter scribbled in Tomo's handwriting. If I went to live with Nan and Gramps, if I left Japan for good, maybe Tomo would be better off. There was ink trapped in me, *kami* power that didn't belong, darkness that caused Tomo's power to spiral out of control. But even if I distanced myself, it wouldn't put the *kami* in him to sleep. He'd struggled before I'd even arrived here. And if he left the country, who knows what would happen? He could run, but the power would still lurk in him. I didn't think it would work.

And the second on the list wasn't an option, not at all.

How to put a dark power to sleep, one that whispered in your ear that you were a demon, one that gave you nightmares and brought your drawings to life with teeth and claws?

"Maybe a really good lullaby?" I suggested. Tomo rolled his eyes. We were slouching on either side of his living room couch, our backs curved against the arms of the sofa and our knees flopped against each other's in the middle. Tomo mashed the buttons on the TV remote, cycling through the channels over and over.

"Or a bedtime story?" Tomo teased back. *"Goodnight Moon?"*

I shoved his knee with mine, gently, but he still winced. The bruises from his fight with Jun hadn't faded yet. They hadn't even had *time* to fade.

Only a few days ago we'd learned the truth, that the *kami* Amaterasu, goddess of the sun, wasn't the only one with descendants. The power to make ink drawings come alive, the nightmares that plagued Tomo and Jun and the others who could control the ink...that power could come from other *kami*. Tomo had sketched Amaterasu in his notebook, and she had revealed the truth to us—that Jun was descended from Susanou, the *kami* of storms, snakes and the World of Darkness. Yomi, or, you know, Hell. Susanou was Amaterasu's brother and most dangerous rival.

And worse, Tomo was descended from not one but two *kami*—Amaterasu, the imperial ancestor, and Tsukiyomi, the god of the moon, her scorned and vengeful lover. The two bloodlines fought within him, which meant that Tomo often lost control of his drawings and himself, his eyes growing large and vacant and deadly. It had become so bad that he couldn't enter shrines anymore; going through the Shinto gateways knocked him out cold. Jun had called him a land mine; he could go off and cause mass destruction at any time. And then Jun had decided it was up to him to destroy Tomo, right then and there. It had been like both of them had lost consciousness, taken over by the ancient hatred between Susanou and Tsukiyomi. Ikeda and I had barely pulled them apart in time before they killed each other.

"Funny," I said. "But I don't think *Goodnight Moon* will cut it."

I wished I could go back to the time I'd arrived in Japan, when the cherry blossoms had rained through the sky and Tomo had just been an annoying senior classmate, when neither of us had awakened the sort of forces we now faced.

I sketched a cherry blossom in the corner of my paper, thinking back on that spring. I wasn't the artist that Tomo was, but I still drew a mean stick figure and flower bud.

Tomo lifted the remote to flip the channel again. The tiny gust of air spun the sketched cherry blossom in circles. I stared at it, my eyes wide.

When Tomo's drawing of Amaterasu had come to life, so had the ink trapped in me. When Mom was pregnant with me, she'd been accidentally poisoned by a *kami* drawing. We'd both barely survived, and now the ink ran in my veins—Jun called me a manufactured Kami, a man-made descendant. I was nowhere near as powerful as Tomo and Jun were, but the ink in me called out to the ink in them. And now it was going totally haywire. I pressed my pencil against the edge of the sketched petal, stopping the blossom from twirling.

"Yurusenai yo," Tomo said in a high, clipped voice, and at first I thought he was talking to me. *I won't forgive you.* But then he made a peace sign with his free hand, holding it up to the side of his face. God he looked adorable. I wanted to reach over and ruffle his hair.

I glanced at the TV, anime sparkles and canned music blaring at me from the screen. A group of magical schoolgirls in a rainbow of skirt colors pulled elaborate poses, peace signs cupped to their faces like Tomo. They blasted a bunch of monsters with their special powers as they backflipped and whirled around the Tokyo Skytree tower in ridiculously high heels.

I rolled my eyes. "How can they fight in those? Where are all the broken ankles?"

The leader of the girls got a close-up now, tilting her head to the side as she posed. *"Yurusenai yo!"* she squeaked, and Tomo looked smugly pleased.

The scene cut to one of the girls smacking a monster in the face with an *ofuda*, a paper scroll that banished evil. Wait. "Hey, would that work in real life?"

"I don't look so great in high heels and a miniskirt," Tomo said. "Unless you're into that kind of thing."

I smacked his knee again. "I mean the *ofuda*. That's a Shinto scroll, right? Couldn't it stop a *kami*?"

He frowned. "I doubt it. They usually invoke the help of a *kami*, not banish one. They're more for expelling demons. Like a larger version of the *omamori* I gave you."

I pulled out my phone, looking at the soft yellow pouch Tomo had risked entering a shrine for, just to give to me. The charm read *"Yaku-yoke Mamoru,"* embroidered on the fabric in soft pink kanji. *Protection from Evil.*

The last time Tomo had entered a shrine with me, he'd collapsed in a pool of ink, attacked by some kind of *kami* alarm system as a threat to the sacred place. *I am evil*, he'd told me. *I'm the demon lurking in the shadows.* But even now, knowing he was descended from Tsukiyomi, I couldn't believe it. He was descended from Amaterasu, too, right? And wasn't she supposed to be the protector of Japan? The little bell on the charm jingled as I put the phone back in my pocket.

"If you remember, the *omamori* didn't work so well," Tomo said.

I chewed on my bottom lip and said nothing. It had worked. The *omamori* had fallen out of my pocket and clinked against the floor when Jun had kissed me at his school. It had broken me out of the moment; it had protected me from the awful mistake I'd made. I still wasn't sure if Jun had actually liked me, or had just been using me to get to Tomo. It didn't matter—I'd screwed up big-time, and almost lost Tomo. Heat prickled down my neck as I shook the guilt away.

"We've got to have more options than leave Japan or die," I said, trying to get back on track.

Tomo closed his eyes. "What if I draw Tsukiyomi, and then rip the sketch in half?"

I stared at him; he'd lost his mind. "You're joking, right? Ripping the drawing of Amaterasu nearly killed me. Ripping Tsukiyomi in half might kill you."

He frowned. "There's never been a constant way to stop the *kami*. Sometimes it overpowers me and I collapse, and sometimes I can get startled out of its control, but... I can't see a connection. Maybe I just need to live under a torii and stay unconscious."

I groaned, scribbling out my list. We weren't getting anywhere this way.

Tomo rested the remote on the side table and sat up, resting his hands on my shoulders. "Hey," he said. "Don't worry. I'm sure we'll think of something." He pulled me gently toward him, turning me so my back was against his chest. I leaned into the warmth of him, the scent of miso and vanilla around me, his heart thudding gently against the back of my shoulder.

The paper list slipped off my lap, floating toward the floor and slipping halfway under the couch. The cherry blossom in the corner spun like a pinwheel, and Tomo went rigid beneath me, his breath catching in his throat. "Is that—is it moving?"

I sat up as he grabbed the paper. He frowned as the flower shriveled before us, crumpling into a scribbled ugliness in the corner. "Katie," he said, his voice deep and troubled.

"I know," I said. "Ever since your drawing of Amaterasu

came to life it's been happening. But my sketches don't come off the page like yours. They seem pretty harmless so far."

"Yeah, but this is…" He ran a hand through the copper spikes of his hair. "Katie, I don't want this for you."

"Maybe it'll stop," I lied. "It's not a big deal. We need to worry about you right now. And what'll happen tomorrow."

He dropped the page and leaned back into the couch. I curled up on top of him, my shoulder pressed to his collarbone and my nose tucked under his neck. When he spoke, the vibration tickled against my skin.

"Tomorrow," he said. "Did you talk to your aunt?"

I nodded, my chin grazing his warm skin. "They want her to come in, too."

The day Tomo had discovered his connection to Tsukiyomi, there had been horrible ink messages dripping from every chalkboard in the school, things like She Must Die and Demon Son. Then ink had poured from every sink in the boys' change room by the gym. It was a huge mess, and the headmaster was convinced it was Tomo's fault because of the way he'd reacted. Well, true, the ink probably *was* his fault, but there's no way it was the horrible prank they were accusing him of. He'd been just as shocked as any of us to see it. Headmaster Yoshinoma had arranged a meeting for tomorrow with Tomo and his dad, and my aunt Diane and I had to attend, too, seeing as I had been in the change room with Tomo and given the ridiculous excuse that Tomo had been framed. Tomo had said my eyes must have given me away. *They're always earnest*, he'd said, which had made my stomach flip over a little.

"Is she still going to let us see each other? Your aunt?" Tomo laughed, but it was dry and empty of humor.

I tried to smile. "So far you're not making the best impression, no. What do you think will happen, though?"

"Suspension, maybe. Or off the kendo team."

"They wouldn't do that. You're one of the top students, and they need you on the team."

Tomo reached for my hand and laced his fingers between mine, squeezing with their warmth. "We'll face it together, whatever it is."

The colorful anime on the screen blinked off, replaced by a stark newsroom and a bowing reporter in a black suit.

"The news already?" I sat up, pulling out my phone to check the time. "I've got to get home."

"I'll take you," Tomo said, but then his eyes went wide and round as he stared at the TV, his hand suddenly limp in mine.

I glanced at the bold white kanji on the screen, at the reporter who rattled off Japanese almost faster than I could follow.

"Sano Chihaya, known as Hanchi, Yakuza *oyabun* and leader in Shizuoka, aged fifty-seven, found this morning in a puddle of blood..."

My body seized with fear. I couldn't move, completely immobilized by the memory. The Yakuza boss who'd kidnapped us, who'd forced Tomo to sketch money at gunpoint to save my life. The same one who'd exploited Jun's father, making him draw drugs and weapons and money, the one who'd tried to recruit Jun after his father's death. *After Jun had killed his own dad,* I remembered with a chill. His father had had an affair with one of the Yakuza, and left Jun and his mother with nothing after he took off. Devastated and desperate, Jun had scribbled down horrible messages, words of ink that had instantly and accidentally killed his dad.

"Sano was in Ginza district, Tokyo—" Ginza, the same place Jun's father had been discovered dead "—when he had what seemed to be a stroke. Collapsed on the sidewalk..." They showed images of the storefront, the police tape and the traffic being redirected. "He appears to have hit his head," the reporter babbled on, her words like syrup in my ears, thick and almost beyond understanding. "He was found in a significant amount of blood."

They showed it then, a pale blue plastic tarp stretched over the shape of a body underneath, the blood seeping out the sides, unwilling to be contained, to keep the secret of what had happened.

"Police can't identify a person of interest at this time. It appears to be accidental, but due to the suspicious circumstances and his Yakuza connection, he will be undergoing an autopsy at the NTT Forensics Center in Shinagawa, Tokyo..."

My heart pressed against my ribs with every beat.

This couldn't be happening. I could see as clear as day that wasn't blood.

It was ink.

Tomo squeezed my fingers in his, both of us unable to speak. *Jun...did you do this?*

2

I found my voice after a moment, my words dry and barely above a whisper. "Was it...was it Jun?"

Tomo shook his head. "Hanchi was still trying to recruit a Kami after he realized I was too unstable to be useful," he said, his voice scratchy and hollow. "Maybe he approached one who fought back." But Jun had told us over and over how he wanted to rid the world of Yakuza. He'd told us he didn't need Tomo anymore, now that he knew his true power as a Kami descended from Susanou. The words he'd said echoed in my thoughts. *I will make the world cry.*

I didn't want to believe it. I didn't know what to believe.

"Maybe it was really an accident?" I said. Tomo's eyes met mine, and we both knew. It hadn't been blood pooled around Hanchi. The ink was all the proof we needed that a Kami was involved.

I pulled my phone out of my pocket. "I'm going to call Jun."

"*Da-me.*" Tomo shook his head, pulling the phone out of

my hands. "It's too dangerous to confront him. If he really had something to do with this, we're not safe."

My pulse buzzed in my ears. How could this happen? The world had cracked; everything would shatter. "We should call the police."

"And tell them what? That Jun murdered someone on a piece of paper? We can't prove anything. We don't even know if it was him."

I drew my knees up tightly, wrapping my arms around my legs. I hadn't thought Jun was capable of this. I still didn't believe it. And yet, a small piece of me, a tiny butterfly in the corner of my heart, fluttered with a dark thought. *Good. I'm glad Hanchi's dead.*

I didn't want to think like that. I didn't want to be glad this had happened.

But he would never hurt us again.

Hanchi got what he deserved, the voice whispered.

I squeezed my eyes shut. Life is precious, I said to myself. Just like losing Mom. Hanchi was someone's son. He had family who loved him, right?

Even though he kidnapped you and Tomo? He was willing to kill you both. He had to be stopped.

Yes, but not like this.

How, then? He's been stopped.

That's...that's true. He hurt so many people.

Who's the monster now? In the end, there is only death.

The butterfly had grown too large, its wings enveloping my every thought. My mind grew dark and tinged with shadow. I could hear the whispers as if they were real. I shook my head to try and empty it, to escape.

"Katie." Tomo's voice snapped me back, and I blinked at the brightness of the room. His hand was on my cheek; the warmth of the pads of his fingers pressed against my skin.

I whispered, "What happened?"

"Your eyes," he said. His face was ghostly pale. "Your eyes changed. Just for a moment."

My heart was pounding like I'd just sprinted all the way to Shizuoka Station. It was the Kami blood that had awakened. It had enveloped me, just for a moment. I had lost myself. *"Daijoubu?"* Tomo asked. *Are you okay?* I nodded. The darkness felt far away now. There was nothing but light and his warmth around me.

The reporter droned on about Hanchi, and the chill of her voice frosted around the edges of us. Tomo clicked the TV off and wrapped his arms around me.

"Let's get you home," he said. "You don't have to be afraid. If it was Jun, he won't hurt you. I know it."

But he might hurt you. And even without Jun, Tomo was still in danger if the ink took control. Ikeda had said Tsukiyomi was a *kami* more deadly than Susanou. Didn't that mean Tomo was more dangerous than Jun?

I closed my eyes and breathed in the warm smell of Tomo, let the tickle of his copper hair against my neck sweep away the fear. I'd always known the world of the Kami was dangerous. But with Tomo, I still felt safe. We would be all right if we clung to each other. I had to believe that, no matter what.

Seeing the Yakuza boss who once kidnapped you lying dead on the streets of Ginza takes the fear out of a reprimand from the school headmaster. Yet here we were, Tomo and me, Diane and Tomo's dad, sitting in four tiny chairs squished into Yoshinoma's office. I folded my hands in my lap, squeezing my own fingers as I looked down at the floor. Tomo and I sat in the center, surrounded by the parentals, surrounded by adults who were *disappointed in us.* I wished Tomo would reach out and take my hand, but I knew he would try to distance himself to protect me from any fallout.

Tomo's dad rose to his feet; the edges of his suit were so crisp you could probably slice *kamaboko* loaf with them. He looked agitated and kept checking his watch; I wondered what meeting he was missing for this. If Tomo's mom was alive, his dad wouldn't even have to be here. Was he thinking that, too?

He bowed deeply to Yoshinoma. *"Moushi wake gozaimasen,"* he apologized. "I can't believe my son would do such a thing. School has always been his top priority."

"Please, Yuu-san, sit down," Yoshinoma said, motioning with his hand until Tomo's dad complied. "We were surprised, as well. He's mostly been a reliable student, an example in his studies. He's still maintaining his grades, and he's advanced further than ever before in his kendo tournaments. But we cannot accept this disrespectful prank on our school." The headmaster leaned back in his chair. It creaked as he pressed the back of it toward the wall. "I can only imagine that he must have become *distracted*."

Tomo's hand squeezed into a fist. "Kouchou, Katie had nothing to do with this," he said, his voice tense. This was wrong. He had to stay calm, or we'd be in more trouble. Surely he knew that.

"Neither did Tomohiro-senpai," I said. I figured now was a good time to put my slightly more formal Japanese into practice. "He didn't do this."

"I'm afraid it's too late for that, Miss Greene," said Yoshinoma. "It's true that we don't have proof that Tomo painted those offensive kanji on the chalkboards, but he was visibly upset about them, and he does have a background in calligraphy. Not just anyone could have written those in the style they appeared. Furthermore, the change room…well, it was full of ink, and students saw him go in. We're sure he went there to wash up."

"You don't know that," I said, my voice rising. "It wasn't him. He arrived at school the same time I did that morning. It wasn't him!"

Diane rested a gentle but urgent hand on my arm, and I hesitated. Was the way I was talking back to the headmaster not okay in Japan? I was probably out of line, but so was Yoshinoma. Tomo hadn't done any of it—well, it had sort of been him, but it was the ink, the *kami* blood in his veins. He hadn't meant for it to happen. He didn't deserve to suffer for Tsukiyomi's sake.

Diane's voice was calm and reasonable as she spoke. I'd never heard her sound so collected before. "Yoshinoma-sensei, these two are good kids. Katie's working so hard on her kanji to stay at Suntaba and catch up to the other students. The last thing these two would do is jeopardize their future."

"I agree," the headmaster said, leaning forward and resting his folded hands on his desk. "But part of growing up is learning there are consequences to your actions."

Tomo's dad nodded like he approved, but he kept sneaking peeks at his watch.

Yoshinoma let out a slow, whistling breath between his teeth. "To be honest, some of the teachers have called for expulsion."

A small gasp escaped Tomo's lips, his eyes round and horrified.

Tomo's father wasn't checking his watch anymore. "Yoshinoma-sensei!"

Yoshinoma's voice was grave and monotone. "This isn't the first time he's caused trouble. He's been in many fights since his first year."

Tomo's father blurted out, "Because his mother passed away, and..."

"That was seven years ago, Yuu-san. And there have been rumors that he fathered a child with a girl from Kibohan Senior High. Is that the kind of student we want to represent our school?"

So, the Shiori rumor had reached the teachers, too. Tomo clenched his hands into tighter fists as his father's face went white. "That's not true," he said, looking down until his chin pressed against the knot of his uniform tie.

I could remember it now, when that knot had been loosened around his neck, his top button undone. Tomo looking up at the wagtail birds as he spread out on the warm field of Toro Iseki, when I'd first stumbled on his secret drawing place. I wanted to take his hand in mine, to pull him to his feet and run back there where we were safe, where no one could reach us. Where we could fly.

Yoshinoma sighed. "Even so, your friend Ishikawa Satoshi was shot this summer, Tomohiro. Yuu-san, do you know what kind of life your boy is up to?"

I looked away from Tomo's dad, frightened of the emotions he tried to rein back on his face. His voice came out shakily. "Kouchou, I assure you, Tomo is not involved in the way Ishikawa is derailing his life."

"However," the headmaster continued, "Yuu scored the highest out of the Third Year boys in the first term exams. And he's earning quite the spotlight for himself in kendo. It's good for our school to gain such national recognition." He cleared his throat. "So I am going to override the teachers and ask Tomohiro to stay at Suntaba."

The relief washed through me, and I let out a breath I hadn't even known I was holding. Tomo's dad bowed his head to the headmaster.

"He will have to be suspended, of course. You understand this cannot go without punishment."

"Of course," Tomo's dad mumbled.

"One month, Tomohiro," Yoshinoma said, and I flinched. A month?

"But his entrance exams," Tomo's dad protested.

"He will have to spend the effort at home if he hopes to pass them when he returns. This was a serious offence to this school, Yuu-san. And a month will give him time to refocus on his work and forget any distractions."

Oh. They wanted to separate us, thinking that time apart would make us grow apart. I took a deep breath, trying to stay calm. It wouldn't work. They couldn't stop us. We were something greater together than they could ever understand.

Tomo's face was blank, unreadable. "What about kendo practices?"

"You'll be back in time for the serious training for the tournament, Tomo. But in the meantime, Watanabe-sensei and Nishimura-sensei have recommended you do your exercises at home. They don't want you to be out of shape when you return."

"And for Katie?" Diane said. Her hand was still on my arm, and she squeezed it to reassure me. I was glad she was there with me. Even if she lectured me later, I knew she loved me. Did Tomo feel that way about his dad? They seemed so distant as they sat side by side, as if they were worlds apart, as if they couldn't really see each other at all.

"Katie hasn't given the school any other trouble," Yoshinoma said, "and we believe she was likely dragged into this. She—I apologize, but—she lacks the skill to have written those kanji on the chalkboards."

My own illiteracy had saved me. I guess I should've felt relieved, but mostly I just felt annoyed.

"We just think it best that she be...separated from Tomo-hiro for a while, so they can both refocus on their futures."

There it was again, that patronizing we-know-what's-best jab. *You're just kids. You don't know what love is. You're blind. You're wrecking your own futures.*

We bowed to Yoshinoma-sensei and parted in the hallway. I tried to catch Tomo's eye, but he didn't look up. He just stiffly followed his father out of the school. It didn't matter, though. I could feel his thoughts as if they were my own.

They didn't know us, not at all. They didn't understand what we had. We belonged together. What I felt was real, and I felt it with every fiber of my being.

They couldn't break us. Nothing could.

3

The dream began with a soft sigh, a whispering sound in the distance like the swell of the ocean. I'd seen glimpses of the edge of the sea that lapped against Japan, once in Miyajima with Yuki, and once looking over Suruga Bay with Tomo. But long ago, Mom and I had visited the shore of the Atlantic when we'd traveled to see friends in Maine. The sun had beamed down on the water, glistening so brightly that I'd had to squeeze my eyes shut, to make the scene almost vanish completely in order to see it at all.

"Look at that, Katie," she'd said with a smile. "Stretching on like it has no end. Sparkling and full of life." It had looked limitless and inspiring, warm and vibrant and blue.

This ocean was nothing like that one. It was dull and opaque, gray-tinged as the shore came into view. It looked as if it bordered on nothing—limitless—but the idea was frightening, like the whole world had drowned. There was nothing left but this earthy coast I stood upon, the sand gritty and sharp against my bare feet.

I was dreaming, I realized. The vague feeling that something wasn't quite right overwhelmed me, like I was squinting to see the whole picture.

Everything was pallor and faded. The shore behind me seemed to stretch on for miles, but I knew it was the last refuge of earth—the seas were empty and void. The land was gone.

I began to walk along the shore. The sighs carried across the waves toward me, whispering in discord, some voices carrying so that I could almost make out the sound of them. Almost, but never quite.

Wreckage lay along the shore, pieces of bent wood that once curved around the bow of a ship, nails stuck into them that no longer attached to anything but air. A cracked turtle shell, belly-up, with kanji carved into it. The waves lapped through it like a tunnel, spilling through the other side like a fountain. Pieces from a distant storm, scraps that had lost meaning.

A bright orange torii appeared from the shadow, the Shinto gateway towering above as though the grayness had just lifted away and left color in its place. The sighs were louder now, except they sounded mournful, like wailing.

I wasn't alone in this strange place. Someone was crying.

I fought the urge to run. Fear prickled down my spine; I didn't want to disturb whoever it was. I didn't want to be involved.

I turned my head to look back at the shore I'd walked along.

A beast stood in the shadows, his angular ears pressed tightly against his head. His eyes gleamed with a ghostly green.

A wolf. No, an *inugami*, the vengeful wolf demons that hunted Tomo, that had mauled his friend Koji and nearly cost him his eye. The *inugami* crouched, watching me, a challenge in his eyes.

I couldn't go back, so I turned once again to the bright orange torii. The grains of sand stuck to my soles as I walked, miniature daggers that pricked me with their warnings.

"Machinasai," a voice said, ordering me to wait. I stopped.

I heard the sound of fabric scraping over sand, and looked to my right. She wore a kimono of gold embroidered with elaborate phoenixes, an obi red as blood wrapped tightly around her waist.

Amaterasu, the *kami* of the sun. She looked like she had in the clearing with Tomo and Jun, but different somehow. Larger, more real. She exuded power about her. She smiled, and yet somehow it was terrifying.

Her headdress of beads jingled as she tilted her head, speaking in a haunting voice that seemed to echo in the vast and empty space. It sounded like Japanese, but I couldn't make sense of it. Her speech was too formal, too ancient.

"I'm sorry," I said. "I don't understand."

"I have tried to speak to you for so long," she said, "that my voice is dry from effort." She was speaking modern Japanese now, graciously but with a subtle distaste, like someone who pretends to be glad to accept a gift they already have.

"Who's crying?" I asked, looking toward the gateway.

"The *kami* have need of tears," she said. "We have cried so long that we have drowned the world."

I tried to grasp the questions I'd had when I was awake. It was my chance to ask, but my head was hazy from sleep, barely able to remember the real world or the fact that I was dreaming.

"Tsukiyomi," I managed. Was that it? It didn't sound quite right asleep. "How can I stop him?"

"Tomohiro is the heir of calamity."

"What can I do?"

"There is no hope for you," she said, like she had said over and over to him. "There is nothing to be done."

I looked over toward the torii, toward the back of a figure on her knees in the sand. She wore a kimono of white, the black obi draped in an elaborate bow across her back, and her body shook with the quiet sobs.

I hesitated, watching for a moment.

"But Tsukiyomi," I said. "Tsukiyomi is trying to take control of Tomo."

Amaterasu tilted her head to the side, her eyes deep pools of blackness. "Tsukiyomi is dead. Long ago he left this world."

I saw another figure beside the crying girl—a boy on the ground in front of her, slumped with a leg bent strangely to the side.

"The mirror has seen it," Amaterasu said. "It cannot be undone."

I stepped toward the girl and the boy, walking slowly as my bare feet slipped in the sharp sand.

The girl wore a *furisode* kimono, with long sleeves that draped over the body of the boy and into the sand, the ends of the soft white fabric stained with ink. The girl had tucked her arm under the boy's neck, and his head lolled back unnaturally, his copper spikes speckled with sand.

My stomach twisted as I looked down at the familiar face.

"Tomo," I breathed, falling to my knees in the sand. Trails of ink carved down his face and across the elaborate silver robes he wore, collecting in the fabric like pools of dark blood. His eyes were closed, his face expressionless as he rested in her arms.

The girl looked down as she wept. Her long black hair had come out of the coils she'd tied them in at the base of her neck, and they tumbled in a tangle over her face. She looked up to take a breath and I realized she, too, was Amaterasu. There were two of them. I looked past her to see the Amaterasu in gold, and she stood there, watching, as she clasped her hands on the rim of a huge bronze mirror that stretched from her hips to her feet. I'd seen that mirror before, the one she'd held up to Jun in the clearing to show him the truth of who he really was.

The girl let out another sob, and black tears ran down her cheeks. Tears made of ink. I reached a hand toward her.

"Katie!" a voice shouted. I jumped, frightened to be recognized in this strange world. I wanted to wake up. I pinched my arm, twisting the skin back and forth. I didn't want to know any more.

"Katie," the voice said again, and the shadowy fog pulled back.

It was Jun, hunched over on one knee and adorned in broken armor, his face streaked with ink. He wore a helmet on his head with golden horns, but one had broken off in a jagged cut and lay in the sand and tangle of brush grass at his feet.

No, that wasn't the horn in the sand. It was the wrong shape, too…too sharp.

It was a sword, stained dark on the blade.

My blood turned to ice. My world turned black.

"Katie," Jun said quietly. *"Gomen."* *I'm sorry.*

No. It can't be.

"Abunai," Jun warned. "Look." I heard the sound of sand shifting under paws. I looked up to four pairs of glinting eyes, four mouths filled with sharp and angry teeth. *Inugami* had advanced while I was looking away; they'd found us. They growled and crouched low to the ground, ready to spring, ready to destroy us all.

I reached for Tomo, stroked my hand through the copper spikes of his bangs, the ink sticking to my fingertips.

This was the end of everything. I closed my eyes, unwilling to see any more.

The *inugami* pounced.

I screamed into the darkness of my room, so disoriented that I barely heard the slam of my door sliding into the wall as Diane stumbled in and threw her arms around me.

"It's okay, hon, it's okay," she soothed as my scream turned into sobs. My arms burned like fire; I could still feel the wolf teeth sinking into my flesh, like I'd been torn to pieces. "It was just a dream," she said, smoothing my hair as I tried to calm down. "It's not real."

But it had felt more real than anything I'd dreamed before. Were these the kind of nightmares Kami had? Did Tomo suffer with these every night?

I gasped in air, trying to focus on Diane so the room would stop spinning.

"Do you hear me, Katie? You're safe. You're okay."

I nodded, wanting to believe her. My heart pounded so hard against my chest it ached. My eyes had adjusted to the darkness of the room, but Diane reached for my lamp and clicked it on, banishing the gray shores of the dream to the corners of my mind.

"Thank you," I said, tears streaming down my face.

Diane frowned, her lips pursed together, her hair a disheveled mop on her head. "Was it about your mom?"

I shook my head. "I don't want to talk about it." I wanted to forget everything. The sound of the lapping waves, the sharp grains of sand digging into my knees. The smell of *inugami* ripping into flesh...

"It's probably the stress from all this school nonsense. Getting suspended when they don't have proof he did it." She shook her head. "They just want someone to blame."

I smiled a little. If only it was just that. Diane was always on my side, no matter what. I was so glad to have her here with me.

"You must think I made a bad choice, but he's not like that," I said. "He's not like that at all."

"Well, you need to bring him here so I can meet him for myself, okay?"

I wrapped my arms around her tightly and she took a short breath. I'd startled her. "You can stay home today if you want," she said. "No need to face school right away after that."

"That's okay. I think I'll get up." I didn't want to risk going back to that dream, that world drowned in *kami* tears.

Diane stroked my hair for a bit and nodded. "I'll start on breakfast," she said. "Come on out when you're ready."

She slid my door shut, and I swung my legs over the side of the bed, pressing my feet against the cool tatami floor.

It had seemed so real. *The mirror has seen it*, Amaterasu said. Did she mean it would happen, no matter what?

That ancient sword that had lain at Jun's side in the grass, the blade covered in ink. Did that mean Jun would... Would he kill Tomo?

Had he killed Hanchi?

I padded across the cold tatami and opened the drawer of my dresser, pulling out a pair of dark kneesocks and throwing them on the bed.

I didn't want the ink to dictate my life. I wanted us to choose for ourselves. But were we really free to choose? Tomo had always said he didn't have a choice.

It was just a dream, anyway. A frightening one, but nothing more.

I grabbed my navy uniform skirt and slid the drawer shut with a thud.

I hesitated, the dream still living vividly in the corners of my mind.

Amaterasu had said Tsukiyomi died long ago. That must mean there was a way to stop him. He had been stopped before.

I looked at my fingers, remembering the slick feel of the ink spreading through Tomo's hair, pooling on his lifeless body...

I had to figure it out. I was running out of time.

★ ★ ★

I knew Tomo wouldn't be at school, but it didn't stop me from scanning all the students as they entered the front gates. They entered in groups, laughing and chatting through the chill of the crisp autumn morning. I tugged on the end of my fuzzy plaid scarf, my breath turning to fog in the air. It wasn't like Tomo and I had any classes together, but knowing that he was at home, that he wasn't welcome at school, made the crowded space seem empty.

"Katie!"

I turned, and saw Yuki darting toward me, clutching her book bag to her black wool coat. She pressed the bag against my stomach and I folded my hands around the handles without asking. Hands free, she grinned and leaned over, tugging at the kneesock that had coiled around her ankle on the way to school.

"I'm glad to see you here," she said, straightening again. "I thought you might get suspended!"

I handed back her bag and she smiled. Our shoes crunched the *momiji* leaves that had fallen off the courtyard trees.

"I'm sorry," I said, pressing the tips of my fingers together. "I should've called you to let you know how it went."

She waved her hand back and forth and pursed her lips. "I know you've been busy," she said. Truthfully, it wasn't that. It was that I had so much on my mind I'd become forgetful about the people that mattered.

"I am really sorry," I said, and her smile brightened. "I didn't get in much trouble, which is fair because I didn't do anything."

"But Yuu-senpai," she said. "I don't see him here."

"Ohayo!" Tanaka pressed his face between ours suddenly, and we jumped back, Yuki screaming as my book bag dropped to the ground.

Yuki sighed. "Tan-kun, you can't go around terrorizing people on a Monday morning."

"I'm only terrorizing my favorite people." He grinned. Yuki shrunk into the coils of her scarf and looked away, her cheeks blazing.

I reached down for my book bag but someone else grabbed it before I could.

"Greene," Ishikawa slurred. He scratched the back of his bleached-white hair with a hand, the other lazily extending my leather bag to me. "Just the person I wanted to see."

"*Ohayo,*" I said, rolling my eyes. *Morning.* But part of me felt just a little relieved. If I couldn't see Tomo, at least I could see his best friend. Ishikawa was in on the Kami secret now, and as long as he stayed away from the Yakuza for good, maybe he could be someone we could rely on.

His eyes gleamed. "It's only my second week back. Did you miss me?"

"Not sure," I said, pulling open the door to the school *gen-kan.* We squeezed past the dozens of students placing their outdoor shoes in the stacked cubbies. "Maybe if you go away again I can let you know."

"Funny," Ishikawa said. "But I won't go away until you tell me what you've done with Yuuto. I called him five times yesterday, and he didn't answer."

"*Five* times?" Yuki said.

I swore Ishikawa's cheeks tinged pink as he offered her a sour smirk. "So? I worry when my sparring partner doesn't show up for practice. Especially after a nasty prank has been played on him." His eyes caught mine, and I knew what he was really asking. Was the ink his fault? What had happened with Jun? But it wasn't safe to talk about it here.

"He's been suspended," I said. "For a month."

Ishikawa's eyes widened. "*Ee?*" He reached down and

pulled a shoe off, even though the Third Year cubbies were on the other side of the room. "A month? Do you know how out of shape that shrimp is going to get in a month? He'll lose the nationals!"

"Suntaba's never placed in the nationals," Tanaka said. He tapped his toes against the floor to fit on his school slippers. "That's nothing new."

"Yeah, but this is Yuuto we're talking about," Ishikawa said. "I want to see him beat Takahashi to a pulp." But he kept looking at me, and I knew he wasn't talking about kendo.

"You should be careful, too, Ishikawa-senpai," Yuki said, pulling on the end of her pink scarf until it tumbled down from her neck into her waiting hand. "I heard you almost got suspended for your injury this summer and the fight outside the kendo match."

"That's none of your business, First Year," he sneered, and looked at me. "Do I even know this *kouhai*?" he asked, hooking a thumb toward her.

"She's my best friend," I said, "and she's right. You're treading a fine line yourself."

"*Maa*, whatever," he said, running a hand through the white spikes of his hair. "I don't need to be lectured by juniors."

The school bell chimed, and Tanaka and Yuki headed down the hallway toward our class. I turned to follow them, but felt Ishikawa's warm fingers tug on my sleeve.

"Hey," he said quietly, his voice a hot whisper against my neck, his eyes deep brown and gleaming. "Is Yuuto okay?"

I hesitated. Was he? The nightmare flashed through my mind, and then thoughts of what had happened a few days earlier—fighting Jun in the sky with a rain of ink falling, learning he was linked to Tsukiyomi, that Jun was out for vengeance. I pressed my tongue to my lips, the knowledge of it swirling together in the pit of my stomach. "I don't know."

"Let me know what I can do."

"Hanchi's dead," I said.

He looked surprised that I knew, his fingers stiff for a moment before they relaxed their grip. "Yeah."

My voice was barely there. "I'm scared it was Jun." *I'm scared Tomo is next.* I didn't say it, but Ishikawa looked like he knew, like he was thinking the same thing. His other hand slipped into his blazer pocket. He wouldn't be stupid enough to bring his switchblade to school, would he? But this was Ishikawa, after all. He *would* be stupid enough.

"Meet you here after class," he said, and then he was gone down the hallway, and there was nothing for me to do but get to my homeroom and start the school day. I slid in the door just before the class rose to bow to Suzuki-sensei, my thoughts whirling.

How could I stop Jun, if it was him? And how could I stop Tomo if Tsukiyomi headed down the same destructive path that Susanou was leading Jun?

My phone buzzed in my bag, startling me out of my thoughts. When Suzuki-san turned to write on the board, I smuggled the phone up and behind my textbook.

Still in my pajamas. I think I got the better deal.—Tomo

I grinned and slid the phone back into my bag. With all the darkness closing in around us, I was glad to see Tomo still shining.

Ishikawa was slumped on the floor, one leg bent with his arm draped over it, the other leg stretched into the hallway, forcing students to step carefully around him. The spikes of his hair were pressed flat against the wall, his eyes closed.

I stepped forward, kicking at the calf of his outstretched leg.

"Rude," I said, and he turned his head to look at me. "You're tripping everyone up."

He grinned, his teeth as white as his hair, and rose to his feet. "Your fault, Greene. If you'd gotten here sooner, I wouldn't have fallen asleep waiting."

"How'd I get stuck hanging out with you, anyway?"

He smirked, sliding open the door to the *genkan* so we could put on our shoes and coats. "That would be Yuuto's fault. As always, he's the source of all my problems." He zipped up his dark green coat, the dark fur trim around the collar looking a little ridiculous around his pale face and hair. "What?" he asked, and I realized I was staring.

"You look like a temaki roll," I said.

He rolled his eyes. "Ha-ha. Green coat, white hair, looks like sushi. Let's move." He pushed open the door to the courtyard and a gust of cold air swirled around us. He didn't have on the standard school loafers, but wore shiny black shoes that were slightly pointed at the toes. "So," he said, "fill me in."

I walked alongside and told him everything. I figured it didn't matter how much he knew. He wasn't the enemy anymore; no matter what, he was on Tomo's side. So I told him about the fight with Jun on Mount Kano, about the fact that Tomo was linked to two *kami*, Amaterasu and Tsukiyomi—the sun and the moon, lovers turned enemies. I told him about Jun and how he'd killed his own father by drawing with hatred, and that I thought the same thing had happened to Hanchi.

He stopped on the top stair of the Shizuoka Station tunnels. "Well, fuck," he said.

"Exactly."

He turned on his heel and headed north. I had to hurry to keep up with his wide strides. "Wait, where are you going?"

"We don't have enough information," Ishikawa said. "If

Takahashi is involved with Hanchi, things are going to get messy, and I need to know."

I felt the blood drain from my face. "Wait, you're not going to sic the Yakuza on Jun's Kami cult out of revenge, are you? You'll start a war."

He shook his head, his cheeks pink from the autumn cold. "If it's true he killed Hanchi, Takahashi's the one who started it, not me. And you forget that I'm not exactly on good terms with them right now. They'd just as likely pound me into the ground as trust me. They'd think I was heading a sting operation or something. But we need to know if it was Takahashi, because if it was, then we have a shit storm to prepare for."

"So you're not on the Yakuza's side?"

"I'm on Yuuto's side, Greene." His voice was soft, vulnerable, and I had to strain to hear him through the wind. "I always have been. *Ikuze.* Let's go."

I wanted to remind him how he'd put all our lives in danger by involving the Yakuza in Tomo's secret. I wanted to remind him of the anger I'd seen in his eyes, the hatred there. But he looked so sincere now that instead I found myself wondering. Had he really thought his actions were for the best all along?

We walked north toward Katakou School, Sunpu Park on our left. Half of the leaves lay in piles at the bases of the trees, but the others clung to the branches, not yet ready to let go, hanging on to what little warmth the autumn held. The wind stung my cheeks and I readjusted my scarf to try and cover them. We were going to see Jun. What would he say? I could hear Tomo warning me in my mind. *Go back. Don't confront him. It isn't safe.* But Ishikawa was on a mission, and it would be worse if I wasn't there to temper whatever stupid thing he ended up saying. And, anyway, I wanted to know. I couldn't stand not knowing what Jun was thinking, or what kind of threat we had to fear from him.

We approached the gates of Katakou and Ishikawa walked through without hesitation. Crowds of students heading home stared as he stormed into their courtyard, but none of them confronted us. Maybe they remembered how he'd pulled a knife outside the kendo match at their school, how he and Tomo had been yanked into police cars with the two goons who'd picked the fight in the first place.

"*Oi,*" Ishikawa grunted at one of the students, who flinched. "Which homeroom is Takahashi Jun's?"

"I... I don't know," the boy stammered, speeding toward the gate and avoiding further eye contact with us.

"Don't scare the wildlife," I said. "He's probably either in the gym or the music room."

"Music room?" Ishikawa said, squinting as he looked up at the six floors of Katakou School.

"He plays cello," I explained.

"When he's not murdering people."

My stomach twisted. "I really hope that's not true."

Ishikawa walked back to the school entrance and strummed his fingers over the iron gates. "It's already true," he said. "He's done it once before."

It had been an accident, though. He hadn't really wanted something to happen to his father. It was another part of the curse he and Tomo had to live with. Their actions could spiral out of control in ways they couldn't imagine.

I spotted Jun's motorbike parked near the bike racks, and motioned at Ishikawa. "We can wait here. That's his bike."

"Let's just go in," Ishikawa said, but he slumped onto the bench where I'd once waited for Jun's help. "I want answers."

I sat beside him, wrapping my hands around the edge of the seat. "Yeah, but do you really want to question him in front of the music club? In fact, this whole thing is a terrible idea." Tomo had warned me to stay away from Jun. Even I knew this was stupid. We were putting ourselves at risk by confronting him. He could be capable of anything.

"You're right," Ishikawa said, tilting his head back to look at the sky. "But leaving him alone is worse. He needs to know that we know."

"Because when you confronted Tomo about joining the Yakuza that ended so well."

"*Uru-se na,*" Ishikawa droned at me, shaking his hair from side to side and inspecting his fingernails. "You annoy me, Greene."

"Likewise, Maki Roll."

We sat for a few minutes in silence, watching the stragglers from the school as they got out of after-school activities and hurried home. The sun had started to set, the nights getting shorter as fall dragged on and winter drew nearer.

I got to my feet and paced for a while in front of the bench.

"You're making me dizzy," Ishikawa said, closing his eyes.

It was like my whole body was buzzing; I couldn't focus. "This is bad. We should go."

A voice sounded from behind me. "Go where?"

Ishikawa opened his eyes as I spun around. Jun stood so close he blocked the wind gusting around me. He wore a dark coat over his school blazer, his motorbike helmet tucked under his arm. His eyes, forever cold, were unreadable as he looked down at me.

"Jun," I breathed.

His voice was stone. "You shouldn't be here."

He was right. I could hear my voice trembling. "I know."

"Does Yuu know you're here? You should stay away." He stepped around me, resting his helmet strap on the handle of his bike.

"What kind of greeting is that?" Ishikawa drawled. He

stood and put his hands on his hips, arching his back as he stretched.

"Ishikawa," Jun said, stepping toward him. "Is he giving you trouble, Katie?"

Ishikawa narrowed his eyes and pressed his index finger against Jun's collarbone. "The only one giving her trouble is you, Takahashi."

I tugged on Ishikawa's arm, trying to pull him away as he and Jun glared at each other. I accidentally pulled him off balance and he stumbled backward, then ran a hand through his bleached hair, trying to act as though he'd decided to step back on his own.

"What are you doing here?" Jun said quietly.

Ishikawa gave a short laugh in reply. "Please. Don't patronize her. You know why we're here."

"Jun," I said. My throat was dry and thick, my heart pounding. "I saw on the news...about...about Hanchi." Jun was motionless, expressionless. "Hanchi is dead, Jun."

He wasn't surprised, that much I could see. At the very least he'd heard the news. *"Sou ka,"* he said. *Is that so.*

"That's it?" Ishikawa sneered. "You had all this talk of killing off Yakuza, you threaten to 'make the world cry,' and now the first Yakuza boss is dead and you say, *'Sou ka'*? What the hell is wrong with you, Takahashi?"

"What do you want me to say?" Jun snapped. "You know more than you should. The Kami aren't a threat, Ishikawa. They're not weapons to be handed over to the Yakuza. They are heirs of heaven. They are protectors of Japan." Jun turned to me, gently wrapping his fingers around my elbows. The feel of his hands sent a jolt of panic through me. "Tell me you aren't glad Hanchi is dead, Katie. He can never hurt you again."

My heart lurched. "It *was* you, wasn't it?"

His icy eyes melted, just for a moment. "Don't ask me that."

I could barely move my lips to speak. "This is wrong, Jun. It's murder."

"What does it matter who did it? He's dead now. You're safe."

Ishikawa grabbed the collar of Jun's jacket and shoved him away from me. Jun stumbled backward, his shoes clicking against the pavement as he regained his balance.

Ishikawa's white spikes flopped into his eyes as he snarled. *"Bakayaro,"* he spat.

My body was ice; my heart cracked under the weight. I blinked back tears, terrified. "Jun, tell me it wasn't you, and I'll believe you. Tell me."

He said nothing, watching me with his dark eyes.

"Tell me," I whispered.

His eyes never left mine. "I can't."

The fear shook through me. He was crazy. I stumbled back, Ishikawa stepping in front to protect me.

"Katie, you can't condemn this," Jun said, his eyes pleading. "It's not so black-and-white. Do you know how many people died at the hands of Hanchi? Do you know what he's done in his life? I know. So many victims cried out, and he never showed one of them mercy. He was in and out of jail so fast it never held him back for a moment. A scumbag like that doesn't deserve to live. His death has saved lives. Can't you see that?"

"You're fucked up," said Ishikawa.

Jun shook his head. "The world is rotting," he said. "Tell me you're not glad he's dead, Katie."

I am glad. I'm glad he's gone.

No. I couldn't think like that, not again.

The ink protects. It marks the world and paints the future. There is no escape from its judgment.

"Greene!" Ishikawa's voice shook me out of it. "Your eyes," he said, his face twisted in confusion.

"Even the ink in you knows," Jun said. "We can't sit by any longer."

"Tomo won't join you," I said. "Neither will I."

Jun laughed. "I don't need Yuu to help me anymore. As the heir of Susanou, I am more powerful. But Yuu is an abomination. He'll blast a hole in the world when he explodes." Jun straddled his motorbike, sliding the helmet onto his head and pulling the strap tight below his chin. "My offer to him isn't open anymore. He will serve me, or he will be purged from this world. And until then, I will continue to do what needs to be done." His motorbike roared to life, sputtering as his words echoed through my head.

I thought back to my dream, the sword on the ground covered in ink, Tomo lying nearby. My eyes blurred with the tears I tried to hold back. "Jun, please. If we were ever friends, please don't do this."

Ishikawa rested a hand on my shoulder. "Forget it, Greene. You act like he has a heart."

There was a sadness in Jun's eyes. "You doubt me, even now. That I ever cared for you."

"Oh, you cared for me all right," I said, my hands curling into fists. "Like a dragon cares for gold."

He smiled and revved his bike. "More than that." He laughed. "And I'm reminded why."

"Creep," Ishikawa said. "Get the hell out of here before I call the police."

"They'd be more interested in you, Ishikawa. All I ever did was sketch." He turned to look at me for a moment, and then lowered his visor. *"Gomen,"* he said, almost below hearing. *I'm sorry.* The same thing he'd said in the dream. And then his bike roared out of the courtyard gate. We listened to the sound of it as the distance grew, as the rumbling faded into the cold wind that swirled around us.

"It's war, then," Ishikawa said, and the tears I'd been holding back spilled down my cheeks.

4

"Well, what now?" Ishikawa said. "What a jackass. Do you want a coffee or something?"

I shook my head, unable to answer.

"Why do you call him by his first name, anyway? You guys close once?"

He didn't know that Jun had kissed me, that Shiori had used her phone to try and drive a wedge between Tomo and me. Everything Jun did seemed to contradict what I knew about him. Did he care for me, or had he really just used me the whole time? I felt like maybe it was a bit of both. And did he really believe he was helping the world by killing Hanchi? He sounded so convinced, like he'd had no choice. Hanchi had destroyed Jun's family; he wasn't a good person, that was for sure. And the criminal system had failed with him. But still…vigilante justice was only a good thing in movies, right?

"Katie?"

Oh god, I'd totally phased out. "Sorry."

Ishikawa shook his head. "It's a lot of bullshit to take in," he said. "No wonder you're confused. That guy is a psycho."

I wanted to agree, but I felt like there was more to Jun. Life had given him so many bad turns—some he'd chosen, some he hadn't. If he wasn't a Kami, things would be different. But he was, and I couldn't keep making up excuses for him. Ishikawa was right—I needed to stay away from him. There was nothing good to gain from being near him anymore.

"Well?" Ishikawa said. "Want to check in on Yuuto?"

I thought back to the text he'd sent me in class and smiled to myself. That glimpse of normal life—that could keep me going. "You're Third Year, too, aren't you? Don't you have some kind of cram school for entrance exams?"

Ishikawa let out a laugh and shoved his hands deep in his pockets. "There's no point for me to study for entrance exams," he said. "I'm going to fail them, anyway."

I looked at him, unsure what to say. I couldn't imagine giving up before I'd tried. "It's only October," I said. "You have time."

He kicked at the ground and started walking away from Katakou School. "Yeah, what am I going to accomplish in four months?"

He was heading toward Otamachi, where Tomo lived. I followed, wrapping my scarf tighter around my neck as the evening darkness fell. "Yeah, but you've been studying all year, right? Don't give up now."

"So inspirational, Greene!" He put his hand to his heart and closed his eyes for a moment. When he opened them again, he smirked. "College isn't for me, anyway."

"What, you'd rather slum it with the Yakuza? That's not a future, Ishikawa."

"Why the hell are you so interested in my future? Not everyone can pull off marks like Yuuto, okay? God, drop it already."

I'd hit a sore spot, I could see that. But Ishikawa didn't strike me as dumb, at least not school-wise. Weren't the exams really just about preparedness, anyway?

We were already talking about them in my homeroom, and I was only a First Year at Suntaba. Oh god…would I pass the entrance exams? Maybe I should reconsider international school, after all. But no; I'd probably have to do entrance exams regardless. And Yuki insisted they were way more brutal than the SATs that had loomed at home. I'd kind of escaped those, too. If I'd moved in with Nan and Gramps in Canada, there wouldn't be any crazy tests to get into university, just a good GPA and all those extracurriculars they asked us to rack up. Kendo and Tea Ceremony Club were good starts, I figured.

What did I want to do, anyway? I'd always thought about journalism like Mom, but in Japan? And Shiori had said a Japanese husband would likely want me to quit my job and stay home. Was that even true? Not all of them felt that way. Or would I make my way back to the States, all alone again, ripping my roots out and starting over? I didn't feel like I was strong enough to do that. It all felt too far away to be real.

"Earth to Greene," Ishikawa said, waving a hand in front of me so close I blinked. "Man, you space out more than Yuuto. You coming or what?"

"Sure," I said. "Let's go."

He shook his head and we continued toward Otamachi, toward Tomo's house looming in the dark, the silver plate that read The Yuu Family illuminated by a tiny light. I pressed the button underneath the plaque, and a fake-sounding electronic doorbell chimed out of the speaker attached to it. We waited, but nothing.

"Maybe he's not home," I said.

"There are lights on, dummy."

I bristled, wanting to shove him. "Yeah, but his dad works so late. Maybe he stepped out to the *conbini* to grab some dinner. Should I try his *keitai*?"

Ishikawa pressed the buzzer again, then stepped backward. He cupped his hands around his mouth and took a deep breath. "Yuuto!" When nothing happened, he yelled again. "Yuuuuuutooooo!" I bit my lip to keep from laughing. I was starting to see why Tomo could be friends with this guy.

A tinny version of Tomo's voice came across the speaker. "Shut up, Sato! I'm pretty sure they heard you on the other side of Fuji."

Ishikawa pressed his lips against the speaker. "Open the door, then, jackass." Tomo yelled out; the sound of Ishikawa's voice must have been amplified inside. The gate beside us clicked open and we closed it behind us.

Tomo was already at the front door when we reached it. *"Gomen ne,"* he apologized, looking at me. "I didn't know it was you at the gate."

"That's what the vid cam is for," Ishikawa said. It sounded like some intense security system, but it was pretty common in Japan to have a doorbell attached to a speaker and camera.

"I laughed at your text," I said as I lined up my shoes in the *genkan* and stepped onto the raised wooden hallway.

"You sent her a text? Man, you didn't send me anything," Ishikawa said.

Tomo smirked at him. "I forgot it was your first full week back at Suntaba after getting shot. I should've sent flowers."

"I'll forgive you this time," he said, wandering into the kitchen. I heard him open and close some cupboards.

Tomo looked at me through his copper bangs, a worried look on his face. "Was school okay?"

I nodded. "Other than Yuki, no one brought up the ink kanji on the chalkboards."

"We have bigger problems than that, Yuuto." Ishikawa appeared in the doorway, shaking a can of soup up and down. I'd seen them before in the vending machines; it looked like a soda can, but you pulled a tab on the bottom and it heated up so you could have hot soup without a microwave. Ishikawa opened the top tab and tipped his head back to drink; the smell of the broth made my stomach growl.

"Bigger problems?" Tomo repeated.

Ishikawa nodded and reached into his pocket, throwing me another can of soup. Maybe I really had been wrong about him, I thought as I shook the soup to heat it. He had his good points.

"Takahashi," Ishikawa said, and Tomo's face scrunched up in confusion. I pulled the tab of the soup back and took a sip; it was like drinking hot creamed corn.

"What do you know about this?" Tomo said. We made our way into the living room, where Ishikawa slumped back onto the couch. He definitely made himself at home here. I sat down on a *zabuton*, a cushion on the floor near the coffee table.

"It was him," Ishikawa said. "He killed Hanchi."

Tomo turned to look at me, his face pale. "You went to see him?"

The soup can radiated warmth in my hand. "I know it wasn't a good idea, but…"

"He could've hurt you!"

"Calm yourself," Ishikawa said, tipping his head back over the couch arm to empty the can of soup into his mouth. "I was with her the whole time."

Tomo rolled his eyes. "Like I said. She was completely defenseless."

"*Oi,*" Ishikawa said, tilting his head upright to glare at Tomo.

I reached for Tomo's hand, slipping my fingers into the curl of his. "We needed to know," I said. "We had to talk to him."

"What if he'd attacked you, or kidnapped you? We can't trust him, Katie. He wants to kill me, and what if he hurts you?"

I stopped, remembering the nightmare. Why had I thought Jun might still be on our side? Of course he was dangerous. I had to protect Tomo. "I'm sorry," I said. "It was stupid to go."

He shook his head and ran a hand through his copper spikes. "I just… I hate to be trapped in here, not knowing what's going on. I don't want to see your life destroyed because of what I am."

"It's not just you," I said. "This affects me, too."

"And me," Ishikawa said. We both looked at him. "What?" he said, putting his soup can on the coffee table with a clank. "I may not be a Kami, but I am Yuuto's best friend. And I have an objective view of what's going on."

Tomo leaned back against the wall. "That's a big word for you."

"*Uruse.*" Ishikawa flipped him the finger. "Here's the thing. It's not just about you lovebirds anymore. Jun's going to set the world on fire, one tree at a time." He rose from the couch and approached Tomo, resting a hand on his arm. "This affects everybody. It's everyone's problem. He's more screwed up than I am, man. He said he wanted to 'purge you from the world.' Who says that?"

Tomo gasped and doubled over like the air had been knocked out of him.

"Tomo!" Ishikawa and I each grabbed one of his arms as he keeled backward toward the hardwood floor. Gravity pulled him down as we tried to keep him upright. We lowered him gently as he shook.

Whispers gathered on the air, a cacophony of voices that

grew louder as Tomo writhed on the floor. I'd heard these voices before, and I checked Tomo's eyes, frightened. His pupils flooded with black, large and vacant.

"*Oi*, Yuuto! Snap out of it." Ishikawa tapped Tomo's cheek, trying to wake him from the nightmare overtaking him. "We're right here. Come on, man."

"Tomo," I said again. "Don't let it win. Find yourself." Tomo let out a cry, and ink welled up underneath his shirt. It poured down his arms, dripping onto the floor.

Ishikawa leaned back, his eyes wide. *"Kuse!"* he swore. "What *is* that?"

He could see the ink, too. Oh god. This was bad.

Tomo yelled, but his voice didn't sound right. It echoed like the voices on the wind. He curled his hands into fists, his fingers slippery from the greasy black ink.

I grabbed his hand, the ink warm on my fingers as I wrapped them around his. "Tomo, it's okay," I said. "It's okay."

He looked at me with those large eyes; he shook with fear. "No," he said. "No!"

Ishikawa looked at me with panicked eyes. "No what?"

I knew then. Not me, but something inside me knew. Tomo and I spoke the words together, as if I'd said them a hundred times.

"No escape."

The ink lifted into the air in a dust of fluttering gold, and Tomo closed his eyes, falling into a heavy sleep.

5

"You guys are freaking me out with your synchronized weird-
ness," Ishikawa murmured. We were sitting on the couch,
watching Tomo sleep on the floor. We'd discussed carrying
him up to his room, but figured it was better to put a blanket
over him and watch him for now.

I sat with my feet pulled up, my toes curled over the edge
of the cushion. "It's the Kami blood," I said. "Amaterasu and
Tsukiyomi warring in him for control."

"Creepy," Ishikawa said. "Like, real *kami*? As in he's pos-
sessed or something?"

"I don't think so. More like awakening to the destiny he
can't escape. He's Kami *and* human. He'll become the whole
person he really is."

Ishikawa sneered. "Don't be an idiot. I know who he is.
He's Yuuto. That's all."

I blinked. I'd never thought of it like that, but he was right.
Tomo had spent his whole life creating his own identity, becom-

ing who he was. To suggest he was some other person, some time bomb that would destroy the world...that wasn't him.

I must have stared into space too long, because Ishikawa frowned as he looked at me. "What, Greene?"

"I was just thinking that you haven't bleached all the brain cells out of your head."

"*Hidoi*," he complained. *That's cruel.*

I ignored him. "What we need to do is silence Tsukiyomi. That's all we need to do, and Tomo's suffering is over."

"That and stop Takahashi."

Tomo grunted and we stopped talking, watching as he slowly turned onto his side and continued to sleep.

"It's getting late," Ishikawa said. "Don't you need to get home?"

I pulled out my *keitai* and checked the time. "Crap!" I'd missed text messages from Diane asking if I was coming for dinner. We both had so many late nights at school—it was common in Japan for students and teachers to stay for after-school clubs until even eight or nine—that we didn't have the chance to eat dinner together as much as we had when I'd first arrived.

"Go home," Ishikawa said. "I'll stay with Yuuto and make sure he's okay." I hesitated, but he just smiled at me. "The worst is over, yeah? And you need to stay on good terms with your aunt so she doesn't stop you guys from seeing each other. As much as that would make my life better, it would make Yuuto's suck, so get going already."

He had a point. "But you'll tell me if something happens, right?"

"Of course. Now get lost."

I texted Diane to let her know I'd eaten and that I was on my way home. It didn't feel right to leave Tomo lying there, but Ishikawa tried his best to look reassuring. Maybe he'd finally listened. Maybe he was straightening his life around. I took a last look at Tomo, who really did look fine now, and headed out the door toward Suruga.

I pulled the ends of my scarf tightly around my neck as I headed home. The streetlights lit the concrete paths of Shizuoka City, autumn leaves crumpled in piles around the lamp poles. It was safe enough to be walking home at this time alone, but I saw nothing but shadows in the darkness, possible Kami in every corner, waiting for me. Or maybe Yakuza. They knew what I looked like, and I was pretty much the only American girl in the city. If they wanted to find me, it would be easy.

I ran down the last few streets, clutching my *keitai* in my pocket. I knew the emergency number now. I'd asked Diane. The one for police was 1-1-0, and for medical and fire stuff it was 1-1-9, which kind of made me mad. Reversed, of course! That made so much sense. I'd told Tomo, who'd just laughed and asked why *we'd* reversed it to 9-1-1. Good point.

I ran up the steps of our mansion—that's what they called certain apartment buildings here—and the automatic glass doors slid away. It was still cool in the lobby and the elevator; our building didn't have central heat like some of the newer ones, so we relied on our heated *kotatsu* table and lots of sweaters to stay warm. It was only late October, though. I remembered how cold that February had been when I'd first arrived in Japan. It felt so long ago now.

I leaned against our pale green door and it opened into the *genkan* with a quiet snick. I opened my mouth to tell Diane I was home, but she was talking to someone, and the tone of her voice made me hesitate.

"No," she said loudly, "I don't think it's for the best. She's just settling in. It's been hard for her."

They were talking about me. I closed the door quietly and

slid my shoes off, sitting on the edge of the raised floor to listen. I didn't hear anyone respond before she started in again—she must be on the phone.

"I know, but this isn't about you. It's about her right now."

I'd never heard Diane so worked up about anything. She was always smiling too much, even when she was nervous. I'd never heard her sound angry, not like this.

"You're not hearing what I'm saying, Steven. It's not a good time."

Steven. The name froze me as I leaned against the wall. My father's name, the one who hadn't stuck around to even meet me when I was born. The one who'd run out of town after Mom had eaten the Kami dragon fruit, after she'd nearly lost me before I'd had a chance to live. Steven had walked out after the doctors had warned them that I might never talk or walk as a result of the food poisoning.

Was Diane... Was she talking to my dad?

"It's been a year, Steven. Where were you?" she said. "When Katie needed you, you weren't there." A pause. "No, I know you didn't know, but...Yes, I get that, but..." Diane suddenly appeared from behind the corner, the phone clutched to her ear. I stared back into her wide eyes, both of us surprised to be caught out.

"I have to go," Diane said. "I have your number...Yes, I know. Okay." She clicked the off button as the phone slowly dropped from her ear.

My mouth was dry, my words thick. "Was that...my dad?"

"Oh, hon," Diane said. Her eyes crinkled up, the corners of her plum-lipsticked mouth crumpled in a frown. "I'm so sorry. I wasn't going to trouble you with it."

"What did he want?" I asked. "How did he even find you?"

"He phoned Nan and Gramps. He got my number from

them. He found out about your mom a few weeks ago. He didn't know you were here with me."

"What does it have to do with him, anyway?" I wasn't trying to be snarky; I meant it. He hadn't been around for me ever. Him surfacing was like someone suddenly digging into the soil of my life and uprooting me, tipped on my side, exposed. Why now?

"He'll be in Japan for a business trip in a couple weeks," Diane said. "In Tokyo. He wants to see you, but I told him I don't think that's for the best."

I felt like my heart had crystalized. I thought I didn't care what happened to him, but I could feel the whisper of it circling through me. I did care. I wanted to know why I hadn't been worth staying around for.

It would be no good getting involved with him, that much I knew. He'd destroyed Mom's life; he'd destroy mine, too.

"Thanks," I said, my voice shaky. "I don't want to see him."

Diane nodded. "I thought so."

But part of me wanted to ask him why he had run off, and why he wanted back into my life now. And part of me wanted to cling to it, because with him, I wasn't an orphan anymore. I'd have a parent again. But that was too idealized. It wasn't going to be some kind of soppy reunion. It would be awkward and painful, and I had more than enough of that going on right now.

Diane rested a hand on my shoulder and attempted a smile. "I picked up some chestnut cakes from the *depaato* on the way home. Want to have one?"

"Yeah," I said, giving her a fake smile back. She nodded and hurried into the kitchen. I could hear the clink of plates and the fridge door opening, the little cardboard flaps on the cake box popping open. Food as a source of comfort—that was Diane's specialty. But after today, it sounded like the best idea ever.

I could bury the idea as soon as it had surfaced. I didn't need to think about my dad right now; I could forget about it, erase it like it had never happened. If only I'd stayed with Tomo a little longer tonight. I would never have known about my dad being in Japan.

It didn't matter, though. Steven could be in the same room as me, and it would feel like the farthest corner of the world, a wall of emptiness between us that couldn't be scaled.

I sat down at the table, smelling the sweet cream on the chestnut cake as Diane hurried around the kitchen.

She was all the family I needed now.

The water was black this time, oceans of ink lapping against the stained shore. There was no orange gateway, no rolling dunes of sand. Instead, the ink waters ebbed against an inlaid stone path that trailed upward, toward a towering jumble of angled rooftops reaching toward the sky. On the distant edge of the black ocean, the ink tipped over in a waterfall that encircled the whole island, the spray sending up a fog of clouds. Were we high up in the sky, or on some cliff? I'd have to wade deep into the waters to look, and I was scared the current would drag me over the edge.

I looked back at the building—some sort of pagoda, maybe, or a fortress like Sunpu but as tall as Himeji Castle, layer upon layer of slanted tile rooftops and whitewashed walls, placed upon one another like tiers of a fancy wedding cake. Simple wooden steps led into the building; there was nowhere else to go on this tiny island surrounded by ink.

I stepped forward, and saw the first victim.

He lay at my feet, nearly buried in the grasses that sprung up around him. He wore armor, like some kind of samurai, but his eyes were empty, staring at a future that wasn't there, his breastplate splashed with ink.

I opened my mouth to scream, but no sound escaped my lips. *A dream*, I thought. Another Kami nightmare.

I looked around the steps of the castle as I moved forward. Dozens of men lay slumped in horrible, lifeless heaps, ink soaking each of them as they lay beside their shattered weapons and snapped bowstrings. My feet moved toward the building against my own will. I didn't want to see what was inside. I didn't want to know what was responsible for this.

The stairs creaked as I went up them. Inside, the room was musty and dark, the only light shining from the windows near the raised platform at the end of the room, where great white curtains billowed out with a wind I couldn't feel. The bamboo tatami mats were cold and hard against my bare feet as I stepped forward. There were fallen soldiers here, too; what horrible battle had taken place?

Wait, that one's alive. I looked and saw him crouched in the corner, a dark shape hunched over his bended knee, a sword on the tatami beside him.

His silver earring glinted as he tilted his head forward, his blond highlights slipping from behind his ears.

"Jun," I said, and he looked up at me. He lifted the sword; it almost looked as though it was made of stone. It was a deep black, like the inside of a cave, and the blade of it dripped with a darkness that must be ink. Or blood.

"It's over now," said a woman's voice.

I turned to the raised platform in front of me, where the voice had come from. A woman knelt on the floor, the folds of her crimson kimono stretching in a pool of red around her. The sleeves of the kimono layered in a dozen different colors, all variations of black, red, gold and silver. An elaborate golden headdress rested on her head, the strings of golden beads tinkling against one another as she tilted her chin to the side.

"Okami Amaterasu," I said, stepping over a long smear of ink on the tatami. I glanced at the fallen soldiers in the throne room as I walked toward her. "Who did this?"

"You did," she said, and the world went cold with fear.

I shook my head. "I could never do something like this. And I only just got here."

"There is only death," she said. "There is no escape."

Tomo had said those words so many times. He heard them in his nightmares, too.

"No escape from what?" I said. "Fate as a Kami?"

Amaterasu smiled sadly. "No escape from the past." She twisted her knees to the side, the fabric of her red kimono swishing as she moved away slowly, and I saw one more body beside her.

"Tomo," I whispered. I wanted to throw up; I wanted to wake up. I pinched my arm, hard, to remind myself this wasn't real. *It's just a dream.* But there was no comfort from seeing him there, lifeless, drenched in ink.

"Tsukiyomi," she answered, and I saw then that his hair wasn't copper, but black. I'd thought it was ink staining his hair, but he looked different—older, more worn and...less human than he'd ever looked, an almost angelic beauty that left me feeling terrified. He looked like a trickster fairy, the kind that was too beautiful to trust.

He was, and wasn't, Tomo. I couldn't explain it, except that dreams are strange and never quite right.

"I don't understand," I said. Was this all meaningless nightmare stuff? Why was I seeing this?

"I loved Tsukiyomi," Amaterasu said. "And so I killed him."

Ikeda had mentioned the story to me before, that Amater-

asu and Tsukiyomi had once been lovers, before Tsukiyomi
lost his mind.

"I had to stop him, before he destroyed everything the August Ones had made."

"The August Ones?"

"And now he's dead. But he lives in the shards of his soul
that carry on." She motioned at the ground, and I saw shattered pieces of glass in every color.

"Like Tomo," I said.

"Taira no Kiyomori, Tokugawa Ieyasu, Yuu Tomohiro, all
of them magatama of one soul," she said.

I tilted my head. "Magatama?"

She motioned again to the broken glass. "Susanou shattered
it," she said. "Only the sword remains." I looked to Jun and
the stained sword at his side.

"Listen to me, child," Amaterasu said to me. "Green means
an eternal circle. You will betray Yuu Tomohiro, just as I have
betrayed Tsukiyomi."

The heat rose up in my cheeks. "I would never hurt him."

She leaned back, the golden beads jingling on her headdress.
"You will kill him, before the end."

My mind reeled. I wanted to retch. Kill him? Me?

I fell to my knees. "No," I said. "This is just a stupid dream.
I don't have to do what you tell me. We make our own fates."

"There is only one fate," she said.

I looked down, my clothes soaked in ink.

I woke to my own screaming, to the sound of Diane thump-
ing across the floor to hold me tightly in her arms.

"Why didn't you tell me sooner?" Tomo said, his eyes wide
and filled with concern. We were hiding inside one of the
Yayoi huts at Toro Iseki. His dad was asleep at home, after
stumbling in from overtime work sometime in the middle of

the night. Considering the whole separating-us-for-a-month business, this had seemed the best place to meet without anyone knowing.

"I didn't want to worry you," I said. "Anyway, I was pretty sure these were just typical nightmares. I mean, they don't mean anything, right?"

Tomo pulled me toward him, wrapping me in the warmth and smell of him as we held each other. "They don't," he said gently, his voice against my ear. "I've been fighting them my whole life. Don't listen to what they tell you. I never have." But that was only half-true. He fought against it, sure, but he believed it, didn't he? He believed he was a monster, that he only had a short time left, that in the end, there was only death.

I hadn't told him everything about the dreams. It sounded stupid, but I was scared that if I said it out loud, that Tomo had died, that it would come true. I didn't want to tell him Amaterasu had said I was the one who would betray him. Maybe she'd only meant the stupid mistake I'd made kissing Jun? But Tomo had forgiven me, and, anyway, Amaterasu's face had looked like the topic was a whole lot more serious than a kiss.

Instead, I'd told Tomo about the castle and the dead samurai, about Tsukiyomi dead beside Amaterasu. "What did she mean by the Magatama?" I said as Tomo and I sat on the packed dirt floor, our backs pressed against the wall of the straw hut. "What is that?"

"It's a curved jewel," Tomo said. He lifted his hand palm-up, and I could see the ribbons of scars peeking out from under his soft wristband. "I've seen it before in my nightmares, too. Like glass in my hand…" He closed his hand slowly, remembering. "It shatters, and the shards dig into my skin. *Kuse*, they burn like fire."

"It was broken in my dream, too," I said. "There were sharp pieces all over the floor."

"The Magatama is one of the Imperial Treasures," Tomo said. "But I don't get what it means. Maybe it doesn't mean anything. Maybe it's just *kami* memories, from when they ruled Japan."

"Imperial Treasures?" I wrapped my arms around my knees. "Like mythical, or real?"

"Real," he said. "Well, sort of. They're called the Sanshu no Jingi. They're real, but I don't know if the myths surrounding them are. There are three of them—the mirror, the sword and the jewel. I think they're kept in the palace in Tokyo. The mirror is linked to Amaterasu. Not sure about the sword and Magatama."

The large brass mirror, the one the paper Amaterasu had held in front of Jun in Nihondaira—it had revealed the truth about all of us, that we were tied to some kind of awful tragedy that kept repeating itself with the *kami's* descendants. Jun and Tomo would always be enemies, because Susanou and Tsukiyomi were. And Amaterasu and Tsukiyomi, in love until... until what, exactly?

I shivered in the morning cold. "What happened between Amaterasu and Tsukiyomi?"

Tomo pulled the top of his knit hat until it snapped off his head, his copper spikes flopping around his ears. I felt the warmth from the hat as he gently pressed it onto my head, smoothing it over my hair and pulling it down over my ears. "Better?" he said. I nodded, and he grinned. "I don't know what happened, Katie, but it doesn't matter. They aren't us. They're long gone."

"You're right," I said. "But we still have to deal with their drama." The mirror, the sword and the jewel. The sword...was it the one I had seen beside Jun? How did these treasures tie into all this? Were they really just fragments of *kami* memories?

Tomo took my hand in his and pulled me up from the ground. "We'll beat this," he said, his deep eyes searching mine. "You'll be just fine."

"So will you," I said, and he smiled, but I saw the sadness in his eyes, the disbelief. Amaterasu's threat echoed in my thoughts.

I will never hurt him again, I thought as I pulled him toward me, as I pressed my lips against his. *We will make our own future.*

I grabbed Yuki's arm right when the bell rang. "Yuki-chan, I need a favor." She looked at me, surprised.

"Everything okay?" she said.

I nodded. "I just… I was wondering if Niichan is still in town."

She raised an eyebrow, puzzled. Behind her, Tanaka started fake laughing, flipping his chair on top of his desk before walking over to us. "Hu-hu-hu," he said in an over-the-top voice that the drama club could probably hear from here. "Does Tomohiro have a rival?"

"Ew," Yuki said, smacking Tanaka in the arm. "My brother? He's, like, six years older than us."

"Maybe she's seen enough of Tomo-kun's immature side," Tanaka grinned slyly. "She wants an older man."

I flushed with awkwardness. *"Chigau yo,"* I stammered. "Not even close."

Yuki put a finger to her lips and blinked slowly, looking thoughtful. "He has a point, though. Boys our age are totally immature."

Tanaka's face drained of color. *"O…oi!* That's not…" His shoulders slumped and he headed toward the blackboard, grab-

bing a cloth and starting to clean. Poor guy. He'd been asking for it, though.

"Niichan's back in Miyajima," Yuki said, "but I can give
you his number. Everything all right?"

"I just wanted to ask him something about my history assignment," I lied. "He knows a lot about *kami* myths."

"Oh, yeah, he knows all that stuff. Here." She took out her
keitai and sent the number to me.

"Thanks."

She grinned. "No problem." I helped her push the desks out
of the way while our classmates mopped the floor, and then
I dashed to kendo practice. I'd call Niichan as soon as I had a
chance, I thought. He'd be able to help me understand how
the Imperial Treasures were caught up in this mess.

"*Oi*, Greene!" Ishikawa drawled from across the gym as I
opened the change room door. He wore his gray *hakama* skirt,
the *dou* chest plate already tied overtop. The colorful swirls of
his tattoo slipped from sight as he slid on his *kote* glove. "Still
taking kendo when Yuuto isn't here?"

I reached for his other *kote*, still on the floor, and smacked
his arm with it before passing it to him. "I don't take kendo
for Tomo, *baka*." Maybe at first I had, to spy on him, but the
sport of Japanese fencing had given me an outlet to deal with
my grief over losing Mom. I loved the way I felt when I held
the shinai, when the world was silent except for the shouts
of opponents and the shuffling of feet. There wasn't room to
think about anything else.

"You're tougher than I thought." Ishikawa grinned. A lick
of white hair pressed against his forehead, and he tucked it
under the cloth *tenugui* wrapped around his head. Our club's
headbands were stamped with the black kanji that made up
our motto: The Twofold Path of the Pen and the Sword.
The last time I'd looked at the motto, it had been covered in

Tomo's blood as he'd pressed the *tenugui* against a bite from the dragon he'd sketched. My stomach twisted at the memory of the blood in the rain, the limbs dropping from the dragon as it tried to lift into the sky.

"Greene," Ishikawa said, and I snapped out of it. "Man, you phase out a lot now. You okay?"

"Fine," I said. "Thanks for staying with Tomo the other night."

"You're all right, for a *kouhai*," Ishikawa said, ruffling my hair with a strong hand before getting into line for push-ups. "Juniors," he mumbled.

"Hey!" I called out, but he didn't look back. I grinned and dropped to the floor, ready to sweat and spar my troubles away, to escape just for an hour.

6

The dial tone sounded tinny and strange in my ear. I couldn't call Niichan long-distance on my *keitai*, so I was using the house phone. Diane wasn't home yet, but as long as I kept it short, she probably wouldn't mind me calling. I was allowed to call Nan and Gramps anytime—that was different, but still.

I punched in Niichan's number and waited, my thoughts drifting to his small place on Miyajima Island in Hiroshima. I remembered how Yuki and I had slept in his one-room apartment on the tatami floor, how we'd whispered and chatted in our soft futons while the ocean outside lapped against the beach. It had only been a few months ago, but it felt like ages.

The ringing sound cut out, and a woman's voice recited ultra-politely that the customer was unavailable. I left a short, awkward message, and then hung up. Guess my questions would have to wait.

I opened the lid of my laptop, putting it on the low table by my bed, and sat down on my *zabuton* cushion beside it. Might as well find out what I could about the Imperial Treasures.

It turned out they were just about as mysterious to the rest of Japan as they were to me. They were called the Sanshu no Jingi, the Three Sacred Treasures. Only the emperor and his close aides had ever seen them, and even then only for special occasions. No one was even sure what they looked like, or if the treasures kept by the royal family were the originals.

They had really long, fancy names. The Yata no Kagami, for one, was Amaterasu's mirror, the same one that had haunted Tomo's nightmares and sketches. The one I had seen for the first time in my dreams a few nights ago.

Tomo had been wrong about their location, too. Only the Yasakani no Magatama jewel was kept in the palace in Tokyo. The sword, Kusanagi no Tsurugi, was in Nagoya, about two hours west of Shizuoka by bullet train. They were thought to be replicas, but Amaterasu's mirror was supposedly the real one, and they kept it in a shrine in Ise, Mie Prefecture. I pulled up a map to see where Mie was. Southwest from here, past Nagoya and curved around a bay of water.

Outside the rain began to fall, tapping against the sliding door to our tiny balcony. I hoped Diane would be home soon, or at least that she wasn't caught out in this. It was getting heavier by the second.

The breath caught in my throat as I looked at the search page. The real mirror of Amaterasu. Was it really the real one? I knew the Kami were real—I knew the ink lived in me and in Tomo—but it was still a scary thing to think about, that someone as powerful as Amaterasu had really existed. The paper copy of the goddess, the one whose name I had written with Ikeda in the sketchbook, had already been strong enough to send both Tomo and Jun reeling in the sky. After learning they were descended from Susanou and Tsukiyomi, Tomo and Jun had grown ink wings and fought high above the trees. It was only with Ikeda's help that we'd summoned

Amaterasu's power to blast them apart and stop them from killing each other.

And that was only the Amaterasu that Tomo had drawn. What about the real one? For anyone to have that amount of power was terrifying. And like Ikeda and Niichan had told me, *kami* didn't play by our modern rules of morality. They had their own code entirely of what was right and wrong.

I shut down the search tab and reached for the lid of my laptop, but the news column on my home page made me hesitate. The kanji for death, 死, stared up at me from the headline. I clicked the article, my hand rising to my mouth.

Two more Yakuza found dead in Shizuoka. They showed old photos of them, smiling.

I knew that one. The Korean guy with the Mohawk who'd brought the bottle of green tea over when Hanchi was forcing Tomo to draw. His photo smiled back at me, completely unaware of what awaited him in his future.

I scrolled down the news article, much of it still illegible to me with my current kanji-reading abilities. The page showed a photo of the crime scene, a dark graffiti image painted across the rice paper door in the room where they'd died.

A black viper, tall as a person, with ink dripping down his painted fangs.

Oh god.

I grabbed my *keitai*, my thoughts whirling. I pressed it to my ear, listening to the ring as I held back tears.

His voice was steady, emotionless. "Katie."

"Jun, please," I said, holding the phone with shaking hands. "Please stop."

"I can't do that."

"You can. You have to." The rain swelled, beating against my window as the wind whipped the storm around.

"Katie, these aren't innocent people, you know. We've talked about this. The world is better off without them."

"That's what courts are for," I said, the tears streaming down my face. "I should call the police."

His voice softened, warmth seeping in. "They won't believe you."

"That's why I'm asking you to stop. Please."

A pause. "It's not in my hands anymore."

"I don't get it." And then it dawned on me. His followers. "Wait...is your Kami cult helping you?"

"Katie, I..."

The rain pummeled my window as I jumped to my feet. "I thought you said most of them weren't strong enough for their sketches to lift off the page!"

"They're not, but...when Amaterasu showed me the mirror, the truth about who I really was, I felt the shift. I felt the power of Susanou awaken in me. It's affecting them, too. They grow stronger being near me, the way Yuu and I were affected by you."

Ishikawa was right. It was war, and Jun had his own army. Could you fight death sketched on a page? How do you catch the murderer? How do you protect the victim? My mind raced.

Jun's voice turned gentle and patient. "Katie, the Kami are rising. It's a new world now, and we don't need these scum polluting it. Listen...almost every religion in the world talks of a final judgment, right?" He laughed, the sound of it jarring in my ears. How the hell could he laugh at a time like this? "I'm the heir of Susanou. This is my fate. It's always been my fate." I collapsed onto my bed, the rain outside nearly overcoming the sound of Jun's voice. "I'm the heir to the ruler of Yomi, the World of Darkness. The Judge. I will fulfill my purpose until the end."

"Not like this," I pleaded. "That can't be what it means. You don't have to do this. You can choose your own fate."

His calm voice cracked open, his voice tinged with panic. "It's not like I want to do this, okay? Sometimes you have to do things you don't want to do."

This was the real Jun, now. This was the guy who'd rescued me in Oguro, the one who'd asked me out for coffee. But then I realized, fear creeping up my spine—the other side of him was just as real, wasn't it? They were both him.

"But Tomo is fighting his fate."

"Tomo is the descendent of Tsukiyomi. Don't you get it? Tsukiyomi lost his mind and murdered the other *kami*. What do you think is going to happen with Yuu?" My heart froze; I collapsed onto my knees, the hard tatami pressing lines into my skin. Murdered the *kami*? Is that what had happened to Tsukiyomi? Is that what would happen to Tomo? "It can't go on forever like this. You always knew it would end. He's a monster that should never have existed. A monster who wished to be human. *Sore dake.* That's all."

I clutched the phone as the rain poured. Everything was changing. Everything was ending.

There is only death.

I took a deep breath. "You're a monster, too, Jun."

"*Gomen,*" Jun said, his voice a whisper lost in the rain. "I'm sorry it has to be this way." And then he was gone, and there was nothing but the sound of the rain washing away the only world I'd ever known.

7

I woke to the sound of my *keitai* buzzing beside my laptop. I blinked, trying to orient myself in the dark room. Had Diane come home? I hadn't heard her. The rain was quiet now; the storm must have stopped. The phone screen was too bright to look at with my tired eyes, so I lifted it to my ear as I stretched out my legs.

"Hello?"

"Katie-chan?" It was Niichan, Yuki's brother. I realized my mistake then, that I'd answered the phone in English.

"Oh, hi," I said, switching to Japanese.

"Sorry, is it too late to call? I think I woke you."

"No, no," I mumbled, rubbing my eyes. "I was in the bath." I stopped midrub. That was more embarrassing. "I mean, um, the rain is really something, huh?" Bath was *furo*, and the verb for raining was *furu*. Maybe I'd get away with it.

Niichan sounded like his face was bright red. "Uh, I…don't know," he said. "It's not raining in Miyajima."

"Right," I said, squeezing my eyes closed.

"Is everything okay? I was worried about calling so late, but you sounded nervous on your message."

I shook my head and flicked on my bedside light so I wouldn't crash into anything as I talked. "I need to talk to you about the *kami*," I said. "Things are out of control, Ni-ichan, and I don't know how to stop them."

"You didn't stay away from him, huh?"

"It's more complicated now," I said, sliding my door open and stumbling into the hallway. I was relieved to see Diane's shoes in the *genkan*. She must have figured I'd gone to bed and so she hadn't woken me. "There's a rogue Kami out there and he's trying to take over the world."

Niichan hesitated. "Are you joking?"

"I wish," I said. "I need to know how to make the ink go dormant, Niichan. For Tomo's sake, so he doesn't...lose himself. And I have to make this guy Takahashi Jun's power go away, too, or he's going to destroy everything."

"Wait, wait. Takahashi Jun, the kendo champ? He's a Kami? Katie, tell me everything."

I grabbed a mug and held it under our hot water dispenser as I filled in Niichan on the details. "Jun told me there are two kinds of Kami, right? Imperial ones, descended from Amater-asu. That's the royal line, all the emperors and stuff. But there were also Kami in the samurai families, and they showed up through a bunch of different ways. Marriages, affairs, even different *kami* ancestors than Amaterasu."

"Right," Niichan said. "You said to me that day you were scared Yuu was descended from Susanou."

"I was wrong," I said, dipping a *genmai* tea bag into the hot water, smoothing the little string attached over the ceramic lip. The side of the mug burned my finger and I pulled away, the string slipping into the cup. "It was Jun—Takahashi—that got his ink bloodline from Susanou. Tomo is descended from Amaterasu on his dad's side, and Tsukiyomi on his mother's."

Niichan was silent for a moment, and then he let out a shaky breath. *"Maji de,"* he said. "That's impossible."

"It's true," I said. "And I need a way for the power to go dormant. There's got to be a way, Niichan."

"Maybe, but I… I'm sorry, Katie. I don't know."

My heart sank. I curled my fingers around the handle of the mug. "Not even any ideas?"

"No pleasant ones," he said. His list was probably about the same as mine. 1) Leave Japan. 2) Die.

"Well…can you at least tell me more about Tsukiyomi?" I said. "Jun said he went crazy and murdered *kami.* Is that true?"

"They're myths, Katie. How do we know what's true? And remember what I told you about judgment calls—times have changed. You can't judge what the *kami* did by the way society works now."

"I know," I said. "I just need to know what happened. Maybe there's some detail that can help us, Niichan. Please."

"Ee to," he said, deep in thought. I could hear a sound across the phone, like a pencil tapping against a chair. "Well, Amaterasu, Tsukiyomi and Susanou were all created at the same time by the August Ones."

August Ones. Where had I heard that before? The vision of the dead samurai snapped back into my memory. Amaterasu had mentioned them. *I had to stop him, before he destroyed everything the August Ones had made.* What had she meant? "Who are the August Ones?"

"The first *kami,* Izanagi and Izanami. They created Japan, and then they gave birth to all the other *kami.* Well, a lot of them. The three you mentioned were created by Izanagi."

"So Tsukiyomi was going to destroy Japan?"

"Destroy Japan?" Niichan's surprise reminded me I hadn't

told him about the nightmare. "I don't think that's in the legends."

"Then what happened?"

"Let me think. It's been a while since I studied it. So Amaterasu and Susanou fought, that I remember. She hid in a cave—solar eclipse, *ne*? And they tricked her back out again. They threw a big party and fooled her into glancing at herself in a mirror to draw her out, and they hung the Magatama jewel in a tree to tempt her out, too."

The Imperial Treasures. That was two of them linked to Amaterasu and Susanou. But it didn't make any sense. How could the treasures be involved? "What about the Kusanagi?"

"The sword? It belonged to Susanou." That made sense. Jun had always had the sword beside him in my nightmares.

I remembered Tomo in the nightmare, unconscious, dripping in dark ink. Jun's head bowed, his apology.

Oh god. What if that hadn't been ink spilling from Tomo's wounds?

I was an idiot. A complete idiot. But it was just a dream. I couldn't let Jun hurt him.

"How does Tsukiyomi fit in? He was Amaterasu's lover, right?" I yanked the cutlery drawer open and dug for a spoon; my tea was already way too strong, but I dipped the spoon into the mug to chase down the tea bag, anyway.

"At first. But then he killed another *kami*. Amaterasu banished him from the heavens. That's why the sun and moon are separated, right? Night and day. It's just a creation myth, Katie."

But the Amaterasu I'd met hadn't banished him. She'd killed him. Why? "She didn't...hurt him?"

"I don't think so. She had a lot more trouble with Susanou, but she was a gentle ruler. She's always been considered benevolent, a protector of Japan."

"She gave the first emperor the Imperial Treasures," I said. "I looked it up."

"Yeah," Niichan said. "They each represented a trait she wanted him to rule with. The mirror is honesty, the sword is bravery and the jewel is love. She gave them to Jimmu, her descendent, and I guess one of the first humans to have the powers of the *kami.*"

Emperor Jimmu. I tried to picture him, an ancient figure who was half myth himself. What had he thought when his ink kanji had started to move on their scrolls? Or had Amaterasu explained to him how to control it? Was that knowledge somehow lost over time like Jun had said?

"I'm sorry I can't help more," Niichan said. "I don't know enough about how this all ties in."

"It's okay," I said. "I'm really glad you called me back, Niichan. You've helped, really." At least I understood the stories a little better. The Imperial Treasures had been handed down through the line of Kami. They had to be linked. If only one of them had been a paintbrush or something. That would've made a lot more sense as a starting point.

"Katie? Be careful, okay? For your sake and Yuki's, too. There have been powerful Kami in Japan's history, and they always changed the landscape. I don't know what Takahashi is up to, but stay back. At the kind of power level you're suggesting, the ink is uncontrollable. He may just burn himself out."

I took a sip of my tea; it had gone cold as we'd talked. "I hope so."

But somehow, I didn't think it would be that easy.

8

Yuki and I sat with our backs straight and our knees folded underneath us, our hands barely touching the tatami of the school's traditional room. It was our weekly Tea Ceremony Club meeting, and we sat in a row along the wall while Yuki's friend Ayako whirred the bamboo whisk through the milky green tea.

It was getting harder to go through the motions of everyday life when I felt like the world hung in the balance. Diane had passed me the newspaper that morning to practice reading my kanji, and I'd pushed it away, too frightened to see another headline about dead Yakuza. It was almost impossible not to hear about it, since it was the most sensational thing that had happened in Shizuoka City in a long time. Theories abounded among my classmates before homeroom had started; what did the ink snake mean? Was it a rival gang, or a Yakuza civil war?

I wondered if Jun would reveal himself or his motive at some point. What was the point of a revolution if no one knew it was happening?

Ayako shuffled toward me and placed a *chawan* of matcha tea on the tatami in front of me. I bowed gently, my face to the floor. *"O temae choudai itashimasu,"* I recited from memory, reaching for the teacup and placing it on my palm to admire the cherry blossoms drifting around its ceramic surface.

I thought of Tomo in Sunpu Park, the cherry blossoms swirling around him.

The tea was always more bitter than it looked. The taste of it surprised me every time.

"So?" Yuki whispered next to me. I looked at her with warning—we weren't supposed to talk while receiving tea— but she looked straight ahead, as if she hadn't spoken. Ayako was serving the next girl in line, and the teacher hadn't seemed to notice us talking.

"So what?" I whispered back, tilting the *chawan* toward my mouth to take another sip.

"Did you and Tomohiro do it yet?"

I choked on the tea, coughing and sputtering as I clunked the cup down on the floor. Ayako looked over with wide eyes, and the teacher shook her head disapprovingly. Yuki pulled out her hand towel and passed it to me. I wiped up the tea spatter on my chin.

"I'll take that as a no," Yuki said. "What's taking you so long?"

I could feel the heat as it spread across my face. I guess saving the world had taken priority over other thoughts, for once. *I see you finally have your priorities straight, Greene. Better late than never.* "I'm just... I'm not ready yet."

Yuki frowned, reaching for her *kuromoji,* a tiny bamboo stick she used to carve a bite off of the pink bean cake in front of her. "You're thinking about it too much. You're not in America anymore, Katie. It's not such a big deal here. Just go for it."

The heat spread down my neck. I was in Japan, yeah, but I was still myself.

"You like him, right?"

I stared at her like she was from another planet. "Yeah."

"Then just do it already."

"You say it like it's such a casual thing," I said. I lifted the *chawan* up to my lips so I could hide behind it. The other girls had to have heard her. Whispering or not, there's no way they wouldn't hear her.

"Yeah, but you two make a cute couple," she said. "Tan-kun tells me Tomohiro's a good guy. So what's to think about?"

"I don't know," I said, spearing a piece of my pink flower cake with the *kuromoji*. It wasn't really the thought of it that was tripping me up. It was the way Yuki could talk about it like it was no big deal. To me, it felt like something that should live in the quiet shadows of conversations with Tomo, not in a sunlit tea ceremony room at school surrounded by other students.

Of course I'd thought about it, but I didn't trust my own judgment. My heart and my mind couldn't agree. What did I really want? Would I regret it? Would I regret not doing it? What exactly was I waiting for, and why? It was so hard to know what was true when I was already drowning in an ocean of ink, when the waves were already thrashing us against a nightmare shore.

"The first time's the hardest," she said. "After that, it's easy. Anyway, I'm sure Tomohiro's done it before. Lots."

"Oh my god. Do you listen to the words that come out of your mouth?"

"What?" Yuki said. The teacher glared at us and we looked straight forward, not speaking for a minute. Then Yuki added in a whisper, "He's a Third Year."

"Yuki!" The last thing I wanted to picture was Tomo with

another girl. It was embarrassing enough to think about him with me. Had he really done it before? Had he done it with Myu? Great, so if we did go through with it, he'd be all experienced and I would completely humiliate myself. Anyway, the fact that I couldn't even think about it without choking on my tea just reinforced that I wasn't ready, right? It was easy to put off the idea back in New York, when the dates I'd gone on hadn't been serious, when nothing had sparked for me. But Tomo was made of sparks and embers, every touch of his skin against mine burning away thought and reason, lighting the darkness with stars.

No, I knew how hard it was to stop with Tomo—how hard it was to think straight when he was all warmth and softness and sound. God, that sound he made in his throat when we kissed. And the tickle of his spiked hair on my neck. Being with him always felt right. Maybe Yuki was right. I was overthinking it.

Yuki leaned toward me, her shoulder bumping mine. "You're imagining it right now, aren't you?"

"Stop." I giggled, shoving her with my shoulder. She pressed her lips in a tight line as Ayako shuffled in front of us to receive our teacups. She eyed us suspiciously as we shook with the effort not to laugh. The *chawan* rocked on my palm a little as Ayako took the cup from me, and then from Yuki. The minute she turned her back, we burst into laughter.

Under the glare of the teacher, Yuki and I helped collect the *washi* papers, oily from the imprints of the flower-shaped bean cakes. "Do you think Tan-kun's done it before?" Yuki asked.

"Ew," I blurted out. She raised an eyebrow. "It's not that *he's* gross," I clarified, tossing the *washi* in the garbage bin. "It's just that I don't want to think about my friend like *that*."

"Well," Yuki said, "I don't mind if he hasn't."

I turned to look at her; her cheeks looked a little pink, but not much. I admired how she could talk about all this without getting as flustered as I did.

"Yuki, are you and Tanaka going to…?"

"Probably not in this lifetime." She sighed. "He has yet to ask *me* out on a real date."

We walked down the hallway together. She and Tan-kun had always been a unit, although when I thought about it, I'd never asked her to clarify exactly what that unit was. Best friends? Couple? Unrequited love? No, that couldn't be it. Yuki was awesome, and Tanaka spent all his time with her. He had to feel the same, so why hadn't he made a move?

"Love is way too complicated," Yuki said.

That was the truth.

Yuki slid open the door to the *genkan* and jumped down all three steps in one go. "*Ne*, did you fill out your Future Plan assignment yet?"

I followed her over to our cubbies; they were on opposite sides of the aisle, but close enough that we could still chat while changing shoes. "Not yet," I said, holding the wall to keep from falling over as I slid the slipper off. "I don't even know where to start." It was an assessment they did with all First Year students at Suntaba. They wanted to make sure you stayed focused on an end goal, that you thought about where you were headed after high school. So much of our time was focused on entrance exams that you needed to have a plan early so you could have enough time to prepare.

"You don't know what you want to do?" Yuki said, blinking at me.

There was so much to face in my life right now that I couldn't think so far ahead. "Well, I'd always thought about journalism. My mom did that."

"Hey, you could be the first blonde reporter on NHK

News!" Yuki giggled. "Or maybe you can play the token blonde extra in every café scene in the dramas."

"There isn't always a token blonde," I said, tapping my toes against the floor to hammer on my black loafers.

"Well, the airport scenes, then. Or if they do a scene where the main characters travel abroad. I saw this one that was supposed to be set in France, but I could tell it was Tokyo."

I shook my head. "I don't really want to write 'Professional Token Blonde' on my Future Plan assignment."

Yuki smiled again. She always seemed so cheerful, so full of energy. I smiled back; I couldn't remember ever having such a best friend in Albany. I'd had some close friends, but they hadn't stuck by me when I was depressed after Mom died. I didn't blame them, of course—they had their own stuff to deal with, and I couldn't pull myself out of my despair—but one of the things I loved about Yuki was how she just accepted me as I was. Who I was and how I was feeling was always okay with her.

"I put down 'Fashion Designer,'" Yuki said. "I really want to own my own shop and work on my designs at night, when the store closes."

"Fashion?" I said. Yuki had told me before, but I hadn't really mulled it over as a viable option. "Can you go to university for that?"

"Sure you can. One university in Osaka even has a specialization in textiles."

Osaka. The name hit me with more finality than I could have imagined. This life I was living would change so dramatically in two years. Everyone would go their own direction, and I'd have to start all over again. And Tomo? Where would he be, even next year? He'd pass his entrance exams, and would he go to Osaka, too, or to Tokyo? Wherever he went, he'd leave me behind.

Too far ahead, I reminded myself. Right now I just had to make sure he wouldn't get hurt. After Tsukiyomi was put to sleep forever, then I could worry about long-distance relationships and where my future was headed.

We stepped into the courtyard, and he was there, suddenly, like a dream. He wasn't supposed to be at school for a month, and yet he leaned against the school wall near the gate, his copper hair pressed in spikes against the cool stone, his arms folded and his head bowed. He stood out from the rest of us, not dressed in his school uniform but instead in black jeans and a deep crimson coat. The memory of the nightmare flashed back to me, the dark black liquid pooling on Tomo's skin. I shook the thought away. He was here, and alive. It was just a stupid dream.

"Tomo," I said quietly, and Yuki looked over.

She frowned. "He'll get in trouble if he's seen. He's not supposed to be on school grounds for a month."

I walked toward him, Yuki trailing behind me while cautiously peeking for teachers. A stray maple leaf fell from the *momiji* tree in the courtyard, spiraling on the wind as it floated toward Tomo and smacked into the stone wall at his feet.

"Tomo," I said as I reached him, and he looked up, his arms still folded.

"*O,*" he said, a casual Japanese hello.

"*O?*" I repeated. "All you can say is '*O*'? You'll get in trouble if the teachers notice you." I grabbed his arm to pull him through the nearby gate, but he didn't budge.

"Yuuto!" Ishikawa shouted across the courtyard, and Yuki turned to shush him. He shrugged, his green coat pressed up against his mop of white hair. He leaned his shoulder against the wall beside his friend. "Did you come to flaunt your suspension at us? Strike a little fear into our hearts?"

Tomo didn't say anything, but he smirked. He was putting on his school act again, I could see that. Ishikawa had hit on the reason right away. He probably knew Tomo better than anyone.

"Yuu Tomohiro!" The voice startled me, and the smirks slid off Tomo's and Ishikawa's faces. Yuki and I turned to see Headmaster Yoshinoma across the courtyard, a hand on the still-open door to the school. He stuck his jaw out, his face filled with resolve. He was trying to look dignified, like he had authority, but he just looked super angry to me. He let go of the door and walked briskly toward us.

This couldn't be good.

"Tomo, go," I urged, pulling on his arm again. "Quick." He didn't move, his eyes meeting Yoshinoma's.

"You are not allowed on school grounds," the headmaster barked.

I looked at Tomo pleadingly. He pressed his heel against the stone wall, pushing himself upright from the slouch, rising to his full height. Relief flooded the pit of my stomach. I don't know what dumb scheme he'd been up to, but he was going to leave now.

But Tomo didn't turn toward the gate. He leaned forward until he collapsed into me, wrapping his arms around me and pressing his lips against mine.

I froze, shocked, his grip holding me tightly to him. Yuki gasped—public displays like this weren't the norm here, and Tomo hadn't even been one to hold my hand on the way to class. I could only see Yoshinoma out of the corner of my eye. The headmaster turned a deep red, the veins in his forehead looking like they would pop.

How was this even happening? This was the worst decision ever. I wasn't sure what Tomo was trying to prove, but he was only going to earn himself more suspension time. But there was something in his eyes, something that pleaded with me to let him do this. What was he thinking?

I pulled back just as Yoshinoma began to shout. "*Yamenasai!* Stop it right now!"

Tomo narrowed his eyes like he was ready for a fight.

"Tomo, what are you doing?" Was he a total idiot? He had to know he'd get in more trouble for this.

Tomo stepped toward the headmaster; he was slightly taller than the man, and leaner from his kendo training. Yoshinoma wasn't all that old or heavy, but compared to Tomo, he looked insignificant, already defeated.

The headmaster wagged his finger in Tomo's face. "Do you want another month's suspension, Yuu? This is absolutely unacceptable!"

Tomo looked straight at him, unmoved. "Kouchou, being accused of something I didn't do is what's unacceptable. I didn't write those kanji on the blackboards. I didn't spill ink in the change room. It wasn't me."

I frowned. Technically it was him, though, wasn't it? Tomo's abilities to control the ink had spun out of control. We were responsible, but we hadn't meant for it to happen. Tomo hadn't done it as a prank; it was an accident, and punishment was unjust.

"You think I don't know the style of your calligraphy, Yuu? If you didn't do it, name one student in this school who could have painted kanji like that."

Tomo's face flushed red, his hands curling into fists.

"Get off school grounds, and use this time to prepare for your entrance exams, and to think properly about your actions." He pointed at me, the severity of the action knocking me back a step. "And no more displays like this. You've only proven to me how childish you're being. Put some distance between the two of you. You can't fight your way out of this one, not with me. It's time you start taking responsibility."

"You can't bully students into doing what you want," Tomo snapped. Yuki looked like she was ready to pass out; only Ishikawa had an amused smirk on his face.

Yoshinoma looked confused, like he couldn't believe what he'd heard. "What?"

"You can't stop us," Tomo said, reaching for my hand. "A month isn't going to change what we are. She's not distracting me. For the first time in my life I know exactly where I want to go, and who I want to be." He took a slow breath, his fists trembling, just a little. "I know what's important to me. And I'm not going to let you change that." He lowered his voice, his eyes cast down to the courtyard. "It's my choice."

Tomo. I wanted to reach out to him, but I didn't want to make things worse.

The headmaster sighed again, rubbing the bridge of his nose with his thumb and index finger. "I'm not trying to change anything," he said. "Only giving you time to calm down. So go home. And calm down. Stop setting a bad example for your *kouhai*."

Tomo flinched, his eyes meeting Yoshinoma's. Because no matter how hard he tried to be badass without a care in the world, it wasn't who he really was. He cared a lot. Too much.

He stepped back, lowering his eyes to the courtyard, walking slowly through the gate and disappearing onto the street.

"Insolent," Yoshinoma muttered, and turned on his heel toward the school. The students in the courtyard let out an audible breath as the *genkan* door swung shut.

"*Kuse*, what the hell got into him?" Ishikawa said. "He used to like skulking in the shadows at school. Now he's the fucking center of attention all the time."

I ran through the gate and alongside the school wall. Tomo

had his hands shoved deep in his coat pockets, his eyes cast to the ground. I stopped in front of him and he looked up, his eyes searching mine from under the fan of his copper bangs. "Care to tell me what the hell that was about?"

He reached slowly for the sleeve of his coat, lifting the shirt underneath with it as he scrunched it up his arm.

I gasped.

The hundreds of old scars that trailed up his skin—they had torn open, bleeding trails of black ink that dripped and crisscrossed as they made their way down.

"What...?" I pressed my fingers against one of the welts. It was warm to the touch, the ink slippery on my fingertips. I looked at the ground around him and saw the tiny droplets of black, like darkened stars on the pavement, pinprick constellations that foretold his doomed fate.

"I don't have much time left to be me," Tomo said. "So I want to spend it doing the right thing." He shoved the sleeve down, the ink dripping to the pavement in tiny beads that splattered with puffs of golden dust. "I want to be with you. I don't want to hide anymore. And I don't want to be in trouble for things I didn't do."

"I get it," I said, "but you can't fight Tsukiyomi from the detention hall."

"Katie, do you know where I woke up this morning? Here's a hint—not my own house."

The wind held a sharp bite, and I buttoned my coat around me. "You're sleepwalking again?"

He nodded. "This time to Toro Iseki. By the museum and the rice field they've planted, the one with the black rice." He opened his right palm again, and now I saw the faint red marks all over his skin. "There was a Magatama jewel in the water. It shattered in my hand before I woke."

The museum had a ton of magatama-shaped jewels found at

the site, but I knew the jewel Tomo meant. The one I'd seen in my nightmares. The Yasakani no Magatama, the one that had tricked Amaterasu out of the cave in the eclipse myth.

"Do you want to get a drink or something?"

He shook his head, but I gently took his wounded hand in mine. "We should at least get out of here before any more students peek around the edge of the gate." He attempted a smile, and I pulled him forward, leaving behind the galaxy of ink droplets. Hopefully no one else would notice them or figure out what they were.

"The Magatama has to mean something," I said. "Tomo, I talked to Yuki's brother last night, about the Imperial Treasures."

I saw the anxious look on Tomo's face. "It's too dangerous to get anyone else involved."

"I just asked about mythology stuff," I reassured him. "Anyway, who cares who knows now? We need help. Amaterasu gave the treasures to the first emperor, Jimmu. Each had a meaning attached to it. The mirror's was honesty. And we saw how her mirror showed Jun his true lineage and power, right? It's connected to the ink."

"Probably," he said. "The imperial family are directly descended from Amaterasu. There's no reason to doubt she gave Jimmu the treasures herself, one Kami to another."

"Right. So, the Magatama's meaning is love."

Tomo stopped walking, and tilted his head at me. "But it's always shattered. That's not a good sign, Katie."

My enthusiasm plummeted like the wagtail he'd drawn that day long ago. Of course it wasn't a good sign. The jewel shattered; love smashed into pieces. It could mean we'd be torn apart, or it could mean...

You know what it means, a voice whispered in my head. *There is no escape from fate. You will betray him.*

"She wasn't giving him treasures," Tomo said. "She was weighing him down with his fate. Ever since the first Kami, we've been doomed."

I walked in silence, completely deflated. So much for my brilliant idea.

Tomo must have felt guilty, because he asked gently, "What does the sword stand for?"

"Bravery," I said.

"That one I like. I need bravery now."

I pressed my fingers against his elbow. "You are brave, Tomo." He needed to believe me. Navigating the world with such a dark secret, always fighting against it to be a better person—wasn't that the definition of *brave*? "Heck, even your last name comes from the kanji for courage."

He paused, like he hadn't considered that. *"Sou ka?"* he mused. "Yeah, *isami*. Courage. And it's the first kanji in *yuuki*, bravery. I didn't know you'd noticed." Kanji had multiple readings depending on what other kanji they were paired with, but every word I'd ever seen that included *"yuu"* had a similar meaning—bravery; courage; valor.

"So you have courage," I said, squeezing his arm with my fingers.

"This courage thing is overrated, then." His voice dropped to a whisper. "Why am I bleeding ink?"

I hesitated. "Do you need to see a doctor?"

"You know I don't have that option."

"Okay," I said. "Then same plan as always. Stop Tsuki-yomi from poisoning your bloodstream. Talk about uninvited guests." I looked down the unfamiliar road ahead of us. "Wait, where are we going, anyway? We should've turned back there for Otamachi."

"I don't suppose you want to be an uninvited guest yourself?" Tomo ran a hand through his hair, and then pulled his phone out to show me a text. "Shiori had the baby."

My jaw dropped. "Today?"

"Last night," he said. "After what she did, I didn't want to go, but...bleeding ink made me think about a lot of things. She's the little sister I never had, and I promised my mom I'd take care of her. I can't leave her alone, no matter how I feel about her."

I paused. Shiori had tried to blackmail me and take Tomo for herself. She'd said I wasn't good enough for him, that I didn't know how to be a girlfriend to a Japanese guy. She'd taken and emailed to Tomo a video of me kissing Jun, for god's sake. She was kind of crazy.

But I couldn't entirely blame her. She hadn't forced me to kiss Jun—that was my own stupid lapse in judgment. And I had sort of swooped in and taken Tomo from her, even if I hadn't meant to. When I thought about the vicious bullying she'd endured, that in the middle of it I had separated her from her only friend, one she cared for on a deeper level...well, no wonder she'd felt desperate. I would've, too.

I took a deep breath. "Do you think she'd be mad if I come, too?"

Tomo grinned. "I need you, Katie," he said, his fingers tucking my hair behind my ear. "You make me brave."

"Likewise."

9

We sat in the stiff, uncomfortable chairs as we waited for the nurse to return. Tomo kept lifting his sleeve to sneak glances at the condition of his arm.

"You should get it looked at," I whispered. "We're here, anyway."

"I already told you I can't," he said. "Bleeding ink? They won't know what to do with that."

I frowned. "I know, but the skin looks so inflamed. It can't be a good thing. At least it's stopped dripping." I ran my finger along the wound. The ink stuck to my fingers, but it didn't drip off his arm.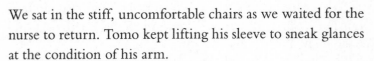

The automatic doors in front of us slid open and the nurse reappeared. Tomo rose to his feet.

The nurse's voice was quiet and gentle, her hands clutching a clipboard. "I'm so sorry, but there have been complications with delivery. At the moment, she can't have any guests outside of family."

"Complications?" Tomo said, his eyes wide. Oh god. Was Shiori okay? Was...was the baby okay?

"Not to worry," the nurse said quickly with a forced smile. "Both she and the baby are all right, but it's better for only family to go right now."

"He is family," said a voice, and I turned to see an older woman standing there, her hair pulled into a messy bun and a soft pink scarf wrapped around her beige coat.

"Yamada-san," Tomo said to the woman. *Oh,* I thought. Shiori's mother. It wasn't hard to tell, really. They had the same eyes, and who else could it be, anyway, here at the hospital?

"Tomohiro," she said, pulling him into her embrace. I felt out of place as I watched them. Why had I agreed to come, again? But I put on a big smile when Shiori's mother turned to look at me.

"My girlfriend, Katie," Tomo said, and Shiori's mom held out her hand as she bowed forward slightly. I took it and bobbed my head at her.

"Oh," she said, an unsure smile on her face. "How nice. I didn't realize you had a girlfriend, Tomohiro."

"Nice to meet you," I mumbled, feeling so awkward. The look on her face made it obvious she'd been hoping for a spark between Tomo and Shiori.

"Shiori will be so glad you've come to see her," Yamada said. She looked at the nurse, who stepped back and motioned at the doors. We followed Yamada through the Plexiglas entrance into a maze of white hallways.

"Is she okay?" Tomo asked. "The nurse said..."

"She's all right," Yamada said, leading us through the labyrinth. The corridors smelled like cleaning chemicals, strong and unnatural, and the beeping of machines sounded over one another as we walked through. "But the baby is in a bit more trouble." That's where I lost the conversation, the terms getting too specialized for me to understand in Japanese. I assumed the baby was in some kind of intensive care unit or something. The mom didn't sound too worried, so probably it wasn't anything life-threatening. I hated being left in the dark, though. Another channel of Japanese life I couldn't navigate. What if I fell off Diane's bike one day and broke a rib? I wouldn't even be able to explain myself to a doctor, or understand her questions.

We stopped outside a door and Yamada slid it open.

"Shiori-chan, look who's here." She smiled, and Tomo stepped in.

I stood at the edge of the door, uncertain what to do. The room was bathed in afternoon light, the bedsheets almost glowing from the sun-filled windows beside them. Shiori sat up in her white nightgown, which shone just as brightly. She looked angelic somehow, peaceful. Her black hair curled around her shoulders in tangles. I didn't see the baby anywhere, though.

"Tomo-kun," Shiori said. Her eyes widened and her knuckles clutched the sheets.

"How are you feeling?" he said, but I could see the tears welling up in the corners of her eyes. She'd texted him, but I could see the uncertainty on her face if he would come, the relief that he had.

"Go ahead," Shiori's mom said close to my ear, and the words prodded me forward. Shiori noticed me, her cheeks flushing. Was she irritated or embarrassed? Maybe she just felt awkward like me.

"Hi," I said. "I… I just wanted to wish you, um, congratulations."

"Thank you," Shiori said, nodding her head at me just enough that I could catch the movement.

"Your mom didn't tell me," Tomo said. "Girl or boy?"

Shiori's anxiety melted away then, a bright smile overcoming her face. "A girl," she said. "She's beautiful, Tomo-kun."

Tomo grinned and reached a hand to ruffle Shiori's hair. "You did it, huh? Good job." She beamed from the attention.

"Can we meet her?" I asked.

The smile fell from Shiori's face, but it was her mother who spoke up. "Ah, right now it isn't possible. She has *haiketsushou*."

The smile froze on my face. I had no idea what that meant.

"She needs extra care for a while," Tomo said. "But it will give you time to rest up, *ne*, Shiori-mama?" He said it so tenderly, with a cheerfulness that lit up Shiori's face. I loved him more than ever then, seeing his kindness. The boy that had challenged the headmaster melted away. This was the boy I loved.

Monsters can smile, too. And this is the monster who longed to be human.

The words hovered in my thoughts, Jun's words from before weaving through them. *This is the monster who wished to be a man.* I tried to shake the voice away, but it unfurled in my mind, taking over my thoughts. The room started to spin; I felt so hot, too hot.

I dropped to my knees. I could hear Tomo calling out, could feel him as he pulled me up from the floor into his arms, but it was hazy. The dream was clearer than the reality. The voices took over everything I could imagine.

Mukashi, mukashi, they whispered, the traditional opening to a Japanese fairy tale. *Once upon a time, long ago, there was a monster who longed to be a man. And so he took the form of a man, but his mind stayed that of a demon. And one day the demon broke free and gobbled the man up. He cracked open the world and consumed it whole. This was not enough to sate his hunger, so he spat it up again and lured it back. He is still hungry, always, always.*

"Katie!"

I blinked slowly, the vision of the room becoming clearer. Shiori's mouth was open in a delicate O, while her mother helped Tomo lift me from the ground to a chair by the bed.

"I'm so sorry," I said. "I...I must have fainted."

"It's warm in here," Shiori said, and I didn't know why she was covering for me, but I was grateful. "Okaasan, could you get her some water?"

"Of course," her mom said, stepping toward a sink in the corner of the room.

"You're okay now," Tomo said, but he looked different to me somehow, like I could see the horns and wings on him that weren't there, the trails of ink dripping down his hidden scars, the shards of the Magatama piercing the palms of his hands. "Your eyes," he whispered as a warning, but I already knew it. The ink had taken me over. And that didn't scare me half as much as he did right now, in his gentleness.

For the first time, I could see the ancient hunger in his eyes.

10

I tapped my fingers on the small purple couch in our living room. I had my legs curled up tight against me, the TV blaring the latest drama, something about a doctor who had a terminal illness but didn't want to tell anyone. Not exactly uplifting to my mood, but to get to the other channels I had to pass at least one news hour, and I was afraid to watch. Another Yakuza leader had died, this time in Kobe. The mob families were getting paranoid, turning on each other and on smaller rival gangs. At least, that's what the news was reporting. The Yakuza weren't dumb. They probably knew a Kami was hunting them. And they'd fight back.

I watched the two love interests in the drama chase after the doctor for a while. One was a girl from his past who'd rejected him in medical school; the other was another doctor at the hospital, one he'd grown close to over the past few years.

"Doesn't matter," I mumbled out loud. "He's going to die in a few episodes." I watched him stumble in the hospital hallway. The music swelled as he clutched the side railing, as he pressed his head against the wall and cried, as he forced himself one step after another to get to the patient's room. I felt the tears well up in my eyes, too. It was melodramatic, sure, but it still got to me.

The house phone rang, which jarred me out of it. Diane walked in front of the TV toward the headset. She took a glance at me and tossed me the tissue box, which I caught with a loud thunk. I dabbed at my eyes. I wasn't made of stone.

"Moshi moshi," Diane answered cheerfully, while she rolled her eyes dramatically at me. I stuck my tongue out in response, and she grinned; she loved Japanese dramas as much as I did.

The smile dropped from her face, though. "I thought I told you that we'll call you," she said, her tone serious. She paused, looking at me, and then shuffled into her room, closing the door behind her.

My dad. It had to be.

I padded down the hallway in my socks and pressed my ear against the door.

"I know you're only there for another week," Diane said. "But if she hasn't called, it means she's not ready to see you, okay?...No, I know there won't be another chance for a while. Steven..." Her voice started out calm, but grew frustrated. "Steven. Listen. I hear you, okay? But that's the choice you made seventeen years ago. You had the chance...No, I'm not saying you don't deserve—I know people change, but...Steven, you have to think of what's best for *her* now."

I listened to Diane struggle, to try and stand up for me, but my heart sank. He wanted a second chance. He regretted what he'd done. I hated him for leaving us, but I couldn't help but wonder if he was telling the truth. Did he really regret it? Did he really want to meet me? He must have, to keep calling.

I heard the phone beep as Diane turned it off, but I made no motion to hide that I'd been eavesdropping. Diane must have known, too, because she opened her door and showed no surprise at all to see me there.

"Sorry, kiddo," she said.

"He's in Japan now?" I said, and she nodded.

"In Tokyo until next Wednesday. I don't know. He sounds so sincere."

I couldn't believe I was saying this. "Maybe...maybe I should meet him."

Diane wrapped her arms around me and pulled me into a tight hug. "That's for you to decide," she said. "Whatever you choose, I'm here for you, okay?"

"I love you," I said. The words just burst out; they felt right. She hugged me tighter. "I love you, too, hon."

I could face anything with Diane at my side. Even my dad.

"Think about it, okay?" she said, and I nodded, heading for my room. No point catching the end of the drama. I could hear the credits song playing.

I sat down at my desk and my Future Plan assignment stared back at me. I had to focus to read the instructions for each section. Would I ever look at Japanese writing and not have to concentrate to understand it? I'd always taken it for granted in my old life that I could just glance at English and understand without trying.

Future plans. I tapped my pen against the paper. Stop Jun from taking over the world. Stop the Kami power from destroying Tomo. Learn all my kanji perfectly so I don't have to fail the school year and transfer to an international school in English. Confront my dad about how he could've left Mom and me.

I sighed, folding my arms across the paper and resting my head on my hands. It was overwhelming. I lifted my head slightly and scribbled my name in the corner.

The edges of my katakana letters flickered with gold, so

quickly I thought I'd imagined it. But my stomach twisted like motion sickness, and I knew I hadn't imagined it. The ink was moving.

Something tapped against my window twice, and I jumped back from my desk, bumping my knees against the top. We were up on the fourth floor, but I was still scared to look. A small figure gleamed in the window, and I stepped toward it slowly.

It was a raven, its feathers scribbled in black ink, its blinking eye vacant and papery white. It tilted its head and ruffled its feathers as it peered in my window.

"Did Tomo draw you?" I said quietly. The raven tapped again and cawed loudly. It hopped along the windowsill, its feet crinkling like paper as they bent under the bird's weight.

I looked, horrified, as I realized the raven had three legs. I stepped back from the window as it squawked and tapped urgently. What was wrong with it? Maybe Tomo had drawn it from two different angles and they'd combined somehow into this three-legged sketch.

"Poor thing," I said, but its beak looked sharp and vicious. It lunged toward the glass and I called out, jumping back. I yanked my curtains over the window, leaving only the shadow of the bird hopping from side to side. My heart twisted at its incessant caws. What if its sharp beak pecked right through the glass?

After a moment there was a sound like a rush of pages flipping in the wind, and the tapping stopped. The raven cawed once, from a distance.

Why would Tomo send a raven? Maybe it was supposed to be a sweet gesture, but he knew the dark twist his drawings took. It could've tried to peck my eyes out if I'd opened my window.

I clicked off my lamp and lay on top of my comforter, listening to Diane as she shuffled around the living room to the muffled sounds of the TV.

I could feel exhaustion take hold, could feel myself spiraling into sleep.

Mukashi, mukashi, the voice whispered in my head. *Once upon a time there was a boy who devoured the whole world.*

At first, all I could hear was the roar of the ink waterfall all around the island, the world dropping off a sheer cliff in every direction. Then, darkness, as if someone had simply shut off the sunlight.

Then the glow of *inugami* eyes illuminated the darkness, narrow canine slits gleaming turquoise in the distance, a faint growl drifting on the air.

And then, nothing. Complete silence, complete dark.

I took a pace forward, but not even my footstep made a noise. I waved my hand slowly through the blackness, the air thick like water. There was no cold, no warmth. Nothing.

It was stifling.

I took another step, and another. And then my foot landed on something sharp. I cried out, falling to my side.

Dim light began to flicker, hundreds of lanterns catching fire around me. In the distance I heard horses whinny, stifled by the sound of thundering hooves. The castle from before was burning, the flames gleaming in a scorching halo, a thick plume of smoke lifting into the darkened sky.

I held on to my ankle and looked at the sole of my foot in the firelight. Shards of glass had embedded themselves in my skin. With shaking fingers I reached for the pieces, pulling each one carefully as I winced at the extraction. I laid them on the ground like a puzzle, lining up the breaks with one another.

The Magatama jewel.

I heard a rustle of fabric, and looked up. Amaterasu stood

over me, tears in her eyes. The firelight subsided; the screams went quiet. We stood on the small island in the sky, the sun and bright clouds surrounding us. No more horses, and no more fire, just the murky ocean spreading out from us, tipping over the edge of the floating continent in a soft roar of golden clouds.

Another weird dream. I couldn't take them anymore. Couldn't I just dream about taking exams in my underwear or something? Why did I have to be so aware I was asleep? I didn't want to live this anymore.

I scooped the pieces of the Magatama up and spread them in my palm for Amaterasu to see. She reached over, her hand covering mine for a moment, and when she pulled her hand away, a red string unraveled from inside her palm, the Magatama pierced through the top like a necklace pendant. It was in one piece now, a curved teardrop of glass, and she held it between us, where it dangled and twisted on the string.

"They're the key, aren't they?" I said. "The Imperial Treasures."

"I gave them to Jimmu," she said. "So he could survive the cycle."

"The cycle of what?"

She lowered the jewel, resting it in my hand. It felt cold and smooth as I wrapped my fingers around it. "The cycle of fate. Birth, innocence, betrayal, death."

I shook my head. That was too bleak an answer. "I thought they represented love, bravery and honesty."

"Honesty," Amaterasu repeated. "They hung the mirror in a tree to trick me into leaving my hiding place in that cave. Is that not deceitful?"

I tried to slog the thought through my sleep-lagged brain. "No," I said, "because they only showed you who you truly were."

Amaterasu smiled, the tears on her cheeks glistening in the sunlight. "They showed me I could not hide from what I was meant to do. I could not hide from the truth."

I knelt slowly, like I had seen the samurai in TV dramas do. I knew I was probably doing it wrong—bowing like a guy instead of a girl, or at the wrong angle, or something—but I pressed my forehead into the sand, the grains sticking to my skin.

"*Ojousama,*" I said, calling her a princess like I'd heard before on TV. "Please help me. Tell me what happened to Tsukiyomi. Tell me what I can do to stop him from hurting Tomohiro."

Amaterasu bent down, the fabric whistling as it slid against it-self, fold over fold. She took my arms and gently lifted me back up, until we were standing, facing each other. The dream faded away, and we were in a thick bamboo grove, the tall green stalks blocking out everything but the brilliant glow of the sun above us.

"This isn't about saving Tomohiro," Amaterasu said. "It's about saving the world. Already Tsukiyomi's bloodlust claws for control in his veins. He cannot escape his ancestry. It is your task to stop him."

She looked into the forest of bamboo, her eyes gleaming with memory. "Long ago, I pledged my heart to Tsukiyomi, and he promised me his. We were the children of the August Ones, not completely immortal, but neither were we human. Yet we longed to take care of the world, to nurture the hu-mans who were building homes, who were experiencing the first of human life and death. They were our children, and we knew what it was to be lost to our ancestors.

"Alas, Tsukiyomi soon saw nothing but corruption, disease and despair. He became obsessed with his own power, his own vision to change the tides of the earth. He was disgusted with *kami* and human alike. The other *kami* and I wanted to guide the descen-dants, but he wanted to paint a new world, to begin anew. He began to sketch dragons that scorched the skies, *kappa* spirits that drowned livestock and people in the waters, *inugami* that stalked the mountain paths. He was filled with bitterness and blindness."

The sun above us clouded over, the field of bamboo shifting to a deeper, shadowy green. I had never dreamed like this before, remembering her words so clearly. Would I remember them when I woke up? I forced myself to listen, to stay focused.

Amaterasu's arm fell to her side, her closed fingers hidden beneath the twelve layers of colored kimono sleeves. "To quell his anger, I asked Ukemochi to prepare a feast for him. Rice from the plains of what is now Niigata. Tea brewed from the sacred leaves in the valley of Fuji's shadow, now called Shizuoka. Fish pulled wriggling from the grasp of Susanou's raging seas. It was to remind him of the beauty found on the earth, to remind him that not all was lost."

"But...it didn't work, did it?"

Amaterasu shook her head sadly, lifting her hand to hold the Magatama tightly. "He became angry with Ukemochi for serving him dirty food from the earth instead of preparing nectar from the High Plains of Heaven. And so he murdered her, another *kami*. Our kin." Her eyes closed, tears brimming in the corners. "I knew then how dangerous he had become."

I thought of Jun on the tatami, sword by his side. "And so Susanou killed him."

Amaterasu opened her eyes, gleaming like the sun. "No, child. I did."

The thought of it made me dizzy, made the dream break into bleached-out fragments. I willed myself not to wake up. Not yet. "I don't understand."

"He trusted me," Amaterasu said. "He loved me. I was the only one who could get close enough to do it. I betrayed him, Katie, to save the world."

I struggled to stay asleep. I could feel myself lifting, rousing to the real world. "You said I would betray Tomo. Is that what you meant?"

"The mirror shows the truth," she said. "The jewel bears

the marks. The sword saves all. These three, the Sanshu no Jingi, will mark the way."

"But Tomo isn't Tsukiyomi," I stammered. "We only need to keep the ink in him dormant. He doesn't think the world is rotting, Jun does." The sun beamed above us, the bamboo lighting in brilliant flames of white-green.

"Takahashi Jun must be stopped," she agreed, placing the Magatama in my hands. The smooth surface felt cold against my skin. "The treasures will bring Susanou's fate to him. Susanou's descendants were never meant to rule. Nor were Tsukiyomi's."

"But Tomo doesn't want that. He's not like that."

"A monster on a leash is still a monster," Amaterasu said, her voice echoing with the sound of other voices rising on the wind. "You must kill him, before he remembers himself. Before it is too late and he hungers again. Betray him. Kill him."

"No!" I shouted to the voices, and the light burst around me, the morning sun beaming through my bedroom window.

I remembered the dream so clearly. It didn't fade, no matter how many other things I threw myself into. Other dreams became hazy, full of confused feelings or remembrances, but not this one. I remembered it too clearly.

In class, Suzuki-sensei wrote math problem after math problem on the board, but I found myself scribbling the three treasures in the margins of my notebook. The mirror shows the truth, she'd said. The jewel bears the marks. The sword saves all. The Sanshu no Jingi will mark the way. If it was hopeless, why did Amaterasu give the treasures to Jimmu? All this time, the ancestors of Tsukiyomi had survived. I mean, some of them had met terrible ends, but they hadn't died as teenagers. They hadn't destroyed the world.

Maybe the mirror, the sword and the jewel could have some kind of effect. I looked at my sketches, wondering if I needed to cross them out. I carefully ran my finger along the sword in case it was sharp, but it was only smooth, cool paper. But the mirror worked; I looked into it, and a tiny piece of my eye looked back. I held my pen tip over the mirror, watching it reflected in black and white on the page. Creepy. I scribbled out the mirror, drowning it in ink.

My phone buzzed deep within my book bag. I looked around, making sure no one had heard it. Yuki had, but she rolled her eyes. Suzuki-sensei was still lost in the problems he was copying from his paper onto the board, his shirtsleeves dusted with yellow chalk. I lifted the phone carefully out of my bag; it buzzed again in my hand.

Suzuki-sensei heard it this time, and turned around. I crammed the phone under my notebook, praying he wouldn't see.

"Sorry, Sensei," Tanaka said, and Suzuki stopped scanning the room, focusing on him instead. "I'm expecting a call from my parents."

"It can wait until break, Tanaka," Suzuki said.

"Yes, sir," Tanaka said. He reached into his book bag and pulled out his white phone, which he turned off with a great show. Suzuki turned back to the board, satisfied.

I let out a shaky breath while Tanaka turned and winked at me. I winked back—I had the best friends ever. I reminded myself to bring some of his favorite *onigiri* tomorrow from the *conbini*.

I waited a moment, then carefully slid the phone out from under my notebook. A text from Tomo—not so surprising.

I know what to do. Meet me at the gate at lunch.—Tomo

I dropped the phone into my bag and tried to concentrate on the math on the board. He knew what to do? Had he figured out how to stop Tsukiyomi? There had to be another way. There had to.

When the lunch bell rang I grabbed my coat and quickly changed my shoes, running out to the gate.

He was there, waiting, his bangs fanned over his eyes and his bike leaning against the wall of the school.

"What do we do?" I asked, but he shook his head.

"Not here. Let's go get a burger at the station." He offered the seat of his bike, and I sat down and wrapped my arms around his waist as he pressed his feet against the pedals.

"Because it's noisy there and no one will hear us?" I asked.

"No, because I'm starving and want a burger."

Typical.

We sat in a booth at the burger place, and Tomo took a huge bite out of his before he spoke.

"I had a dream," he said, wiping his mouth with the back of his hand. I winced and passed him a napkin, and he grinned. "What, you don't like cavemen?"

"Spill the news, not the toppings," I said, and he rolled his eyes. "I had a dream, too."

"Amaterasu spoke to me," he said. "It was the clearest dream I've had in ages. Finally something makes sense."

My eyes went wide. "She talked to me, too." I took a bite of my teriyaki-and-corn burger.

"*Uso,*" he said. "No way. It must mean we're on the right track. She told me we need the treasures to stop Tsukiyomi."

"That's...sort of what she told me," I said, wondering how much Amaterasu had told Tomo. Had she told him I would betray him? I hesitated. There was no room for secrets anymore. "Tomo?"

"Mmm?" He sipped at his vanilla shake.

"Amaterasu...she told me that I would betray you. But I want to tell you right now, I would never do that."

Tomo looked grim for a moment, but then shrugged. "I know that," he said. "The dreams tell me things all the time that aren't true." He used his fingers to number the things he'd heard, folding them into his palm for each one. "There's no escape, that I'm a murderer, a demon, that there's only death. You know, the usual." He took another sip of his milk shake.

"You're not...freaked out by that?"

"It loses its effect after ten years."

I shuddered. Ten years of dreams like these?

"The dreams are just dreams, Katie. You don't have to live by their rules. But I do believe that the Sanshu no Jingi are involved. The Kusanagi is a legendary sword that could slice through dreams, even cut spirits from bodies. That's what we need, right? To cleave Tsukiyomi from my body."

I narrowed my eyes. "That doesn't sound believable," I said. "How do you cleave a spirit from a body?"

"I dunno," Tomo said. "Maybe like in ancient times. They used to bleed a fever out of someone, right? Use the sword to cut someone, and bleed out the ink. A normal sword wouldn't work, but the Kusanagi would. And maybe you need the mirror to see where to make the incision."

"You sound like a manga plot."

Tomo laughed. "Well, we don't have many leads. Amaterasu said to seek the treasures, so that's what I'm doing. After I finish this burger, of course." He wolfed it down, making a big show of using the napkin. "The treasures are in Tokyo. I think it's time for a field trip."

"Yes and no," I said. "Only the Magatama is in Tokyo. The mirror is in Ise, and the sword is in Nagoya."

Tomo blinked. "I see you've been researching, too. Fine, we'll start in Tokyo, and then make our way to Nagoya and Mie Prefecture."

"Aaand I'm totally sure my aunt will be fine with us traipsing around Japan."

"Let me talk to her," Tomo said.

I shook my head so fast the restaurant blurred. "How do you think that's a good idea?"

"Okay," he said. "Then you could tell her you're going alone?"

"I doubt she'd agree to that, either. And how are you going to get past your dad?"

"He doesn't care much," Tomo said. "Anyway, Tokyo's just a day trip. I can be back before he notices. I mean, dads. Seriously."

My thoughts reeled. "Tomo, wait. My...my dad. He's staying in Tokyo this weekend. He wanted me to meet him."

Tomo tilted his head to the side and leaned back against the red pleather of the booth. It squeaked under the movement. "You want to meet the guy who abandoned you? That doesn't sound like a good idea."

"It's the perfect cover for the trip."

"Katie, you don't have to meet the man who deserted you just to give us a cover story."

I waved my hand back and forth, another Japanese gesture I'd picked up. "It's not like that. I'd been thinking about doing it, anyway, you know. About meeting him."

Tomo looked at me carefully, tilting his head so his bangs fanned into his right eye. "Why would you want to do that?"

"I have a lot of questions," I said. "About why he left. I want closure, Tomo. And, anyway, without Mom, I feel kind of...well, alone."

"You have me," he said, pressing his hands against the table. The sleeve of his shirt caught awkwardly on his wristband. "And you have your aunt."

"I know," I said. "But I can't help but think, *What if?* I mean, why's he in Japan? That's weird, right? It must be the universe telling me something."

"I guess," Tomo said, but he didn't sound convinced. "One stone, two birds, huh?"

"That reminds me," I said, the mention of birds bringing back the frantic tapping of the raven on my window the night before. "Why did you send me a paper raven?"

He leaned forward, his eyes crinkling in confusion. "A what?"

"A sketched crow or something," I said. "You could've at least told me it was coming. It scared the hell out of me. I thought it would break the glass."

He looked startled. "Wait, you saw a sketched raven at your window?" I felt the doubt spread through me, the slow heat of panic. He didn't even know what I was talking about.

"You didn't draw it?"

He shook his head.

"Maybe it was Takahashi?"

"Why would he draw a paper raven?"

Tomo took hold of my wrist, leading us quickly out of the burger place. We turned around the corner, but there was nowhere we could see that was quiet.

"Over there," he said finally, pointing to some trees near the station. Hardly private, but at least it was a less populated corner to stand in. We stood with our backs to the travelers as Tomo pulled his notebook from his bag, fanning through the pages. Sharp teeth jutted out of the book, trying to slice into his fingers as they flipped past. The wagtails beat their wings against the paper, feathers lifting onto the autumn breeze and fluttering away over the station.

He flipped to the start of the blank pages, then carefully turned it over to the last drawing.

A raven, like the one I'd seen.

"That's the one," I said, pointing at it with my finger held safely away from its sharp beak. It pecked at the page angrily, pacing back and forth on its legs. "It even had three legs like that."

"I don't remember drawing that," Tomo breathed. He reached into his pocket and pulled out a pen, scribbling through the raven so quickly the page ripped. The raven let out a strangled noise and sat still; it wasn't dead, though. It watched us carefully with its beady eyes from the ink cage Tomo sketched around it. Tomo swore beneath his breath as he closed the book.

"You don't remember?"

"Like the drawings of Amaterasu—I mean, when I drew you as her," he said. "The ones I did in my sleep. I'm still doing it. I can't believe I drew that."

"A raven's not so bad," I said. "Better than a dragon."

"You don't understand," he said, running a hand through his hair. The way he looked at me, exasperation in his eyes... I knew he didn't mean it, but I felt so different at that moment. I didn't fit in. I couldn't. How could I know what a three-legged raven meant? I came from a different culture. I didn't even know that was a thing. "It's the Yatagarasu."

"Yatagarasu?" I slowly wrapped my tongue around the word.

"It's a special raven," he said. "It's Amaterasu's messenger. It first appeared to Emperor Jimmu. And it was trying to get to you?"

I nodded, my thoughts in a tangle, my stomach in a knot. "Good thing or bad?"

He sighed, shoving his notebook back into his bag. "I'm not sure. Give me your phone."

I passed over my *keitai*, and he started to search for the bird's meaning. "You really need to update your phone," I said. I wanted to think about anything else right now than bad omens.

He snorted. "I like my old *keitai*," he said. "I don't want to use my dad's money. I want to earn my own way."

I didn't know what to say to that. I wasn't sure if that was a good fight for him to pick, or a dumb move that left him back in the past century.

"Here," he said, pointing at the kanji scrawled across the screen. I squinted, my brain working overtime to understand the text. "'The Yatagarasu is the messenger of Amaterasu,'" he read. "'Its appearance signifies the will of Heaven being done, or that the divine are preparing to meddle in the affairs of the mortal.' That must mean we're on the right path, then."

"Or the wrong," I said. "And Amaterasu is trying to correct us."

"Look, we both had dreams about the Imperial Treasures, right? We need them, for whatever reason."

It dawned on me, like a bright light flashing through my mind. "Jun!" I said. "We need the treasures to stop him, Tomo."

He looked at me, startled. "You do realize you called him Jun again?"

"I didn't mean it," I said. "Anyway, Amaterasu said the treasures would stop him, that Susanou was never meant to rule Japan. Maybe the mirror can show him the truth."

"It already did, remember? That's what started this mess."

I bit my lip, trying to think. "But maybe it can restore your power or something, so you can stop him. Or maybe the jewel has some kind of power. And can't we at least use Kusanagi to cleave Susanou's spirit from him or whatever you said?"

"You're right," Tomo said, squeezing his hand into a fist. "With the Sanshu no Jingi, we could win Takahashi's stupid Kami war before it even starts."

"I'll talk to Diane about Tokyo tonight," I said. "I'll find a way to make it work."

Tomo nodded once, taking my hands in his. He didn't usually do that in public, and the feel of his skin against mine send a hot blush up my neck. "We're coming to the end of all this, Katie. There's a way out."

"Yeah," I said. "Our own way."

11

"Absolutely not," Diane said.

"Pleeeease?"

"You're joking, right?" She leaned back against the kitchen counter. "There's no way I'm going to let you go to Tokyo alone."

I'd figured she'd say no, but it was worth a try. "What if I go with a friend?"

Diane smirked. "What's so uncool about me, anyway?"

"It's not that," I said. "Not at all. It's just... I'm so nervous about meeting Dad—Steven. Wait, do I call him Dad or Steven? Oh god. See? I'm a mess."

Diane turned to lift the hamburg steak out of the frying pan and onto my waiting plate. "All the more reason I should come with you," she said. "I don't exactly trust him after he abandoned my sister and you. I know everyone deserves a second chance, but if it breaks your heart..." She sighed. "I don't want to see you get hurt, hon."

"I know," I said, holding Diane's plate steady as she slid the spatula out from under her steak. I carried the plates to our tiny dining table and put them down with a clunk. "But this is something I have to do for myself." I slid the chair out and sat down, resting my head on my propped-up elbows.

Diane followed, cradling a glass salad bowl to her chest. "Well, okay. If it's that important to you, of course I'll wait while you spend time with Steven. But I'm not sending you alone."

"Fine," I conceded. "And the friend?"

She grinned, lifting her chopsticks and resting them in place between her fingers. "As long as it's okay with Yuki's mom, it's fine with me." She clasped her hands together, and we both said the customary *itadakimasu* to each other.

"Thing is," I said between bites of my salad, "it's not Yuki I want to invite."

Diane stared at my frozen, too-big smile. "Is this a friend of the male variety?"

How had she learned to read me so well? She was surprisingly tuned in for someone who'd never had kids of her own. "You said you wanted to get to know him, right? It's just a day trip."

"Meeting your dad is a big deal, Katie. Could we leave the date night until you get back?"

But I couldn't, of course. I needed to find the Magatama jewel, and I needed Tomo to be there to help me. "It's not like that," I said. "He has family in Chiba, so he's not going to be in the way when I'm visiting Da—Steven. It's more of a 'riding together on the train and maybe having dinner all three of us together' kind of thing."

Diane's mouth twisted as she thought it over. "And his dad's okay with this? I thought after that talk with the headmaster... well, he looked pretty upset."

"His dad's fine with it," I said, almost too quickly. She gave me a funny look; please let my smile work this time. I mean, I wasn't even trying to be *that* shifty. We were trying to sneak off to the Imperial Palace, not a love hotel.

"Katie, maybe another time, okay? I just don't think…"

"Diane," I interrupted. "Tomo's really important to me. He's really kind of special, you know? He lost his mom, too. And he's been there for me. I think… I think I could face Dad more easily if he was there with me, too." I wasn't lying. Knowing he was there, too, would give me the strength I needed to get through the meeting.

"I guess I don't see why not, then. But no sneaking off to make out at the top of the Skytree tower, okay?"

"Ew. I mean, not ew making out, but ew talking to you about it."

Diane laughed, breaking off another piece of her hamburg with her chopsticks.

"I'm not planning on it," I added. "This trip is to get things in order in my life, starting with Dad." And finishing with the Magatama. "Having you both there means a lot."

"Fine," Diane groaned, waving her chopsticks in the air. "You're as persuasive as your mom, you know that? I can't say no to you!"

I grinned and shoveled the rest of the food into my mouth. I pushed my chair back with a squeak and carried my dishes over to the sink.

This would be great. Tomo and I could finally get some answers.

The TV droned on from the living room. "Not another one." Diane sighed, and I turned my head. Another Yakuza, this time one in prison. I froze, unwilling to watch but unable to look away.

The reporter shoved her microphone into the face of some kind of spokesperson for the prison, who kept adjusting his glasses nervously up and down the bridge of his nose. "It appears to have been some kind of terrible accident," he said. He nudged the glasses again. "It's hard to believe, but he seems to have drowned."

"Drowned?" the reporter repeated.

He nodded, his glasses slipping down his nose again. "The forensics report has returned an unusual amount of ink in his lungs. We think perhaps he somehow ingested ink from the calligraphy class taught at the prison. Perhaps a suicide attempt."

Diane snorted. "Suicide attempt," she said, flipping the TV off. "I doubt it. They're all linked—they have to be. You know, in the last one, someone had written with ink on the wall?"

I shuddered. I'd tried so hard to block the news out. "What did it say?" I asked, unable to help myself.

"'Kami Arise,'" Diane said, and the fear jolted through me like a shock. "Weird, huh? They think it might be a new gang name."

"Totally weird," I said. I stumbled toward my room, barely able to move my feet.

We had to gather the treasures quickly. We were running out of time.

I watched the rooftops of Shizuoka slip away as the bullet train rushed toward Tokyo. I'd skipped Saturday kendo practice so we could leave earlier—Tomo wouldn't have missed it with the tournament coming, but he was still banned from school. The coaches were starting to shake their heads, though. If he didn't come back soon, he wouldn't have a chance in the competition.

Diane and Tomo had shaken hands at the station, Tomo's hair flopping back and forth as he nodded his head in a casual-type bow. He hadn't looked quite as tough as he had that day when he'd come to the door to say goodbye, before I'd almost left Japan to stay with Nan and Gramps. At least this time he'd spared us the ripped-jeans-and-chain-necklace look. He looked like he had in the headmaster's office, top-student material in a simple dark wool overcoat and a pair of dark jeans. The only problem was that the dark ensemble made his hair look brighter and more rebellious.

Most high schools in Japan didn't allow students to dye their hair, and I'd seen the slight rise in Diane's eyebrows as she'd watched him swagger into Shizuoka Station with that copper hair. She was probably wondering if he was ever going to let the color grow out. Not that Diane likely cared if I dyed my hair—it just signaled something different in Japan, like a revolt against the norm. But at least Tomo had been really polite with her, shaking her hand and even smiling. No tough-guy act today, I hoped.

The bullet train had a pair of seats on either side, facing each other with a short table in between that I kept smacking the top of my knees against. Diane and Tomo had taken a seat on either side and then stared at me. Great. Where was I supposed to sit? What was the choice that would get me in the least amount of trouble? In the end, I'd sat beside Diane, firstly because she was family, and secondly because I didn't want to be subject to her waggling eyebrows at Tomo and me.

The angular roofs and fields of green tea flew past the windows and my ears plugged as we sped up. None of us had really talked since meeting on the platform. The train got faster and the silence more awkward.

The intercom chimed, followed by a stream of polite information about the train in Japanese. A minute later the door between train cars slid open and a lady bowed before pulling a trolley through the aisle, the cart toppling from side to side, loaded down with bags of chips, bentou boxes and bottles of iced tea.

"So, Tomohiro," Diane started, and I winced. I should've invited him for that dinner she'd asked me about a while ago. At least I'd have food to shovel into my mouth so it looked like I was doing something except wringing my hands. At least I'd be sitting across from both of them and I could give them looks when they said awkward things. "How did you and Katie meet?"

I felt the heat flush to my face as I laughed nervously. "Oh, we don't need to talk about that."

Tomo tilted his head, no sign of any awkwardness at all. "Katie watched my girlfriend slap me because my other girlfriend was pregnant."

I opened my mouth, but only a strangled sound came out. I was too scared to look at Diane's face, but she was deathly still.

"That's...that's not exactly true," I finally stammered. "The other girl wasn't his girlfriend at all."

"Right," Tomo said. "And she's younger."

This was not going well. "I mean it wasn't his baby! God, Tomo, what the hell?"

"Is this some kind of joke?" Diane said. My jacket felt too hot; I yanked the scarf from my neck and unbuttoned the top two buttons.

"No, it's true." Tomo grinned. "It wasn't my baby."

"Quit it," I snapped. He raised an eyebrow. "You're not exactly making the best first impression," I said through gritted teeth. What the heck was he thinking?

"The thing is, Obasan," he said, leaning toward Diane, "I think we're already off to a bad start because of the meeting with Kouchou Yoshinoma. You think I'm no good, *ne*? And maybe you're right."

Diane pursed her lips as she tried to make sense of him.

"Listen, bud," she said, "I've taught English at one of Tokyo's more troubled public high schools. If you're trying to impress me with a flashing 'Look, I'm a delinquent' sign, then I don't buy it."

Tomo looked shaken for a minute, then recovered with a grin. "I see where Katie gets her determination."

"Katie knows what she wants," Diane said. "And if she thinks you're worth spending time with, then you better earn it. So enough tough-guy act, okay?"

He fell silent then, thinking back on his actions. His head bobbed up and down, his expression embarrassed. "*Warui,* Diane-san," he apologized. "I wasn't fair to you. And to be clear, I never cheated on my past girlfriend."

"Obviously," I said, rolling my eyes. I fought back the urge to kick him under the minitable. "I wouldn't choose a guy like that."

"Look, let's start over," Diane said. "Try not to be on the defensive, Tomohiro, okay? Some adults are worth trusting."

I hadn't thought of it like that. Was he used to adults rejecting him as trouble? His dad definitely did. Is that why he was putting on this uncomfortable show? And here I thought he'd be on his best behavior with Diane.

Monsters bite when cornered, said a whisper in my mind. I could feel the voices gathering on the wind. *No,* I thought, shaking the feeling away. *Not now.*

"So, Katie tells me you have family in Chiba."

He nodded, folding his arms across his chest as he leaned back into his chair. "My aunt," he said. "And two cousins."

Diane smiled. "Same age?" She was way more forgiving than I thought I could be. I was still dwelling on the awful fallout that could've happened from Tomo's story.

"Younger," he said. "Two boys."

I hadn't known this about him. It was strange to think

about his life this way, that he had a normal family outside of his life as a Kami.

"And is that why you're going in today?" Diane said.

Oh. This is where this was going. She was skeptical about why Tomo was on this trip with us. Well, I didn't blame her. We were up to something, after all. Just not whatever it was she was thinking—like, possibly, a love hotel. My cheeks burned.

"I'd promised to look in on them for my dad," Tomo said, unfazed. He'd been ready for questions like these, prepared by a lifetime of lying. "My uncle died a few months ago."

"I'm so sorry," Diane said, shifting in her chair and glancing out the window.

The train ducked into a tunnel, the light blotting out around us. My ears plugged from the pressure, but just as quickly the tunnel was gone, and the bright light of early morning flooded in the windows again. Fields of rice and colorful houses spread out behind the constant fence of electrical wires that followed alongside the train tracks.

"It's okay," Tomo said. "We weren't that close. I don't see them that often."

"Then you must be looking forward to today."

Tomo dropped his hands into his lap, folding them as he looked down. "Actually, the main reason I'm coming to Tokyo is for Katie." What was he doing? He was so used to lying. Was he really cracking under Diane's friendly interrogation?

I tensed, trying to gauge Diane's reaction from the corner of my eye. Why the sudden truth from him?

"I know she's going to meet her dad, and I don't want her to get hurt." My cheeks flushed pink as Diane folded her arms across her chest. "I was thinking about what you said earlier. If I start this off by lying to you, I'll be screwing up." Tomo reached up and brushed his bangs out his eyes with his slender fingers. "I don't know what you really think about me, but...I don't want you to be mistaken."

"Mistaken?" Diane repeated.

"That's not me," Tomo said, his eyes defiant. "I'm not who Yoshinoma made me out to be."

"You need to know something about me, too, Tomohiro," Diane said, a smile growing on her face. "I make up my own mind about things. But you also have to know that I'm her parent here, and so if you want my trust, you have to earn it. Telling me all this is a good start."

Oh god. "While this is heartwarming," I said, "it's also mildly awkward and totally embarrassing. I'm still here, guys, in case you didn't notice."

"Oh, I know," Diane said. "I was just thinking we should get to the group hug and stirring emotional number on the intercom." She pointed up at the speakers, as if they would burst into some cheesy music, and Tomo grinned. I pushed down the awkwardness and smiled back. This could have gone so much worse. Diane was so awesome; I should've given her more credit from the beginning. She looked past Tomo's tough-guy exterior and saw what I saw—someone kindhearted, someone determined to make it against all odds.

Suddenly the window beside us darkened in a rush of wings, and a loud bang shook the side of the train car. A passenger screamed as we ducked into another tunnel, immersing all of us in darkness.

I stared at the window; something black pressed against it, the intermittent tunnel lights glowing like haloes around the shape as we passed them.

"What was that?" Diane said.

"A bird?" Tomo said, but there was no way to know until the train left the tunnel. We listened to the *click-clack* of the tracks as the train swayed slowly from side to side.

The train burst into the sunlight again, our window still blotted out with blackness.

It was a huge ink splatter, dripping down the window in streams like thin paint. Black feathers smeared with the liquid stuck to the window as they dried in the sunlight, tendrils of scrap paper curled around their quills. The feathers were spread on the window like an explosion of plumage. No sign of a bird body—just ink, feathers and little scraps of paper.

I looked at Tomo. Was it the Yatagarasu, the three-legged raven of Amaterasu? Had it tried to attack us, and left only the scars of its attempt?

He looked back at me, his eyes alien and dark. Oh, no. Not here, not in front of Diane. He couldn't lose to Tsukiyomi on the train, in front of everyone. They'd call the police—they'd lock him up in a lab.

He saw the panic in my face, and he started to breathe slowly, his eyes cast downward at his hands.

"Poor bird," Diane said, looking around the train car. "Let's move to another seat. It's hardly full today, and there are only a few stops until Tokyo. If someone comes on with a reserved seat number, we'll just move again." She stood up, grabbing her purse and my backpack as she shuffled toward another set of seats.

"Come on, Tomo," I said, taking his hands in mine to help him stand.

"Get away from me," he snapped, pulling his hands from mine. The rejection stung; was he embarrassed in front of Diane? But no, that wasn't it. It was the alien eyes, the ones that didn't know me. He breathed harder, his upper body slumping over as he struggled against it.

"Tomo," I said, squatting down in front of him.

Ink trickled down his forearms, staining the cuffs of his shirt black.

"Not here," he gasped, squeezing his eyes shut as he gulped in deep breaths.

"Katie?" Diane called from the new seat. "Tomohiro?"

I stood up, putting on my best smile and cheerful voice. "In a minute!"

She smiled, thinking we wanted a minute alone, a stolen kiss. If only it was just that.

I ducked down again and pressed my hands against Tomo's wrists, willing the ink to stop. Tomo's pupils grew like black puddles of ink; he heaved in each breath now, shuddering as the ink dripped horizontally along the windowpane.

"Tomo," I said, but he was losing himself. Inside his bag, on the seat beside him, I could hear a scraping sound, the claws and talons of creatures trying to escape from the prison of the notebook. "Remember where we're going. We're going to collect the Imperial Treasures, okay? We're so close—don't give up now."

Tomo let out a small moan, and Diane looked over. "Everything okay, kids?"

I swore under my breath and reappeared over the back of the seat. "Fine. He's just a little motion sick."

"I'll get some tea from the cart lady," Diane said, rising to her feet. "Be right back."

"Thanks," I said, only the dread took hold of me then—she'd come back, tea bottle in hand, and see him in whatever state he was. "Come on, Tomo," I said quietly. "I need you right now, okay?"

"I can't," he moaned, twisting his head against the seat. The ink dripped from his fingers onto the train floor. "It feels like I'm being ripped apart," he rasped.

The voice on the wind whispered, *Because it's almost time.*

"Because it's almost time," Tomo said, and I jerked away. He'd heard the voice, too.

"Remember what you told me," I said. "You don't have to listen to the voices. You don't have to listen to the dreams. Make your own fate, Tomo. Fight it."

He blinked a few times, his breathing slowing. I stared into his alien eyes, listened to his sketchbook as it shook the bag on the seat.

"Shut up," I shouted, slamming my fist onto the bag. The notebook stopped shaking, and Tomo snapped out of it. "You okay?" I said. He nodded, looking faint.

"Here," Diane said, passing Tomo a bottle of unsweetened green tea. That stuff was bitter, but exactly what he needed.

"Thank you," he said. I looked at his hands, worried, but the ink was gone from them and from the floor; only his shirt cuffs were still stained, matching the drying inkblot on the window. His hands shook a little; I grabbed the bottle before Diane noticed and unscrewed the cap for him.

Diane smiled. "Tough guy who gets sick on trains, huh?"

Tomo smiled back, chugging back the tea before he replaced the top, not attempting to tighten it. He knew his cover of something more serious was nearly blown. "You've discovered all my secrets," he said.

"Somehow I don't think that's the last of them," she said.

"You're right," Tomo said, and I tensed. He was walking on the edge. If Diane knew about the Kami…but wait. Would she even take him seriously? But then Tomo added, "I like to cook."

"See, that I wouldn't have guessed." Diane laughed. "Come move seats when you're feeling better, okay? No making out—I can see you guys from over there."

"Diane," I said, my neck flushing with heat. "You're to- tally embarrassing me."

"That's what family is for," she said, walking away.

12

Tomo's color had returned by the time the train reached Shin-Yokohama Station, and by now the skyline of Tokyo was all around us, pulling us in to the futuristic dreamlike city. The bullet train pulled up to the platform of Tokyo Station next, and the doors opened with a gasp of air. I hadn't been back here since I'd first arrived in Japan and Diane had led me through the packed platforms. It had all felt like a maze then, an entirely new world that I couldn't fathom. That was last February—nine months ago. Enough time to birth a new life, for the world to go from cold to warmth and back into cold.

I wasn't ready to face my dad, just like I hadn't been ready to let go of Mom. But time went on, not caring whether I was prepared or not. Tomo and I didn't have much time, either.

We followed the signs for the Yamanote line, weaving through the passengers in the station and following the trail of green signs. But Diane stopped at a fork in the hallways, a series of blue signs leading toward the right passage.

"You need the Sobu line, don't you?" she said to Tomo. "To get to Chiba."

"I'll see Katie off first," Tomo said. "I can connect through Yoyogi after."

"Hmm," Diane answered, her face twisted into some kind of grimaced smile. She was trying to decide if he was supportive or pushy. I smiled to let her know I was grateful. I wanted him to stay with me.

She turned and headed for the left hallway to the Yamanote train.

Tomo brushed his shoulder up against mine, tilting his chin down as he spoke quietly. "I bought tickets for the Imperial Palace tour," he said. "I just have to show ID when we show up at the palace."

"What time?"

He shook his head. "If you need more time with your dad, I'll understand. But if you're ready, I booked them for two-thirty."

"Two-thirty?" I said. "And Diane won't wonder at all where we are?"

"Hopefully she'll just think things are going well with your dad. Or you could tell her we went for bubble tea in Harajuku. It is our first time in Tokyo as a couple, after all." The way he said "couple" sent a shiver through me. They used the same word in Japanese, but the pronunciation was a little different. *Kap-pu-ru.* And you didn't use it in the same way in English. You might say some made a cute couple, but you wouldn't really refer to yourself that way. *We're a couple.* There was something charming and antique about it, something that made the warmth in me bloom like a flower.

We reached the ticket machine, a sprawling wall of screens and buttons and rainbow train routes plastered from one side to the other. We fed our tickets into the gates, which beeped and sent the tickets soaring out the other side for us to pick up and take with us. This train was a lot smaller than the bullet train, but because the Yamanote line circled all of downtown Tokyo, we had to cram onto the popular route with a ton of other passengers.

We had to go as far as Harajuku Station. Of course my dad would stay in some outrageous area of the city like Harajuku, with all its bizarre fashions and strange stores. He'd leave with the weirdest impression of what Japanese life was like. Life in Shizuoka was totally different than Tokyo, just like life in Albany was different from New York City. But somehow tourists came away with the idea that Tokyo was like the rest of the country, that everything in Japan was the same.

I wondered about life up north in snowy Hokkaido, or south in Fukuoka, or the tropical Okinawan islands. There was no way life there was the same as the rainbow of colors in Harajuku.

Harajuku Station itself looked like some little ski lodge in Switzerland, all paneled white-and-brown wood and cute country charm. Around us, skyscrapers in all kinds of architectural shapes sprawled across the horizon like a living dystopia novel. I half expected to see bands of disheveled teens roaming the city for canned foods and LED lights or something. Instead, there were guys with hair that was way crazier than Tomo's copper hue—rainbow Mohawks, bright pink spiky deals with frosted blue tips and girls in frilly pink Lolita dresses with strappy vinyl shoes like doll heels on bow steroids. One girl had a giant star on her cheek made of tiny sticker gems. They caught the sunlight as she walked around under a lace parasol, despite the colder weather. Then again, I knew girls back in Albany who sacrificed warmth for fashion, too. I guess it wasn't really that different.

We walked toward Takeshita Street, the huge expanse of Yoyogi Park on our left. The trees were bare, the grass tinged brown, but it made me think of Toro Iseki and Nihondaira, of those quiet forested areas that belonged only to Tomo and me. On the right, the street flooded with people and chaos.

I stopped suddenly. I was going to confront my dad. This was it; this was what I'd wondered about for so long. The chance I never thought I'd have.

Diane squeezed my hand. "You can still go back if you want."

But I shook my head. "I need to do this."

"Dekiru zo," Tomo said, his head tilted back as he looked at me with confidence. "You can do this."

"Thanks for coming the whole way," I said. My eyes were filling with tears; I could see the colors and shapes starting to blur in the corners of my vision. I tried to blink them back—I didn't want to give Steven the satisfaction of seeing he'd hurt me, or seeing he was important to me. It would be a lot easier if I could keep him guessing. I could start a relationship, or shut it down and get closure—whatever might happen, I'd come out on top.

I could see the curry restaurant from here, the one he'd promised to be at for "12:00 p.m. exactly." I don't know why it mattered so much down to the minute—I'd been waiting my whole life for him. I bet everything was always to his convenience, to his benefit. The one thing I knew about him was that he was selfish. He'd left us to look out for himself.

"I'm meeting with a couple English teachers I know for lunch," Diane told Tomo. "Unless Katie changes her mind and wants me to come with her."

"I'm fine," I said again. Maybe I'd start to believe myself.

"Keep me posted," Diane said. "I'll come get you the minute you ask, okay? Train back is at seven. Should we meet for dinner?"

"Sounds nice," Tomo said.

Diane looked at him, suspicious again. "You won't have dinner with your family, Tomohiro?"

He shook his head. "Shouta has a swim competition today," he said. "I doubt I'll be able to visit for long."

Shouta. Tomo has a cousin named Shouta. Add it to the list of things I didn't know about him. But I wanted to. I wanted to know everything.

"Say hi to Shouta for me," I said.

Tomo grinned, his eyes crinkling in the corners. "Okay."

He wasn't going to Chiba, of course. He was here for the Magatama. A wave of guilt rose up in my throat. I'd almost forgotten.

Diane squeezed my hands and kissed my cheek. "You're strong, Katie. You go in there and show Steven what he missed."

Tomo nodded, but he didn't hug me, or even take my hand. *Some Japanese boys are too shy to do that,* Yuki had told me. *It doesn't mean they're not thinking it.* And the way he was looking at me now, his brown eyes gleaming through the fan of copper bangs...it said everything I needed to hear.

If Diane wasn't here, if the crowds of Harajuku-goers weren't here, I would've pressed my lips against his.

Instead, I turned toward the curry restaurant, and stepped forward toward the glass door. I pressed the gray button handle and the door automatically slid open, the comforting smell of curry radiating from the warmth of the restaurant air.

"Wait," Tomo said, and I turned to see him in the doorway, a slip of folded paper in his hand. I looked at it nervously, but he shook his head. "It's not a sketch," he said. "Just...look at it if you need to remember." He pressed the note into my hands.

"Remember what?"

"That you're not alone." He stepped back, and the door closed between us. Just behind him, I could see Diane watching.

I slipped the note into my pocket, Tomo and Diane on the other side of the door. Tomo was right. I wasn't alone. I could do this.

"Irrashaimase!" An employee at the front of the restaurant shouted the greeting at me to let the whole restaurant know I'd arrived. Why my dad had chosen a curry restaurant, I didn't know. Most people wanted the famous sashimi and sushi Tokyo had to offer, or the eccentric-themed cafés you could visit. But my dad hadn't asked where I'd like to go or what I might like to eat. He'd just instructed Diane in a message he'd left on her phone—*"Koko Kare Restaurant, Takeshita Dori in Harajuku, 12:00 p.m. exactly."* Yeah, really warm and encouraging. I guess that's the tone of a father who leaves his pregnant wife and critical prenatal daughter.

I nodded as the man started to motion me to a table, but explained that I was meeting my dad. He didn't seem surprised that I spoke Japanese, probably because I still spoke it poorly, and because there were a ton of foreigners in Tokyo, especially in the touristy areas. This visit might be life-changing to me, but it was just everyday business to him. "He's already arrived." The man smiled, stretching his arm out as he asked me to follow him. I wound through the tiny restaurant until I reached the table.

My dad.

I'd seen pictures of him, but it was the weirdest thing. He looked the same, and yet completely different. It was like when I'd seen a baby picture of myself. There was something in the eyes that was the same, something about the smile, but life had a way of altering everything else.

His blond hair was thinning on the sides, with a spray of white throughout. He had a large nose, too, but his eyes seemed warm enough, and his hands were clasped as he propped his chin on them. He was wearing a lab coat of all things, white and pristine and awkward in a curry restaurant. All I could think was how awful it would be to get curry sauce on that lab coat.

He hadn't noticed me yet, thank god, because I was staring at him like an idiot. He was just a person, I thought. Just another human being walking and breathing and living. He didn't look like someone who'd abandoned his family.

"*Hai, kochira desu,*" the restaurant guy said, and my dad looked up. His eyes connected with mine, and I tensed. The moment was here.

My dad jumped to his feet, his chair pushing back with a loud screech. His hand knocked the plastic specials sign off the table and it clattered on the floor. "Oh, sorry," he mumbled in English as he reached down for the sign. The restaurant guy politely motioned him away and replaced the sign on the table before returning to the front of the restaurant. "Thanks," my dad shouted after him. "Uh, *arigatou.*" He sounded strange, like he was trying to speak Japanese with a New York accent. When Diane spoke Japanese, she used the same intonations they did, and I tried to do the same.

I guess I'd been here too long—judging another *gaijin*, like I wasn't one myself.

"Kate," he said, sidestepping around the table toward me. Was he going to hug me? He held out one hand, and then both, nervously smiling as his lab coat swished around him. "Uh," he said, like he wasn't sure what to do. I wasn't sure, either. But then he wrapped his arms around me and held me in an awkward hug. It felt strange; not awful, but just strange and unfamiliar. The thought made me sad. I didn't know what it was like to hug my own father.

We separated, and I forced a smile onto my face.

"Look at you," he said, holding both my hands as he stepped back and studied me. "Just like your mother. My god, I thought it was her walking in here for a minute."

"Um," I said, noticing the Japanese in the restaurant who were politely ignoring us. "We should sit down."

"Oh, yes, of course," he said, going around the table to his chair. He hesitated and came back around to put a hand on my chair.

"That's okay," I said, wishing he would stop. "I can do it."

"Sure, sure."

We sat, and I opened the menu, wanting to escape. He wasn't threatening or cold like I'd expected. He was flustered, like he wanted to make a good impression. For his benefit or mine? I wasn't sure.

"I want to thank you for coming, Kate," he said, his eyes scanning the menu. "I'm really glad you decided to come."

"Me, too," I said, because it was what I thought I should say. The waiter arrived and bobbed his head at us, ready to take our order. "Go ahead, first," I told my dad.

Dad pointed to a photo in the menu of a katsu curry don, a bowl of rice with vegetables and breaded pork drenched in sauce. He used his English-accented Japanese again to order. *Ko-ray o koo-da-sigh.* It wasn't awful, it just didn't sound like it fit. At least he was trying. I ordered my meal next, a chicken curry set that came with a melon soda.

"Kashikomarimashita." The waiter nodded, and then he was gone toward the kitchen.

My dad stared at me, his eyes wide. "Listen to you," he said. "You're fluent. Amazing!"

"I'm not fluent," I said, taking a sip of the water the waiter had brought. "Not at all."

"You sound like it, though," he said. "Wow."

I struggled for things to say. "So…what's with the lab coat?"

He looked down and tugged at the side of it. "This? I'm an oncologist. Didn't you…? Well, I guess no one would've told you. I'm on my lunch break actually. I'm in Japan working on an experiment with Tokyo University."

"Oh," I said. I knew my dad was some kind of doctor, but

I hadn't really thought about it much. Mostly I just thought about his other role: abandoning jerk.

There was a silence, then. I wasn't sure what to talk about. Was he impressed by my Japanese because I was supposed to be brain damaged? Mom had been deathly ill from the ink dragon fruit she'd eaten while pregnant with me. That had been Dad's fault, indirectly. He'd brought it home from Japan as a souvenir, one that nearly claimed my life.

Dad let out a slow sigh that sounded like a hiss between his clenched teeth. "I bet you have a lot of questions for me," he said.

I did. "Not really."

"It's okay," he said. "I... I made a huge mistake, and I'm so sorry. I want you to know that, Kate. If I could go back..."

"It's fine," I said. It felt too hot, and my appetite was gone. I wanted to leave. "And it's Katie, not Kate."

"Katie," he repeated. "It's not fine. Hell, it's terrible, really. I don't deserve your forgiveness. But you're here, and I'm so, so glad."

I shifted in my chair, looking into my glass of water. Now that he was here, the questions I'd had felt dry and useless, stuck in my throat. Who cared why he abandoned us? He did. There weren't any answers that would make up for it.

The waiter brought my melon soda, and then our curries. I dipped my fork into the sauce and watched it drip off the tines.

"I love this place," my dad said, putting his napkin on his lap. "I come here for lunch every time I'm in Tokyo. Which isn't that often, I guess, but a few times. I never thought Japanese food would include curry. Most people think of sushi, right?"

I sipped at the melon soda, and it was like the fizz sent my thoughts bubbling up. "You know it was the dragon fruit that made her sick. The one you brought back from Japan."

He hesitated, his spoon drowning in the runny curry.

"It was your fault that we both nearly died."

"I know," he said, lowering his head. "I... I'm so sorry."

"You can't just come in after seventeen years and apologize," I said. I bit into a piece of chicken, the spices of the curry flooding my mouth with familiarity. Japan and Diane gave me roots, gave me courage to speak up for myself, even if I was shaking as I did. I could feel my heart pounding in my chest. I hated conflict.

"You're right, Kate," he said.

"Why'd you do it?"

He opened his mouth and closed it, staring down at his curry. After a moment, he said quietly, "It was my fault, and I couldn't face what I'd done to you both."

"So you just abandoned us? Because that's so much better."

"I know," he said. "If I could go back, I'd build up the courage to stay."

"Courage? What, because I'm brain damaged?" I was getting too loud, and I lowered my voice. I didn't want to cause a scene.

Dad looked horrified. "You're not brain damaged. And I wouldn't care if you were in a wheelchair your whole life and you didn't talk or walk or eat goddamn curry. You'd still be my daughter."

"But you left," I said. "You can't say you wouldn't do that, because you did."

"Not for that reason," he said, and the way his eyes looked, I almost felt sorry for him. Almost.

I wanted to get out of here. The curry was sour on my tongue. I wanted to run into Tomo's arms, to forget all this. It was better when I'd been an orphan. "Your reasons don't matter," I said, placing my napkin on the table. "Your actions matter." I stood to leave.

"Kate, wait," he said, reaching an arm out toward me.

"Please don't go. You have every right to be angry, but I want to make it up to you. Please. Please stay."

I stopped, looking at the concerned faces around me. Creating a scene was one of the worst things you could do in Japan. I was involving the people around me who didn't want to be part of this. I flushed pink, humiliated to once again break the social code here. I sat back down, and as I did, the paper Tomo had folded up fluttered out of my pocket and onto the side of my chair. I grasped it with nervous fingers, my palms sweating. *You're not alone*, he'd said. I grasped his words with all my might.

"Thank you," Steven said quietly. "Thank you for staying."

I opened the paper slowly, the first fold, and then the second. It wasn't a drawing, but a couple sentences Tomo had written in his elegant hand.

一人じゃないよ。君は愛に包まれているよ。*Hitori ja nai yo. Kimi ha ai ni tsumareteiru yo.*

You're not alone, it said. *Love envelops you.* I could feel it, like a warmth circling me, engulfing me in vanilla-and-miso-scented peace. He'd sent me the strength I'd needed. *Tomo*, I thought. *Thank you.*

"What's that?" my dad asked, looking at the paper.

"Oh, nothing," I said. I quickly crumpled the note toward the lip of my pocket, but a sharp pain stung my finger and I dropped the paper in surprise. *Seriously? A paper cut?* The paper floated down to the floor, and I ducked under the table to reach for it. My dad did the same.

When the paper hit the ground, a flurry of snowflakes lifted from the page, ghostly white with crisp black edges. It was like a tiny snow globe under the table, the flakes whirling in a spiral as they drifted back to the page. The paper soaked through where they touched, the kanji going limp and transparent as the snow melted into water.

"Oh my god," my dad whispered, and I froze, horrified at his discovery.

I grabbed the note, the paper cold as ice as I put it in my pocket. I looked down at my curry, unsure what to say. Laugh it off? Pretend I didn't see anything? Blame it on the weather outside? Maybe someone had opened the door and...and it had snowed only in the small space below our table. I'd waited too long to speak now.

I opened my mouth. "I..."

My dad's eyes took up half his face. "Kate, was that... Did those come off the paper?"

I didn't understand it. Tomo hadn't even drawn anything. Why had it happened? "I don't know what you mean," I said. "That was weird, but...it wasn't..."

My dad leaned into the table, his voice hushed. "Have the Kami come after you?" he said.

The world around me stopped. I couldn't hear. I couldn't see.

My dad knew about the Kami.

I breathed in the fresh air of Yoyogi Park, glad to be out of the curry restaurant. My dad sat on the bench beside me, watching as a group of teens walked by in a mismatch of rainbows and high-heeled combat boots. We'd sat for a few minutes, with neither of us saying anything.

At last, I spoke. "How did you know about them?" I was too shocked to make up stories to deny it.

"Are you safe?" he asked. "Do they know you're my daughter?"

I blinked. "What? No. What are you talking about?"

He sighed, pinching the bridge of his nose. "I wanted to protect you from this."

The autumn breeze blew past us, and I felt cold, colder than

I'd ever been. I pressed my hands against my legs, my scarf tied tightly around my neck, its fuzziness soft against my lips. I wanted Tomo here with me to face this, but instead I had to face it alone.

Hitori ja nai yo. You're not alone. I remembered the thought gently, like I could hear the words on Tomo's lips.

"What's going on?" I said.

My dad pursed his lips, readying himself for whatever it was that he was going to say. "Almost seventeen years ago, I came to Japan for the first time," he said. "They called me in because of some research I'd been working on. I was still pretty green out of residency. I was just a kid then...damn. But they were dealing with a stomach cancer patient with a really strange strain of bacteria."

"Strange?"

He waved his hand around as he spoke. "Yeah, you know how the bacteria interact with..." He stopped, seeing the confused look on my face. "Well, anyway, it doesn't matter—something wasn't right with her tumors. I'd published a paper on the behavior of long-term infections, and they asked if I could come and take a look. It was stupid, you know. I didn't know anything back then. There's still so much we don't know about it. But they were desperate because of the patient." He put his head in his hands. "Lovely girl. She was only twenty-one, far too young to have to deal with cancer."

I shifted in my seat, tucking my legs under the bench and crossing my ankles. I felt bad for this girl I didn't know, but I didn't understand what it had to do with Kami. The cold breeze blew again and I reached my hand into my pocket for my gloves. The lining was damp from Tomo's snow globe note.

"I looked at the cancer cells for a whole week trying to

gather the courage to share my findings with the other on-cologists," he said. "They...they looked like congealed ink."

I stared at him, narrowing my eyes. Tomo had been bleeding ink lately, yes, but it's not like he had actual physical ink sloshing around his veins all the time. Kami born with the power could make drawings come to life. They held the power in their ancestry, not in physically black blood or anything like that. "That doesn't make sense."

"I know," he said. "And her fiancé looked so nervous that I started to suspect he'd had something to do with it. I confronted him first before I told the other doctors. And he burst into tears and told me about the Kami. I didn't believe it, at first, but how else could I explain this strange ink? So he showed me. He sketched a dog and I saw it running on the page." He put a hand on his head. "I thought I'd lost my mind. He said he was a Kami, and that she'd ingested the ink."

Like Mom. I shuddered. "Ingested it?"

"He'd drawn a plum," he said. "He was working on his paintings. But she hadn't realized. She'd seen the fruit bowl and picked the plum out to eat."

"Wouldn't she realize it was painted?" I said. "Black and white, right?"

He shook his head. "But she didn't notice. Maybe it was dark, maybe she was distracted. The fact remains that she ate it."

But she should've been all right. Mom had survived. Jun had said someone who swallows the ink would probably be okay after a while, right?

But it had stayed trapped in me. Who knew what it would do to someone else?

"As far as I could tell, the ink swarmed her body and attacked. It turned into aggressive tumorlike inkblots, infecting her in a way the doctors had never seen before, leading them to believe it was gastric cancer. Her fiancé begged me not to tell, but to hell with that. I had to save her life, even if he got in trouble with the law, even if this Kami secret came to light. I tried telling the oncologists, but they thought I'd lost my mind. They insisted it was cancer. I didn't know what to recommend. How do you heal someone from some kind of ancient magic attack?"

The thought of what might have happened to her knotted in my throat. This couldn't be good.

"When she died, her fiancé brought me some fancy packaged souvenirs as a thank-you. All tied up with ribbon. Fruit from Hokkaido, he said, in appreciation for keeping his secret and for trying to save her. I was heartbroken, but I brought the fruit back with me. How could I refuse?"

The dragon fruit. Oh god.

"Mom," I said. "Mom ate it."

"Yeah," he said, a hollow, heartbroken word. I looked over at him as he seemed to crumple into himself. Tears streaked down his cheeks, and he wiped at them with the sleeve of his lab coat. "'Here,' he'd said to me. 'Let me share how I feel with you.' I thought he meant he was grateful. I thought he knew how much I'd wanted to save her."

I paused, my hands gripping the side of the bench. "You mean…he did it on purpose? To Mom?"

Dad didn't look up, merely wiped at his tears again. "He wasn't grateful," he whispered. "He wanted revenge."

The tears flowed from my eyes. I didn't even try to stop them. Mom had been poisoned on purpose, so Dad could share what that guy had gone through.

Dad's voice was raw, cracked. "I heard he jumped off a building the week after."

More deaths from the ink, a power humans were never meant to possess.

You survived, a voice whispered in my head. *And now you have to complete the cycle.*

I shook the voice away. I had my own life to worry about right now, not the desires of some stupid destructive power that was ripping my world apart.

"I'm so sorry," Dad sobbed. "I didn't want to abandon you. I left because I couldn't stand what I'd done to you. I panicked. I was too young. I knew there was no cure, nothing I could do. It was all my fault. If I could've saved the girl...if I'd listened to myself about the odd glint in the boy's eyes..." He pressed his forehead into his hands and shook.

I reached into my pocket for a tissue, handing it to him silently. "Mom always said you'd run off with someone else."

He shook his head. "I only said that when Diane cornered me on the phone after. I wanted to make it all go away. I couldn't face you after."

He'd left us out of guilt, a secret we'd never believe. It didn't make it less pathetic, though. "We didn't care about all that, Dad," I said, trying to blink back my own tears. "We just needed *you*."

"I know that," he managed, dabbing at his eyes. "I know that now. If I could go back... I'd do it all differently. I would."

My phone buzzed in my purse, the sound of it breaking me out of the moment. Crap. What time was it? The text message was from Tomo, letting me know he was waiting for me at Otemachi Station near the Imperial Palace. I texted back that I'd be there soon.

"Is it Diane?" Dad asked, and I shook my head.

"A friend."

"So things here are okay for you? How is that you have a Kami paper?"

"Things here are great," I said, but he could see the worry in my eyes. "The Kami...it's complicated, but it'll be sorted out soon. Don't worry." Which is why I had to go see Tomo now, to stop all this before the ink caused any more grief.

Dad nodded slowly. "Stay away from them," he added. "I don't know much about it, but I know they're dangerous. They took you from me once—well, no, it was my fault but—listen. I know we're just meeting, and I don't want to rush anything, but…if you want to leave Japan, Kate—Katie—you can come stay with us, you know?"

"I can stay with Nan and Gramps," I said.

Dad smiled weakly. "I know. But, I mean, even for a summer vacation." He twisted on the bench and reached for my hands, clutching them in his, loosely, so I could let go if I wanted to.

I didn't want to, not yet.

"We live near the lake," he said. "You'd love it. Do you like swimming and fishing? Camping? We go camping every year and Alison…"

I stumbled over the name. "Alison?"

He didn't say anything for a minute, which was answer enough.

I slid my hands out of his. "You ditched us and found some other girl?"

He shook his head. "It's been almost seventeen years. Did you want me to exile myself to a life of grief and loneliness?"

Yes. Kind of. "That's not the point," I said. "You're off having this happy camping fishing life while Mom and I were struggling. You think her journalism gigs paid that much?" I rose to my feet, shoving my hands into my pockets. "You know what? It was a mistake to come."

"Kate, I tried to find you again, I swear. Your mom…she didn't want to see me. She wouldn't answer my calls."

I snorted. "I wonder why."

"It's not like that. I waited ten years until I moved on. Did you want me to be unhappy forever?"

"It's Katie," I snapped. "And I really don't care about your happiness because you sure as hell didn't care about ours."

"Listen, I'm sorry. I… This is all wrong. Let me make it up to you, okay?"

I was shaking, my heart beating in my ears. I knew I was being harsh, but so what? Someone had to stand up for us. But seeing his face crumple like that…he looked like he meant it. And I started to feel a little mean. "I'm… I need time, okay? It's too fast."

"Sure," he said, nodding. "Sure. I'm sorry. I don't mean to bring all this trouble into your life. I just wanted you to know that I want to try again. On your terms."

"Okay," I said. "On my terms."

My phone buzzed again.

"You have somewhere you need to be?" he asked, and I nodded. He let out a slow sigh, rising to his feet and combing what was left of his hair back. "I hope I haven't screwed this up too badly. I really am so glad to see you. I am."

"It's fine," I said, because I didn't know what else to say.

"If anyone knows about that boy and his fiancée…if anyone bothers you, I'll get you a ticket to the States right away, okay? You tell me, and I'll make it happen. I'm serious."

"Okay," I said, and turned to go. I didn't want to hug him, but I might never see him again. The two feelings clashed in me. What was the right thing to do? What was the right thing for me?

"You're a beautiful young woman," he said. "I'm going to spend the rest of my life showing you how sorry I am, okay?"

"Yeah," I said, but I was thinking, *We'll see.* He reached out a hand, and it looked so feeble, so pathetic, that I took it.

I couldn't feel through my mitten, but I imagined it was cold from the weather, cold and worn.

"Bye for now, kiddo," he said.

My hand slipped from his, and I left him behind in the dying greenery of Yoyogi Park.

13

Tomo was waiting by the entrance to Otemachi, the subway stop just outside the redbrick European-looking hub of Tokyo Station. I'd never seen it from the outside before. The whole neighborhood looked like it could be straight from New York City, with its gleaming skyscrapers of glass and metal and the busy traffic, except the cars drove on the left, the roads painted with white kanji and the traffic lights turned on their sides, hanging horizontally. You'd never guess an ancient palace stood only a couple blocks away.

It was easy to spot Tomo as he hunched against the wall of the subway entrance. He was staring at the screen of his old-style flip phone, squinting at the small display. The way he hated using his dad's money for anything, the way he distanced himself from him—I kind of understood the feeling now.

I ran toward him and threw my arms around him, holding him tightly. He tensed under my grip, his eyes wide.

"*Oi,*" he said, trying to push my arm away, but I still clung to him, anyway. He stopped struggling, and then, his voice gentle and deep, asked, "How did it go?"

I let my arms fall from him, and wrapped them around myself. "Fine, I guess. I don't know. He was an okay guy, but... I kind of hate him."

Tomo grinned, and reached a hand up to ruffle my hair. "Of course," he said. "He abandoned you. It's not going to be all rainbows and puppies."

I butted him with my shoulder as we started walking. "I want it to be all rainbows and puppies, though."

"Hmm," Tomo said, nodding his head and crooking his finger against his lip, making a big show of thinking it over. "So you'd choose puppies over me?"

He was trying to take my mind off it; I smiled. He understood me. "Well, how many puppies are we talking about?"

"A basketful."

"It was nice knowing you."

He grabbed at his heart, keeling over as he reached toward the sky. "So...cold..." he whispered. The people around us started to stare.

I giggled and grabbed his arm to pull him back up. It wasn't easy; he went floppy and heavy. "Stop it!" I said between laughs.

He suddenly stopped fighting my pull and with all his strength lunged toward me, pinning me to the wall of the building beside us. He stared at me for a moment, his copper bangs nearly hiding his eyes from view, his hands on either side of my face. He was so close his breath trailed across my bottom lip, and then he pressed his mouth to mine. His lips were softness and butterflies and ice—how long had he waited outside for me at the station? I knew this kind of public scene wasn't the thing to do in Japan, but I couldn't bring myself to care just now. We were just two nobodies in Tokyo, the cold breeze swirling around us as the warmth of his body pressed against me.

The cold wind sent the ink snow globe in the restaurant whirling back into my thoughts. I tilted my chin down, away from the kiss. Tomo pressed his mouth against the edge of my jaw, and then my neck. It was hard to focus. "Tomo," I said. "The note you gave me."

I felt him smile against my skin. "You're not alone," he said, and the vibration of his words on my skin sent a shiver down my spine.

"It's not that," I said, and he heard the worry in my voice. He leaned back, his hands still pressed around me on the wall. "It cut me," I said, lifting my finger to show him the paper cut. I'd received so many from his drawings before. "And it sent a gust of snow up in the restaurant."

He stared at me, unbelieving. He narrowed his eyes, tilting his head to one side. "What?"

I reached up and laced my fingers in his bangs, tracing them to one side of his forehead so I could see his eyes clearly. "It came alive, Tomo."

"No," he said. "That's impossible. I didn't draw anything." He pushed off from the wall and stared down the tunnel of the street toward the palace. I dug into my pocket and gave him the damp note. He opened it, a single snowflake springing from it and dancing on the breeze.

"*Hitori ja nai yo,*" he read out loud, scanning the note. "But I didn't write anything about snow."

"I don't get it," I said. "How could the note make things happen that you didn't draw? Is it like how the ink makes wings on your back? It just forms into whatever it wants now?"

"Not on the page," Tomo said. He blinked, pulling the note away from his eyes. "Oh."

"What?"

"Love," he said, turning the note so I could see the kanji. 愛。

"*Ai*," I repeated. "So?"

"So look at what the kanji's made of," he said. "This top part, that means claw or talon." He traced it, and a cloud of golden dust swept off the page at his fingertip. "That's probably what cut you. Then heart. And look at the last part. Look familiar?"

"It's the start of the kanji for winter," I said. It was the radical at the bottom of the character. Of course. Kanji were pictures, too. They'd changed a lot through history, but they were still what all letters were—evolved drawings, trying to make sense of the world. "English is like that, too," I said. "The letters we use all used to mean something. *A* came from a drawing of an ox head, I think. The long parts of the *A* are the horns or something."

"So now my words are coming alive," Tomo whispered. He crumpled the note, shoving it into his pocket. "How am I supposed to write the entrance exams?"

"Let's do what we came here to do," I said. "The answer's in the Imperial Treasures. It has to be, or Amaterasu wouldn't have given them to Emperor Jimmu."

Tomo nodded, and we hurried down the street toward the palace. Was the Magatama really here among all these modern buildings and stores? But Japan was a place of opposites. Ancient temples beside gaming arcades, crumbling castles across from fast-food restaurants. You could never be sure what monument would rise in the distance.

The Imperial Palace rose then, like a dream shifting into reality. At first there was a busy road from left to right, and then a line of trees. And then the sheer stone wall surrounding the palace seemed to materialize out of nowhere, stretching the length of the roadway. A deep moat ran around the wall, like the moat around Sunpu Castle in Shizuoka.

We walked along the edge of the moat toward Kikyo-mon Gate, the entrance to the palace. I couldn't help thinking how the moat and stones were meant to keep out danger—danger like other Kami. Danger like Tomohiro. In another time, we would have been a threat to come after the Magatama.

He's still a threat, laughed a voice in my head. *He'll be a threat until you kill him.*

I shook the thought from my head, and saw Tomo pressing his hand to his forehead, like he had a headache.

"I heard a voice," I said. It would sound totally crazy, except he knew what I meant. He knew the voices were real, the ink crying out to us.

"Me, too," he said. "What did yours say?"

"Stupid threats," I said. "Nothing I believe."

He nodded. "Good. Don't listen to them."

"What did yours say?" The moat curved under a wide bridge in front of Kikyo-mon Gate. A crowd of tourists, Japanese and foreign tourists, stood waiting for the tour to begin.

"It's like someone shouting in my head," he said, combing his hand through his copper spikes. "The Magatama. It's like I need it to breathe."

I rested my hand on his arm, and he reached up and squeezed his fingers in between mine. He was struggling being here, being so close to one of the treasures. Being so close to destiny.

The tour guide bowed and took our tickets, and we follow him into the imperial gardens with the rest of the crowd. He led us carefully down the stone paths as we curved around a set of buildings. The tour guide explained what they were, but in such rapid and faraway Japanese I couldn't understand.

I leaned into Tomo as we walked. "What exactly is the plan?

No one's ever seen the Magatama jewel except the imperial family and their aides, right? How are we going to get near it?"

Tomo's breath was labored, his eyes shining. "I don't know. I looked up everything before we came, but it's probably highly guarded."

"You don't know?" I said.

"Maybe just being near it will be enough," Tomo said. "I don't know how, but I need it, Katie. It's calling out to me." I listened, but I didn't hear anything, didn't feel anything.

The path curved around a group of trees and sprawled over a beautiful bridge that spanned the western side of the inner moat. Pink and white lilies floated upon the surface of the water, crowded by the thousands of green lily pads overtaking the moat. It almost looked like you could walk across them to the other side. The algae-covered stone wall pulled away from the water at a steep angle, toward what looked like a miniature version of Sunpu Castle. Its white-and-black stories built upon one another like a tiered cake.

"Fujimi-yagura," the tour guide rattled off, and then, for the benefit of the foreign tourists, added in English, "Fuji-view Keep."

Tomo pressed his shoulder against mine, his voice quiet and dark. "A tower won't stop me from taking what's mine."

"We're here to look at the Magatama, not steal it," I hissed. "Do you want to get arrested?"

"It belongs to me," he said, and I knew something was terribly wrong. I looked at his eyes...they were normal, not pools of vacant black like I'd expected. The voice was his, too. He hadn't lost control, then. But then why was he talking like that?

"It belongs to the emperor, idiot. You're not Tsukiyomi, remember?"

He looked at me, his eyes filled with hunger. "You don't

understand. It's all starting to make sense. We were always meant to come here. This is the way to stop Takahashi, Katie. Tsukiyomi's goal wasn't to destroy the world. It was to destroy Susanou."

I narrowed my eyes. "What? You don't even make sense."

The group began to cross the wooden bridge into the east gardens, but we hung back from the entourage. "It's like the Magatama's light is shining over everything, like it's all becoming clear. This didn't start with us. It's like Ikeda said—we're the newest warriors, but the war goes back to the dawn of time. We have a chance to settle it once and for all, to put the feud to rest."

"The voices," I said. "They lie, remember? Don't listen to them."

But he shook his head. "It's different this time. I know it. This doesn't feel wrong."

Almost everyone was across the bridge now, and we followed. But as soon as we reached the other side, Tomo yanked on my arm and pulled me down the bank of the stone wall, so we were hidden by the base of the bridge. I slipped on the stones, but Tomo grabbed my arm tightly. The tips of my shoes dipped into the water, the ripples bobbing the lily pads up and down.

"Not a good time to go swimming," he whispered.

"You're crazy!" I hissed back. "They're going to arrest us."

But they didn't seem to notice they'd lost us, not yet. They carried on down the path, and curved around the edge of the trees. When they'd vanished, Tomo grabbed the side of the bridge and pulled us back up. "You have nothing to worry about," he said. "If they find you, speak only English. Cry if you have to. Tell them you lost the group. It's me that has to worry about answering questions if we get caught."

"Wow, thanks for reminding me I don't fit in," I said, and he frowned.

"It's not like that," he said. "Every samurai uses circumstances to his advantage, right? Don't play by the rules. Use your foreigner status to cheat your way out of trouble."

"One, we're not samurai. Two, don't samurai have an honor code or something?"

Tomo paused, scanning the buildings. "Oh, yeah," he said. "I was thinking about pirates." He rushed for a tree-lined path that ran alongside the main route. I could do nothing but follow.

"How did you get pirates and samurai mixed up?"

"This isn't the point," he said. "Look, over there. The Imperial Palace guesthouse."

It wasn't anything like I'd thought a royal building would be. It looked like a very long teahouse, a rectangular building of white, gray and black. It didn't look elaborate at all, but unassuming and, honestly, a little plain. The tour group was just ahead of us, snapping photos of the building as they walked on a strict pathway around it.

Tomo peered ahead. "We'll need to get behind it, to the Three Palace Sanctuaries. We should be able to sneak past when they take the turn up Yamashita Dori. The trees are a little bare for cover, but we should manage."

"You really researched all this, huh?" I said. "You meant to ditch the tour group from the beginning?"

He shook his head. "I looked up where it is, that's all. The rest is instinct."

"Instinct won't get you past security, Tomo."

Tomo took my hand; his body was shaking from the deep breaths he was taking, and his face almost glowed with adrenaline. I'd only seen him look this way when he was in a kendo match, or when he had thrown himself into a drawing. "We need to find the Magatama," he said. "At all costs."

"And you think it's in there?"

"You can't see it?" he said. I stared, but saw nothing. "I don't mean with your eyes," he said, playfully tapping the back of my head. "It's like a sun. It's radiating heat."

I squinted, trying to catch a pulse of flame or infrared light, but nothing. "How can you tell?"

"I can feel the heat, like a burning flame. And, you know, the internet says it's in the Kashiko-Dokoro shrine to Amaterasu, so that helps." I rolled my eyes.

We walked slowly toward the edge of the Imperial Palace guesthouse. It's not like we were trying to break into the actual palace where the royal family lived, I thought, but I'm sure we weren't the first to try and wander the grounds on our own. There would definitely be guards and surveillance cameras.

"We can't do this," I said.

"Turn back if you need to," Tomo said. "The tour group is still there."

"Tomo, you're going to get in huge trouble."

"Only if I get caught," Tomo said. "And I've got a few good excuses ready."

"Like? The police already have their eye on you from that fight with Ishikawa."

"Like I got lost, like I blanked out and didn't know I was here."

"Oh, please, like they'll believe that."

"Then I'll tell them I'm a Kami and that Takahashi is going to destroy the world. I don't know! I'm just not going to get caught, that's all." He let out an exasperated breath, his glance racing across the grounds like we were wasting time. "Katie, this is the answer to everything. The world is changing, and we need the jewel to stop it. I promise we won't take it, okay? I just need to see it."

He took off into the trees by another tower keep, this one larger than the first. Alone, I stared at the disappearing tour group, and then Tomo. I was terrified. But then I thought about Jun. If this could really help us stop him...if this could stop the ink for Tomo...we had to try it.

Go on, the voice whispered to me. *Go see the truth.*

With a deep breath, I ducked into the forested path behind Tomo. He squeezed my hand, and we moved forward together, past the guesthouse, toward the Three Sanctuaries buildings.

It wasn't far to go, but every step sounded in my panicked heartbeat. The imperial family used the Three Sanctuaries for weddings and ceremonies, so it wasn't far from the guest lodgings in the Imperial Palace. A whitewashed wall surrounded the shrines, black paneling running like a stripe around the center. There was a large gateway on the left to enter, and inside I could see three tiled rooftops on the top of three tiny raised shrines of brown and white.

"The Magatama is in the center one," Tomo whispered.

I was nauseous, ready for someone to grab me and deport me back to New York. Any minute now we'd trigger some kind of alarm. Maybe we'd already set off a silent alarm.

"You okay?" Tomo asked quietly.

"Don't they have cameras all over the place?" I said. "It's the Imperial Palace, for god's sake. There's no way they don't know we're here."

Tomo pointed toward the wall of the Three Sanctuaries. "There," he said, and my eyes widened. A security camera. Three of them, in fact, on this side alone. I recoiled, the panic roiling in my stomach. We would be arrested. "We're too far from the tour group to claim being lost idiots now."

Tomo grinned, his expression dark. "We could say we snuck off to make out."

"And just happened to fall into the courtyard of the shrines? Unlikely."

He lifted his hand into the air, like he was reaching for the cameras. He left his hand outstretched for what seemed like ages. "What are you doing?"

His arm began to shake with the strain, his eyes closed as he concentrated. I heard whispers gathering on the wind, the sound of the ink swirling around us. I looked at the wall of the Three Sanctuaries. The security cameras dripped with ink, each of them completely coated.

"There," Tomo said, rising to his feet and walking toward the wall.

I stared. I'd seen the ink write on him before, give him wings or shinai swords or scars that bled ink, but I'd never seen him use it *on* something. His drawings always attacked him; maybe the ink would make the cameras focus on us or something?

He broke from the trees, and I hesitated, waiting for something horrible to happen. But nothing did, and so I followed him toward the gateway.

"The security guard who checks the cameras will notice something wrong," I said.

"Of course he will," Tomo said. "So we need to be quick. Come on." He took hold of my wrist and we raced to the gateway. The doors were locked, but Tomo rested his fingers on the cool brass plate. Ink streamed from inside the lock, pouring down the wooden door. I heard the lock slide under the pressure. Tomohiro pressed the door open, stepping through.

I looked around, waiting to hear the footsteps of guards approaching, of alarms wailing. Nothing. "Something's not right," I said. "This is too easy." But Tomo didn't hear me, already walking across the courtyard toward the shrines.

The ink was spreading in wings on his back, dripping down his coat and swirling around him like a feathered cape. He looked like a giant raven, the feathers lifting as if attached to his arms. Streams of ink dripped off the feathers and lifted into the air, hanging in gravity-defying ribbons around the courtyard. I'd seen them like this once before, suspended around Jun when he'd played his cello.

This wasn't Tomo. It couldn't be. He didn't have such control over the ink, which meant Tsukiyomi must be taking over.

The shrines looked like tiny houses on wooden stilts. Tomo walked up the wooden steps to the central one, swinging himself over the ornamental fence around the edge. He tried to slide the door of the shrine open, but it wouldn't budge. There was no keyhole to flood with ink, no window to squeeze into. After we'd come all this way... I couldn't see a way in.

"No," Tomo said, running his hands along the door frame. "There must be a way."

"I think the only way in is breaking down the door," I said.

Tomo shook his head. "That would be stupid."

"Says the boy who just broke into the palace of the *goddamned emperor*."

"Not the palace," he protested. "The Three Palace Sanctuaries. And we can't break anything, or we'll end up on the news." Tomo pressed his forehead against the door, his palms against the wooden beams of the little white huts. His copper spikes crumpled against the wall as he breathed in and out; his feathered wings continually dripped down and swirled back up like a reverse slow-motion waterfall lifting into the air. It creeped me out to see it collect like that, saturated around him. He had to be on the edge of control.

"We're running out of time," I said. "The door's locked tight, Tomo. What are we going to do now?"

A smile spread across his face, a dark and delighted smile. I shivered.

"We'll make a new door," he said. He reached behind himself and plucked a feather from his shaping and reshaping wings. The ink rushed in to fill the hole the feather left like a wave of dark blood. The plucked quill melted in Tomo's palm as he crouched beside the doorway, rubbing the ink against the base of the floor.

"Graffiti is your big plan?" I said. But he didn't listen. He traced the line up the side of the building and arced it over his head, his fingertips tracing back down to the floorboards.

A door. He was painting a door of ink.

Tomo pressed his palms against the surface of the door, and it opened soundlessly into the shrine.

My boyfriend just walked through a door he sketched with ink. He stepped in, and I followed, unsure what to say.

A voice on the air giggled, then burst into a childish song. *Monster, monster, where are you hiding?* it sang. *In the pit of your stomach, little girl. In the pit of your heartache. I'm hungry, little girl. What can I eat?* The voice stopped singing, and turned to a harsh whisper. *Let him eat the sword,* it said viciously, *or he'll consume the whole world.*

I swatted at the air around me like the voice was a mosquito I could smack away. The ink ancestry in Tomo was reacting to the *kami* treasure. That didn't make him a monster.

So why did I feel so afraid?

Tomo circled the altar, looking for the Magatama. It was nowhere to be found, but then again, it's not like the priests would leave it lying on a table somewhere, right?

"Where could it be?" I whispered, my hand against the wooden beam by Tomo's makeshift door.

"It's hot," Tomo said, running his hand along the altar. "Like a coal burning in the center of a fire." He looked at the wall behind the covered table, to a large locked cabinet door. He touched the lock, the ink dripping onto the floor, and slid the doors open so hard they nearly slammed into the frames. Inside was a small torii-shaped shrine of wood and gold, pennants of white thunderbolts pulled taut across the center beam. At the foot of the miniature gateway rested a sleek black box.

Tomo put his hand on the box and closed his eyes. The ink swirling around him lit with hints of gold, like a cloak of fireflies flashing around him.

"Maybe this isn't a good idea," I said, taking a step back.

The ink curved through his copper hair and spiraled into horns on his head. He looked like an *oni*, a Japanese demon.

The box lid snapped open under his fingertips.

"Tomo, the ink." But he wasn't listening.

He threaded his fingers through a loop of cord, lifting the necklace slowly out of the dark velvet inside the box. The milky crescent-shaped jewel dangled back and forth on the string as he raised it up.

"Yasakani no Magatama," Tomo whispered, and the gem lit like a match, the buttery glass radiating with a fire that licked the insides of the jewel. The light grew, the whole shrine flooding with brilliance. I closed my eyes, the stark white shining through like a flashlight in my face. The world began to rumble, the floor shaking around me.

And then, darkness.

"Katie?"

Tomo's voice echoed in my ears as I tried to rouse myself from the darkness.

"Tomo?" I felt the grasp of his fingers as they curled around mine. I blinked over and over, the light surrounding us too bright at first to focus.

"Can you stand?" Tomo's face was near mine, his hair tickling against my cheek. But something wasn't right.

"Tomo," I said. "Your hair." Two ink-black horns spiraled through his copper hair like a strange crown. Golden beads dangled from the horns, the strings clinking together like part of a headdress. He leaned back from me and I stared at the robes adorning him, blue and purple and white draped around his body like waves of fabric. A thick golden cord tied in an elaborate knot around his waist. He looked like a prince.

His strong arms wrapped around me and pulled me up to stand.

"Where are we?" I asked. "Why are you dressed like that?"

"I think we're inside the Magatama," he said, and I looked at the horizon, the sky made of milky glass like a dome of crystal built around us.

"Inside?" I breathed.

A woman's voice echoed around us. "Inside the memory of the jewel," she said.

I'd know that voice anywhere, and so did Tomo. "Amaterasu."

"Only the memory of her," the voice said. "She has long since left this world for other shores."

"But she gave this jewel to Emperor Jimmu before she left," Tomo said.

"She did," said the voice, radiating all around us. "The jewel bears the marks."

"Why?" I asked. "What marks?"

The sky around us flickered, turning a deep creamy orange. "The tears of Tsukiyomi formed this jewel," she said. "He saw Amaterasu in the sky and loved her at once, but he knew not what to give her as a gift. What could be worthy of her? She had horses and weaving looms and a mirror in which to gaze at her brilliance. He was but a pale ghost of her light—he had nothing of his own to give. And so he wept, and the tears of his poverty formed the jewel which now remembers."

Tomo turned to look at the sky behind them, the movement causing his princely robes to whistle as they slid against each other. His skin seemed to glow in this light, everything clearer and sharper. He made a fine prince, I thought. He was more fit to rule than Jun ever could have been. I was still in jeans and a sweater; no magical transformation for me. Maybe it was his connection to Tsukiyomi that had caused the change?

"This stone was made of his tears?" Tomo asked the voice.

"It was a fine gift. It filled her heart with happiness," the memory of Amaterasu said. "She wore it upon her breast as she crossed the sky."

I didn't like where this was going. I knew where it ended up.

The orange sky grew darker, a burned brown like some kind of oil painting. Thunder rumbled in the distance. Past the glass of the sky, a land of brown and white beams blurred on the horizon…was it the shrine, the real world? Was this a dream, or were we really inside the jewel?

"But then the August Ones flung Susanou down from the Heavenly Bridge," Amaterasu's memory said. "He saw Amaterasu, and desired her. And she feared him, for he was deeply powerful, enough to frighten the August Ones to expel him."

The sky filled with brilliant light, returning to its creamy swirling clouds. I stepped back against Tomo and he wrapped an arm around me, the fabric hanging from his long sleeves. "To show he meant no harm, Susanou made a promise on the banks of the river. He gave Amaterasu his dagger to break, but in turn he demanded the Magatama jewel, the essence of Tsukiyomi's love, his tears, his soul."

Tomo's arm tightened around me, and I held on to the soft fabric of the robe. I shouted at the sky to make sure she heard me. "You gave it to him? A gift that important?"

"She feared Susanou," Amaterasu's memory said. "And so she gave it away, so Tsukiyomi could protect her. Susanou shattered the jewel to birth new *kami*. But it also birthed the seed of Tsukiyomi's rage."

I saw the sharp edges of the Magatama sky, now, the long scars etched into its glass surface. "It was pieced together again," I said, lifting my arm to point to one of the fissures.

"Yes," the voice said. "Amaterasu gathered the glass shards until her palms were raw and broken, and she presented the shards to Tsukiyomi. The fire of his wrath melded the pieces like a hot iron. His love for her was manifest again, but flawed. And so the wound began to fester. The jewel bears the marks."

So that's what had happened to it, why we kept dreaming of the shards digging into our skin. This was the beginning of the feud between Tsukiyomi and Susanou, the wedge driven between the two of them and Amaterasu. This was what generation after generation of Kami had suffered for.

"Seek the mirror and the sword," Amaterasu's memory said. "It is nearly time."

"For what?" I said.

"For the end," Tomo said, and the sky around us flashed with a searing light that knocked us to the ground. The light faded, slowly, until I saw nothing but the dark wooden roof of the shrine ceiling.

14

Tomo and I barely spoke on the train ride to Shizuoka. We'd awoken to a world of gold dust, the ink around us lifting into the air without a trace. Ducking through the door Tomo had made just before it became undone, we'd headed toward the public imperial gardens along an eerily quiet path, somehow not getting caught. I hadn't seen a single guard. Were they just not worried about break-ins here, that cameras were enough? It didn't make sense.

We'd managed some polite chatter over dinner with Diane, who'd wanted to know everything I was willing to share about meeting my dad, but the effort of getting to the Magatama had exhausted everything I had left. Now Tomo and I sat side by side staring out the window, slumped low in our seats as Diane sat two rows away, pretending she wanted privacy to read her book. Did I mention how awesome she was sometimes?

Tomo slept most of the time, his spiky hair pressed flat against the window frame, his face peaceful and quiet. You'd never guess we'd broken into the palace a few hours earlier.

When we reached Shizuoka Station, Diane held out her hand to Tomo, who shook it slowly. "It was great to get to know you better," she said. "Would you come by for dinner next week?"

Tomo's cheeks flushed; it wasn't that common here to get invited over to someone's house. But he nodded, his spiky hair flopping into his eyes with the motion. "Thank you, Obasan."

Diane nodded and glanced at her watch. "Only eight thirty," she said. "There's time for coffee if you want, Katie."

Seriously? She was giving me more time with Tomo after that stunt of his on the train? "Yeah, for sure," I blurted out.

"Be home by ten-thirty, though, okay?"

"No problem," I said. "Thanks."

Diane smiled and turned, slipping from view as she headed down the stairs from the platform.

"She shouldn't trust you with me," Tomo said.

I rolled my eyes. "Why? Because you can't control your manly urges?"

He laughed, but only once. "No. Because I'm the son of a demon, dummy." The platform was almost deserted now, just a few stragglers left like us. I started down the other stairs of the platform, the ones that led toward the café attached to the station tunnels. Tomo walked closely behind me, his footsteps nearly silent. "And I can control my urges just fine, thanks." His arm snaked around my stomach, wrapping around me like a band of warmth. "For example," he breathed, his face tucked against my ear, "I'd like to take control of my urge to kiss you right now." His lips pressed against my neck and I felt like I might fall down the rest of the stairs if he hadn't been holding on to me so tightly.

He leaned away from the kiss, laughing softly as he released me and walked past me. "See?" he said. "It's you who's at a loss."

My cheeks flushed as I chased him down the stairs. "I can play that game, too," I said, yanking on his wrists as I tried to reach up to his neck. He dodged, laughing, and I chased after him. When he reached the metal gates with the slot for his train ticket, he took off at a run, pressing his palms against the gate on either side and swinging his legs up and over the barrier. "Hey!" I shouted after him. "That's cheating!" I fumbled in my pocket for my ticket, feeding it into the slot so the gates would pull back with their metallic grinding sound. I hurried through the gap, chasing after Tomo. I would pin him to the wall and kiss him, and then we'd see who cried mercy first.

Tomo suddenly stopped running by the central hall, the white marble floors reflecting the lights that shone on the pillars holding up the towering glass ceiling. I crashed into him, grabbing his arm, ready to taunt him. But then I saw what he saw, and stopped dead.

Jun leaned against one of the pillars, one knee bent as his foot pressed against the smooth stone. His arms crossed his chest, his spiked black bracelet covering his right wrist, and the blond highlights tucked behind his ears. His silver earring glinted with the station light as he slowly looked up, his eyes cold and unreadable as he smiled, just a little.

"Takahashi," Tomo said, his voice edged with darkness.

"Yuu-sama," Jun said. Was he mocking Tomo by using that lofty honorific at the end of his name? He could technically mean it, if he was elevating Tomo to princely Kami status. But it was obvious by his tone how he meant it. Tomo's arm tensed under my fingers at the insult. *"Okaeri,"* Jun added. *Welcome back.*

Tomo said nothing, but he reached for my wrist with his other hand and pulled my fingers gently from his arm. He started to lead me away across the echoing stone floor.

"Did you find it?" Jun called after us, his voice resonating up to the ceiling. Tomo stopped walking, but didn't look back. I twisted to look at Jun over my shoulder; he still had that sly smile on his face. "The Magatama," he said.

A chill coursed through my veins. How had he known we were looking for it?

Tomo took another step forward, and Jun's voice echoed around us. "Only two treasures left now, hmm?"

Tomo hesitated; this was a bad place to have a conversation like this. The station still bustled with people catching trains and buses; it wasn't that late on a Saturday night. We had to be careful who heard us, but Jun kept shouting things like it didn't matter.

Tomo turned his head to the side, his eyes cast to the floor. "What the hell are you talking about?"

"It's too late for that now," Jun said, opening his arms to the side. He pushed his foot against the pillar and lunged toward us, his black ankle boots clicking against the floor. "We're too far in for lies."

Tomo turned as Jun stepped toward us, closing the distance. If I reached out my arm, it would brush his; he was too close.

"Sometimes you forget you're not the only one who has the nightmares," Jun said.

I tried to swallow, my mouth dry. "Leave us alone, Takahashi," I said, trying to distance him by name. "Please."

Jun shook his head. "If only it were that simple, Katie. We're linked now. The world is changing." He lifted his arm, watching the lights catch on the silver spikes of his bracelet. "You think you could've gotten that close to the Magatama without my help?"

"You followed us?" I blurted out. Tomo squeezed his fingers around my wrist in warning, but it was too late. The words were out before I could stop them.

Jun laughed. "It's too easy to ruffle your feathers. No, I didn't follow you. But didn't you wonder why it was so easy to infiltrate the palace?" He placed his left hand over top the bracelet, twisting it back and forth on his wrist as he grimaced. "You two kept me busy painting all day. Do you know how hard it is to fill twenty pairs of lungs with just enough ink to knock them out without drowning them?"

My stomach twisted with the horror of it. "You flooded the guards' lungs with ink?"

Tomo narrowed his eyes. "You're sick."

Jun shook his head. "If I was sick, I would've killed them. I did what I had to so you could reach the Magatama."

Tomo's voice was edged with darkness. "What about the others you've killed? Got excuses for those, too?"

Jun shook his head, like we were hopeless. "Those murderers I saved the world from? I didn't kill them, Tomo. They chose their own fates."

"Like hell they did."

"Why would you want to help us?" I said.

"Because," Jun said, pointing at Tomo, "the Sanshu no Jingi are the only things standing between him and a gaping, smoking hole in the side of Japan. If you won't be my sword, Yuu, I won't let you be my thorn, either."

Tomo took a step toward Jun, their faces nearly touching as they stared each other down. Tomo breathed out, and Jun's bangs fluttered against his forehead. "Why don't you just kill me, then?" Tomo sneered. "Why don't you just cross me out in your sketchbook like the others?"

Jun smirked and Tomo's bangs flickered. "I can't kill a Kami as strong as you on paper," he said, his eyes shifting as he studied him. "I'd have to use my own two hands."

I shuddered, but Tomo didn't flinch. "Try it," he jeered. "You know I'm stronger than you."

Jun clasped his fingers around his earring, tugging at the metal. "You don't get it, do you?" he said. "This story has happened before. You made the Magatama from your own soul. From your tears and bitterness, from your cry of loneliness." Jun's cold eyes flicked to my face. "You gave it to your love as a token. She willingly gave it to me, after only one glance." Jun's fingertips dropped from the earring and curled around my hand, lifting it up to his mouth. "And I shattered it to pieces." I tried to pull my hand away, but he gripped tighter, brushing his lips against my skin. The cool of his mouth jolted through me.

My hand ripped from Jun's as Tomo grabbed him by the front of his jacket and slammed him against the pillar. He shoved him against the stone so hard that he forced Jun onto the balls of his feet, the neck of his jacket sliding like a collar up to his chin. Everyone in the station looked over at the sound of the impact.

Tomo screamed into Jun's face, not caring who watched. "Don't fuck with her. Touch Katie again and I'll kill you. I'll fucking kill you!"

"Tomo!" I hissed. A security guard dressed in pale blue spoke rapidly into his radio, no doubt calling for backup as the station travelers watched in shock.

Jun grinned, his eyes cold as ice. "What are you going to do, Yuu? The world is watching."

Tomo took one hand from Jun's jacket and squeezed it into a fist. He pulled it back, lining it up with Jun's face.

"*Yamenasai!*" The security guard hurried toward us. "Stop right now."

"I can still get in one good hit before he gets here," Tomo growled.

"Tomo, he's baiting you," I said. "It's not worth it."

The security guard was closer now, wiggling his radio in his hand as a physical warning he'd called backup. He had no idea who these two were.

Jun smiled. "You can't collect the last two treasures in jail."

Tomo's chin jutted out as he let out a frustrated breath. He lifted his other hand from Jun's jacket, and Jun slid down the pillar to the soles of his feet. He straightened the collar of his jacket, coughing.

The security guard reached us and spouted rapid Japanese at Tomo. Crap. He'd already been arrested for fighting with Yakuza, and had been under suspicion with the police for breaking Jun's wrist. This could be really bad.

But Jun smiled a winning smile, his eyes melting like a warm spring day. "Everything's fine here, sir," he said in a cheerful voice. "Just a publicity stunt."

The security guard and I spoke at the same time "Publicity stunt?"

"Just some healthy rivalry to get everyone excited for the nationals," Jun said, slicking back his blond highlights.

The security guard's eyes widened with recognition. "Oh!" He pointed a shaky finger at Jun's nose. "You're Takahashi Jun! I watched you on TV."

Jun smiled as the security guard canceled the backup, as he pulled out his business card and asked for Jun's autograph. It was like watching a snake devour a mouse—it made my stomach crawl. I rubbed at my hands, trying to rid myself of the ghost of his lips on my fingers. Tomo looked at the ground, his shoulders shaking as he tried to calm down.

The guard waved as he walked away. He actually waved.

Jun stepped forward, so that he and Tomo stood side by side, facing opposite directions. "Don't forget," he said, his head tilting forward as his eyes gleamed like ice. "I hold your life in my hands. You'll live when I want you to live." His high-lights slipped from behind his ear, curtaining his face from view. "And you'll die when I want you to die."

He stepped forward and was gone, lost to the maze of pillars around us.

We didn't speak until we were halfway to my place, our footsteps trudging through the crackling maple leaves that had drifted onto the roadways of Suruga Ward. We weren't sure what to say.

Tomo took a deep breath, and turned to face me, his silhouette lit by the buzzing vending machines behind him. *"Gomen,"* he apologized. "I shouldn't have lost it like that."

"How do you expect to control the ink when you can't even control yourself? You can't let him get to you like that."

"I know," he said, running a hand through his hair. "But he just lights this fire in my blood."

"Maybe because of the old feud between Susanou and Tsukiyomi," I mused.

"Or maybe because he's a jackass."

I couldn't help it—a small smile escaped me. "That, too."

Tomo sighed slowly, kicking at a maple leaf and flipping it over with his toe. "He knew about the Magatama. He knows the Imperial Treasures could hold the keys to his destruction, and he doesn't even care. He *wants* us to find them."

"Then we should stop," I said. "Maybe he knows something we don't."

"He said the treasures will stop me being a threat," Tomo said. "They'll silence Tsukiyomi in my blood and render me useless. That's enough for him."

"But in my dream, Amaterasu told me the treasures could stop Jun, too. I don't get it."

We were silent for a moment, the only sound the whisper of the breeze, the humming of the vending machines.

"We have to keep going," Tomo said. "We don't have any other options. Maybe Takahashi doesn't know the treasures will affect him, too."

I bit my lip, thinking it over. "It's possible. Amaterasu is on our side, right? She wouldn't tell him if she was planning to destroy him."

"Why do you think she's on our side?"

I stared at him. "Why don't you? She's been in our dreams helping us, right?"

Tomo crouched to the ground, reaching for a dried leaf. "Has she helped us? Every night is torture. Death around every corner, threats, names on the wind."

"But she wanted to protect Japan," I said. "She gave Emperor Jimmu the treasures. She stopped Tsukiyomi from creating a new world by destroying this one."

"Yes," Tomo said. "She protects Japan. But it doesn't mean she cares about us." He rose to his feet, twirling the leaf by its stem before dropping it to the ground. It sailed between us, dropping with a small crunch. "We're just pawns to the *kami*. I can be Takahashi's weapon or Amaterasu's. Either way, I'm still just a pawn." He squeezed his eyes shut, his head tilting forward. "I want to be free from all this."

Every fiber of me wanted to hold him, to take away the pain on his face. I reached my hands up and intertwined my fingers with his. "We will be," I said. "We just need the last two treasures, and we'll be free."

He nodded, and we continued walking. He watched me walk up the stairs of the mansion, waited until the glass doors of the lobby slid closed behind me and separated us.

I rode the elevator up and tiptoed down the hall. I slid my

key into our door to let myself in. Everything felt like it balanced on the edge of a cliff. How was I going to get to the other two artifacts we needed? Tokyo had been an easy day trip with a good excuse. What excuse could I come up with for going to Nagoya? And Ise was almost a four-hour trip. I'd need some kind of miracle, like Diane leaving for a conference for a week or something. Like that would happen.

At that moment, Diane popped her head into the hallway. *"Okaeri."* She smiled. "I'm just sitting down to watch that doctor drama you like. Want to watch?"

I shook my head. I couldn't deal with any more drama right now. I had enough of my own. "I'm pretty tired."

"You must be," she said. "It's not even ten yet. I'll record it for you. You and Tomohiro didn't go to the café?"

"I'm sort of overwhelmed with everything that happened today." It was the truth.

She smiled and made us tea, and we stayed up late talking about my dad. She bristled at the mention of Alison, just as I had. It was good to know I wasn't crazy to feel the way I did.

She shook her head, leaning back into the purple leather couch. "I hope he really does mean it, that he's sorry," she said. "He did the wrong thing, and he hurt you. You can't tell what people are going through by looking at them, you know? Look at you, for example."

I felt the heat rise up the back of my neck. "Let's not."

Diane laughed. "What I mean is, you're tougher than you look. You've been through a lot, and you keep going. You don't give up. And it's up to you to decide how much of a role you want Steven to play in your life, not him." She sipped her tea. "And your friend Tomohiro. He looks tough, but he cares about you, and the Japanese he used with me was ultrapolite." She shook her head with a smile. "He's not fooling me. I can see exactly what he is."

"And what is he?"

"A good guy."

I grinned. "I think so, too."

"But take your time with him, okay? I gave you freedom tonight to show you I trust you. Please show me the same respect by deserving that trust, okay?"

Oh god. The awkward talk again. "So no love hotels, huh?"

Diane's face turned crimson. "Absolutely not."

"I was joking," I said. Kind of. I didn't know how I felt about being alone with Tomo, but I knew I felt safe with him. I knew he wouldn't push me.

I'd barely hopped into my pj's when my *keitai* rang. Yuki. I pressed the phone to my ear.

"Where have you been?" she asked me frantically. "I've been waiting!"

"Sorry?"

"You promised me you'd tell me all the details about your Tokyo trip."

I squinted, trying to remember. "I don't think I promised that."

"No, but you should have. What did your aunt think of Yuu? How much trouble did you get in when she saw him?"

I grinned. "Not much. She liked him."

There was a pause. "I guess she had low expectations."

"Hey!" I leaned back on my bed, staring at the ceiling. "You're my best friend, Yuki. You shouldn't talk about my boyfriend like that."

She sighed, like I just didn't get it at all. "It's *because* I'm your best friend that I should talk about him like that," she said. "You're the starry-eyed one, so I'm the voice of reason."

"So he's no good, Voice of Reason?"

"I didn't say that exactly. In fact, he's...actually kind of nice."

"See? I do all right for myself."

"Did you finish your Future Plan assignment yet?"

I glanced over at my desk, where the paper sat untouched. "Why do we have to do it this year, anyway? We have two more years until graduation." More than that if I flunked out and had to repeat a year.

"Two years isn't much to plan ahead," Yuki said. "You should work on it soon, okay?"

"Yeah." I stared at the paper, wishing it would fill itself out. I could live in Canada with Nan and Gramps. I could move back to the States with Dad and this Alison who made him forget us. Or I could stay here with Tomo and Yuki and Diane. Even if it felt impossible, it still seemed so right. "Okay. I promise to look into programs here."

"Great. Try for a school in Osaka, okay? Or even Nara or Kyoto. Then we can be neighbors. Or even roommates! Where is Yuu trying to get in?"

I'd seen papers on his desk I wasn't supposed to, entrance exam info for Geidai, one of the best arts schools in Japan. Problem was, it was in Tokyo. Could he even live a normal life there? *He could if we could end this,* I thought. *If we don't stop Jun, there may not even be a normal life by then.*

"Maybe Tokyo," I said.

"Him, too? Tanaka is talking about Todai. Seriously. I know he's supersmart, but Tokyo University has got to be the toughest entrance exam out there."

"I wish we could all get away from this for a while," I said. "Just...all of us hanging out, like that double date you wanted to go on that time."

Her voice slowed down, filled with concern. "It's a lot of pressure right now, right? Taking on all your kanji at the same time as the regular workload."

"Something like that," I said.

"Maybe we could," she said, her voice brightening.

"Could what?"

"Go on a trip. The school always organizes a field trip in December. The student council is taking suggestions right now."

But...there was no way they'd want to go to Nagoya or Ise, was there? But we could spin either one as a really educational trip. I mean, Ise Jingu Shrine was a hugely important monument of the Shinto faith.

"Where did they go last year?" I asked.

"Enoshima, I think," she said. "The year before that was Fukuoka. Tan-kun's sister Keiko was a First Year then and she told me all about it."

Fukuoka was pretty far, on the southwest island of Kyushu. If they would go that far, then Ise might have a chance.

"It's too bad December's so cold," she said. "I wish we could go to Kyoto for the cherry blossoms. It would be so romantic if I could sneak away with Tan-kun. That is, if I could get him away from eating all those *takoyaki*."

"Do you think the student council would consider Ise?" I blurted.

She hesitated, only her breathing coming across the line. "In Mie Prefecture?" she asked. "Why would you want to go there?"

"We were talking about it in history class, right? It's kind of the home of a superimportant shrine."

Yuki let out a peel of laughter. "Yeah, but that's boring!"

"It's not," I said. "Anyway, I bet it's remote, and quiet, and..." I flipped on my laptop, searching the city for something appealing to Yuki. "It has lots of parks and forests," I tried. "And Ise Bay?"

"You don't have to sell *me* on it," she said. I could hear the grin in her words. "You have to convince the council."

"Okay."

I guess my tone was too serious, because she hesitated. "I don't know why," she said slowly, "but this sounds important to you."

My mouth felt dry, the truth caught in my throat. "It is."

"Then I'll vote for whatever you choose," Yuki said. "And I'll rally as many votes as I can."

Tears welled up in the corners of my eyes. How was I so lucky to have a friend like her? "Thank you," I said. "You're the best."

"On one condition, though." She started to giggle. "You have to help me get alone time with Tan-kun, so he can figure out how he feels about me."

I grinned. "I promise."

We hung up and I tossed the phone onto the low table beside my bed. December was only a few weeks away. Could the world hang on until then? I wished I knew what Jun was thinking, how exactly he planned to become the ruler of Japan or whatever he was thinking. He'd have to eventually reveal himself as a Kami, but in such a way that the police wouldn't take him down as a criminal. He wanted the world to embrace him as a ruler, I knew that much. He was too arrogant to take things by force. He wanted the world kneeling, groveling, offering him a crown on a platter.

December. It seemed too far away.

I slipped the Future Plan assignment off my desk and stared at the empty boxes where I was supposed to fill out my answers.

I grabbed a pen and wrote in the tidiest Japanese I could.

"I want to become a journalist like my mother. I want to

stay in Japan and translate for the English newspapers in Tokyo or Osaka. I want to embrace my life here with my Japanese friends.

I want to have a future that matters."

15

Ishikawa shouted at the top of his lungs, his bamboo shinai swinging toward my stomach. My foot squeaked across the gym floor as I stepped back, my own shinai rising up to meet his. They cracked against each other as I defended myself, but Ishikawa was fast. A minute later he swung it around and tapped my arm.

"Point," he yelled, lowering his bamboo sword to the ground.

I hunched over, panting, and rested my shinai on the floor as well, where it rolled and clanked against his. "How can you be so fast?" I said, pulling the *kote* gloves off my sweating hands.

Ishikawa unlaced the back of his helmet and pulled it from his shoulders. He grinned at me. "Speak for yourself," he said. "You're getting faster."

"It's only because of your shoulder," I said, pointing to the spot where he'd been bandaged up after taking the bullet from Tomo's sketched gun. "Otherwise, I wouldn't go so easy on you."

Ishikawa grinned, slipping the soaked bandanna off his head. "Naturally I'd expect you to let me win since I've saved Yuuto's life." He reached for a water bottle on the bench tucked against the gym wall. "He's back at school next week, huh?"

"Yeah," I said, sitting down on the bench as Ishikawa chugged the water. "Do you think he'll have time to get it all together for the tournament?"

Ishikawa raised an eyebrow, the thin line of black brushing against the tips of his white spikes. "You know about the deal with Watanabe-sensei, don't you?" I shook my head, and he leaned in like a conspirator. "Coach has been letting him come in after-hours to practice."

I blinked. "Seriously?"

He nodded, screwing the lid back on his water. "You don't think they'd actually let him go a month without practice this close to the nationals, right?"

"How come he didn't tell me?"

"He probably didn't want you to worry," Ishikawa said. "Breaking the rules of his suspension could've gotten him expelled. Anyway, he's always been the type to keep his secrets close." He made air quotes. "To 'protect his friends,' and shit."

I smirked. "In your case, it was the right thing to do."

He narrowed his eyes, but a smile tugged at his lips. "I'm pretty sure we've had this discussion, Greene." He sat on the bench beside me, his legs sprawled out and his wrists balanced on his knees. "Whether he was right or not, he shut me out. It gets tiring after a while, when your best friend doesn't trust you with his secrets." He ran a hand through his hair, still slick with sweat. He may have won the sparring match just now, but he looked so defeated.

His face was a mix of guilt and pain. I had to say something. "It's not just you," I tried. "He does it to me, too."

He tilted his head back, his white hair flattened against the gym wall. "Yeah, but it's different. He keeps it from me because he can't trust me. He keeps it from you because he cares about you."

"He cares about you, too," I said. "He's protecting both of us."

Ishikawa let out a single laugh. "He's an idiot. He should've let those punks get me after the prefecture tournament." The attack that had got both of them arrested, because Ishikawa had been stupid enough to pull his knife.

"You're joking, right? You'd be back in the hospital again."

He smirked. "Or worse."

His tone sent a chill through me. "Ishikawa," I said, trying to keep my voice steady. "You okay?"

"I'm not worth anything," he said. His eyes were dull as he stared across the gym. "Yuuto...he's so goddamned smart. He can miss a month of classes and still whip the hell out of his entrance exams. It's not like that for me, Greene. While he's studying I'm on the street corner for some kind of shitty job they have me on."

"Then don't go," I said. "Stay home and study."

Ishikawa balled his hand into a fist and bounced it against the bench. "You don't get it," he said. "I'm not smart like you guys, okay? I try to study and it's like I just can't focus." He lowered his voice to a quiet murmur. "There's no future for me, Greene. I can't be who I am. I can't be who I want to be. I'm stuck."

I couldn't believe he was telling me all this. The culture in Japan was to keep your troubles to yourself so you didn't bother others. Sometimes I wanted to speak up, like when things happened on the train, and Diane would grab my arm and shake her head no. It would be embarrassing for them if I interfered, she'd told me. But here was Ishikawa spilling out his deepest thoughts, his shortcomings, without even caring anymore. Was it a good sign he was being so open, or bad?

"It's okay," I said. "You're probably too tangled in your past decisions to feel like you have a way out."

"There is no way out," Ishikawa said, looking down at his hands. "I can't see one."

I folded my arms across my chest and leaned back against the wall. "There is one," I said. "Get off the street and sit at your desk. You going to let Tomo beat you at this? Someone who's fighting with every breath to stay human? Someone who kept his secret from you so you wouldn't get hurt?" I took a breath, trying to find the right words. "He fought those punks right alongside you, Ishikawa. He was arrested with you. You matter to him, and if you give up, he'll never forgive you."

Ishikawa was silent for a moment, staring at me with his head tilted in thought. Then a big smirk crossed his lips as he nodded his head slowly, thinking about what I'd said.

"Yeah." He bit his lip before he continued. "Yuuto's dealing with ancient crap that I can't even imagine. If he can deal with the Kami spirit trying to take over his body, then I can handle some stupid entrance exams and Yakuza wannabes."

"Right," I said. "Tomo's fighting for a world where you get to choose, Ishikawa. So don't screw it up."

He grinned. "I was wrong about you, Greene. I thought you'd distract Yuuto from who he was meant to be. But I'm starting to get it now, that what you guys have is different. Whether it pans out in the end, who knows? But it matters that you have this time, right now." He took a swig of the water bottle, resting it against the bench as he hunched over. "If it can't be me... I'm glad it's you."

Oh. *Oh.* So it was true, what I'd wondered those times when I'd seen him look at Tomo like that. "Have you...have you told him how you feel?"

Ishikawa shrugged. "There's no point. Enough about me, Greene. *Kuse*, you're so nosy."

I must have misunderstood. "What?"

He shook his head, pulling the *kote* gloves from his arms, the colors of his tattoo weaving around his skin in rainbows of ink. "Nosy," he said. "Annoying. Irritating." He laughed. "Just the way it should be. I'm not going to lose my best friend to someone like you. Now tell me what's next."

He wanted to drop the subject; I got it. "What do you know about the December field trip?" I said.

"Field trip?" Ishikawa narrowed one eye, looking at me like I'd grown another head. "Student council voted on that last week. They're going to Nikko."

My heart dropped. "Nikko? But...but Yuki said we could put in a vote for Ise."

"Ise?" he said. "As in Ise Jingu the shrine? Why the hell would you want to go there?" His expression shifted from confusion to understanding. "This has to do with Yuuto, doesn't it?"

I nodded. Around us, the other *kendouka* were starting to pack up the *bogu* armor from practice, so we got up and started unlacing our *dou*, as well. "It...it has to do with these dreams I've been having," I said. "I think it's a way to save Tomo."

"Then it can't wait until December," Ishikawa said, shrugging out of the plastic chest plate. "You need to go now."

"It's four hours away," I said. "My aunt is going to notice I'm missing."

"Then come up with an excuse," Ishikawa said, rolling his eyes. "You going to let the world collapse because your aunt won't let you go to Ise?"

I looked down and smoothed out the pleats in my *hakama* skirt. "I know, but..."

Ishikawa grabbed my arms suddenly, his fingers wrapping

around my elbows, his face too close to mine. "Greene," he said, his eyes gleaming and earnest. "Go to Ise. If there's some way to save him, you've got to chase after it with your last breath." He closed his eyes, thinking for a moment, and then opened them again. "You've got to do it because I can't."

He was right. We had to gather the last two treasures now. We were already out of time.

I nodded. "I'll find a way."

The dream lifted slowly around me from the shadows, the sound of the ink waterfall hissing in my ears. A tall pagoda loomed over me, its curled rooftops stretched out like tiny pairs of wings between the stories of crimson-red walls. Pagodas were usually Buddhist, I'd thought, but nevertheless I saw Amaterasu standing beside it, draped in a simple white kimono and obi. Her eyes were round and red, the tears dried on her cheeks.

I stepped toward her.

"You found the Magatama," she said to me. "Only two remain."

"I will go to Ise," I said, resting a hand against the pagoda wall. "But what's going to happen when we collect the treasures?"

"Tsukiyomi will be stopped," she said.

"And Jun?"

She nodded slowly. "Susanou's heir will suffer the death foretold."

The words caught in my throat. "Jun... Jun will die, too?"

"In the end, there is only death," she said, something she'd told Tomo and Jun over and over.

"I don't want to kill him," I said. "Just stop him from killing others."

"It is not for you to decide," Amaterasu said. "He is the one who stains his soul with it."

I shook my head. "I've had enough. I don't want Jun to die. You said I would betray Tomo. I won't. We're not going to listen to you anymore."

She paused, tilting her head to the side. The golden beads threaded in her hair tinkled as they swung and collided. In the distance, I could hear the ravens calling to one another.

Finally, she spoke. "There is another way."

The adrenaline pulsed through me. *Another way? Why didn't she tell us?*

"I told Yuu Tomohiro," she said as if I'd spoken out loud. "The Sanshu no Jingi will free him, just as they freed the one destined to be emperor."

"You mean Jimmu," I said, and she nodded.

"If Yuu Tomohiro can accept the full truth of himself, then the sword named Kusanagi can cleave the darkness of Tsuki-yomi from him."

The thought sounded vaguely familiar. Hadn't Tomo suggested the same thing, that he'd had dreams where Amaterasu had told him this?

"Then...I don't have to betray him," I said.

She shook her head. "But only if he has the strength to face himself—all of him—once uniting the treasures. Find the mirror, then the sword. They will mark the way to the tangle he wove."

"The tangle?"

The hissing of the waterfalls grew louder. It was ink, wasn't it? It sounded almost like a pit of snakes...

Amaterasu raised the palm of her hand slowly, outstretched toward me. Did she want me to take her hand in mine? I stood, unsure what to do.

Then I heard the growls.

I turned to see a pack of *inugami*, their eyes glowing with turquoise light, their lips curled back as they snarled and bared their teeth. They crouched on their haunches, ready to pounce.

The panic coursed through me like a jolt. If I hurried, I could make it to the pagoda door.

I wouldn't make it.

I might.

I leaped forward, and so did the *inugami*.

The powerful jaws clamped around my ankle, and I screamed out in pain.

The scream sent Diane running, pulling me back into the safety of the waking world.

16

When I woke again to the early Saturday morning light, Diane was already long gone. She had to supervise Drama Club practice, followed by an English club meeting, which meant it was the perfect time to take off for Ise and not have to answer any questions.

The guilt spread through me like heat as I scribbled down a note that I was out shopping with Yuki, that I was going to sleep over until Sunday. I hated lying to Diane when she trusted me so much. There was no reason to lie to her about anything—she listened to me, and she cared. I didn't have to sneak around—she wanted me to invite Tomo for dinner, and she trusted me even when I wasn't sure of myself.

I bit my lip as I forced myself to write the note. A Kami war was smoldering beneath the surface of the day-to-day world. If I didn't go to Ise, if Tomo and I didn't follow this one lead we had, what would happen to Japan? What was Jun truly capable of? I had to go to protect Diane, to protect everyone.

I grabbed the largest purse I had, a soft pink-and-gold one

I'd bought when I really was shopping with Yuki. It had lace and diamond charms dangling down from the strap, the overly frilly style that was popular with a lot of girls here. "You'll fit right in," Yuki had said. I glanced into the mirror in the hallway. *Yeah, right.* Maybe I should dye my hair.

I shuffled into some tan flats that matched the beige wool coat Diane had bought me and locked the door, tripping over the tips of my shoes as I ran to Shizuoka Station. Tomo was already there, a backpack slung over his shoulder and a paper bag from the station coffee shop hanging from his arm.

"*Ohayo.*" He smiled, and my insides lit. I was going on a trip with Tomo, just the two of us. For a moment, I could almost forget that we were going to save his life and stop Jun. It wasn't so much that I'd lost focus on what mattered. I just longed for the normal life we could have had. Not that Diane would ever let me go on a trip with a guy in a normal world.

"Morning," I said, and we headed toward the bullet train platforms. "Are you okay to do this?"

"We need to," he said. "The Magatama lit a fire in me that won't stop burning." He looked at me out of the corner of his eye as we turned toward the wall of ticket machines. "The nightmares. Did they...did they get worse for you?"

I shuddered at the memory of the *inugami.* "Mostly they're clearer. Amaterasu being less cryptic and all that. But...some of it isn't so pleasant, no."

"Clearer?" Tomo shook his head and adjusted the backpack on his shoulder.

"Aren't yours?"

His eyes looked haunted as he hesitated, wondering if he should tell me. "They're worse. A lot more death, for one thing."

"Death?"

He pursed his lips, a look of disgust on his face. "I'm not the only one descended from...from him," he said, lowering his voice as passengers milled around us. "The dreams where I see Taira and Tokugawa—the dreams where I *am* them—they've changed. I'm not just running from the shadows anymore. I'm leading their campaigns."

Campaigns? Oh. My stomach twisted as I thought about what he meant. Taira no Kiyomori and Tokugawa Ieyasu led some serious military actions against the other samurai families, against other Kami. Jun had told me what happened to unwanted Kami back then.

"Tomo?" I said, not wanting to give my question a voice.

I didn't have to. He looked down at his hands, the coffee shop bag swinging from side to side. "I can't take much more blood on my hands."

I shuddered. "Just dreams," I said, but the words felt hollow on my tongue.

Tomo said nothing, but stepped toward a free ticket machine and punched in our destination. We'd take the bullet train to Nagoya first, then switch trains for a smaller line to Ise City. "Should we stop in Nagoya first, to go to Atsuta Shrine?" I said, but Tomo shook his head.

"The mirror next," he said. "We'll get the sword on our way back. It's the order Amaterasu said over and over in her dream. Anyway, it's easier that way to get back to Shizuoka if something happens to Jun after we touch all the treasures."

I thought back to the nightmare I'd had the night before. *Find the mirror, then the sword.* Why? I wondered. I thought about it as we stepped onto the train from the white stone platform. Because the sword will cleave Tsukiyomi from Tomo, I thought. And a sword as powerful as that needs an instruction manual. The truth from the mirror...wouldn't it give us what we needed to know?

I leaned back into the fluffy seat as the train pulled away from Shizuoka.

Sorry, Diane, I thought with a guilty pang.

Tomo placed the coffee shop bag on the minitable in front of us. He opened it with a lot of crinkling, pulling out a bottled of ultrasweet iced coffee and a chocolate croissant.

"Thanks," I said, suddenly aware of how close we sat, of how our legs pressed against each other from knee to thigh.

He nodded, scrunching the bag down flat as a plate for the croissant. "Can't fight the ink on an empty stomach," he said. He unscrewed the iced tea as I reached for the flaky pastry. *"Oi,"* he said, and my hand stopped in midair. He narrowed his eyes. "I get half of that, okay? Half."

I rolled my eyes and stuffed the croissant in my mouth, biting off a little more than half in one go. My mouth full, I asked, "Why didn't you buy two?"

"You did that on purpose," he said.

"You bet I did. Don't buy your girlfriend half a chocolate croissant."

He grinned, and reached into his coat pocket. Another crinkly bag—another chocolate croissant.

I raised an eyebrow. "Were you testing me?"

He laughed, taking a bite out of the new croissant. "More like teasing you. You passed, by the way."

God, he was such a jerk. "You failed."

He just smiled away, taking another bite of his croissant.

The cities passed by as we sped toward Nagoya. I stared at all the houses as they zipped past, each one holding a family I knew nothing about. The trip to Tokyo, and now the trip to Ise, reminded me how little I knew about Japan, how little I'd seen of the rest of the country. Were things the same here as Shizuoka? Were they different?

A flock of ravens perched on the electric wires, looming over us as we rattled past. A dark reminder of Amaterasu's messenger bird, the Yatagarasu. This was no happy vacation I was on.

Nagoya Station reminded me of Shizuoka—the same chain coffee shops and department stores connected to the station, the same platforms, but with a lot more people. As the train had pulled in, I'd seen the two huge skyscrapers that towered over the station. Office spaces, maybe? I wasn't sure, but they were giant. I'd hoped to see Nagoya Castle from the train, too, but a look at Tomo's determined face reminded me how serious this trip was.

We transferred to the Kintetsu Express; like a miniature version of the bullet train, it wrapped around the edge of Ise Bay, flying through stations whose kanji I couldn't read. I wished I had another croissant to eat; this part of the trip would take a while. I pulled out the book I was in the middle of and started reading. After a while, I noticed Tomo peering over my shoulder.

I looked at him. "What?"

"Nothing," he said. "I just want to know what the Magus does when he finds out that the boy is his enemy's son."

I blinked. "How long have you been reading over my shoulder?"

"Look, are you going to turn the page anytime soon?"

I rolled my eyes, but flipped the page. "Shouldn't you be studying for entrance exams or something?"

He didn't answer for a moment, his eyes flicking across the page. *"Tsugi."*

"I'm not turning the page again," I said. "I haven't even read these pages yet."

"Why not?" He shook his head, disappointment gleaming in his eyes. "You're a really slow reader. This is English, and I'm still reading faster."

I smacked his arm and he laughed, the warmth of it taking the fight out of me. "Are you always a jerk?"

"Pretty much."

The stations got smaller and smaller as we curved around the bay, the water sparkling with the morning sunlight. Everything was brown and half-dead here, only another month until winter would take hold. The train tracks went from four, to two, to only a single set as we clacked along.

Finally, we pulled into the smallest station I'd ever seen, a single taxi waiting outside for visitors. I peered at it from the train window as we slowly lined up with the platform. "This is it?" I said.

Tomo pursed his lips. "Not quite the place you'd expect to have one of the treasures of Japan, hmm?"

"It's a bit on the small side."

Tomo leaned over me to peer out the window. The warmth of his closeness filled me with heat, the smell of him bringing memories of being in his house, cooking miso soup for breakfast. Alone, the two of us, after sleeping the night away on his couch.

We were staying overnight here, too. We didn't know what might happen as we looked for Amaterasu's mirror. We weren't planning to make the four-hour trek back until the morning. I swallowed nervously as he leaned over me, as I thought about where we'd stay tonight. He wouldn't ask me to do anything with him, would he? I mean, we were here for the mirror, not for a romantic getaway.

But the sunlight sparkled on the bay, and the autumn wind rustled what was left of the leaves on the trees, and whether I wanted to admit it or not, it *was* a romantic trip. We were here alone, just the two of us. Anything could happen. Everything could happen.

My throat felt dry, my wool coat itchy and too hot as we got up from our seats and shuffled toward the platform. Was he thinking about tonight, too? Had he assumed we would go that far? Yuki had insisted things were different in Japan, that there weren't so many cultural hang-ups about it, but I wasn't sure. Look what had happened to Shiori. She'd been abandoned at school—worse, relentlessly bullied for getting pregnant. If the consequences were such a big deal, then sex must be, too.

Oh god. I hadn't even thought to pack cute pajamas. I'd just brought my comfy ones, fuzzy pants and a T-shirt. The shirt was even fraying along the hem.

I was lobster red now, I was sure of it. Tomo could take one look at me and know what I was thinking. I walked a step behind him, hoping he wouldn't look back.

We slipped our train tickets into the platform gate and climbed down the stairs to where the single taxi waited. A lone bench had been propped against the station wall, I guess in case two people needed a taxi at the same time.

A man on the bench stood up, and stepped toward us, a black news cap pulled tightly over his head.

He stopped in front of us and lifted one hand up as if he was going to push Tomo. I tensed—was he going to mug us? In front of the taxi driver?

Then his other hand reached to pull the cap from his head. His white hair flopped down around his ears.

"Welcome to Ise, Yuuto." Ishikawa grinned, making a peace sign with his free hand.

Tomo choked on his next breath. I mean, he actually choked. "Sato? What the hell are you doing here?"

Ishikawa grinned. "Keeping an eye on you lovebirds."

Tomo's face flushed a deep crimson. "But…how…?"

Ishikawa sighed, shoving his hands in his pockets. "I convinced Greene to bring you here, and then you texted me you were coming, remember? So I just took the earlier train."

"Why?" was all I could manage. "Why?"

"Speechless, huh? Because I thought you might need help, that's all. There are only two of you, you know. Jun's got a whole army of Kami."

"You're not a Kami, Sato," Tomo said, shaking his head.

"Yeah, but at least I'm in on the secret. And that's one more person on your side."

"Jun's army isn't that impressive, anyway," I said. "He's got, what, fifteen kids whose drawings flicker on the page? And Ikeda. I mean, she's the most dangerous of all of them, and she's not that tough."

But Ishikawa shook his head. "See, this is why you two need me. You don't even know."

An unspoken fear unfurled in my stomach. "Know what?"

"Jun's amassing followers who've read the secret signs he's placed in his attacks on the Yakuza," Ishikawa said. "'Kami Arise,' sound familiar? And they've arisen."

Panic fluttered its barbed wings against my ribs. "No."

"The police think it's a gang war," Tomo said. "Some new gang called 'Kami' fighting with the Yakuza over turf."

"You knew about this, too?" I said, exasperated.

He nodded. "Ishikawa told me last night."

"They're trying to keep it out of the news to avoid panic," Ishikawa said. "Lucky for you guys I have connections. Now are we going to walk to the hotel or take that poor guy's taxi?" The driver stood politely ignoring us, his white-gloved hands crisply at his sides.

"Fine," Tomo said, and we filed into the taxi, a white lace doily draped over the backseat.

Wait. Was Ishikawa going to stay with us now? So I didn't have to worry anymore about being alone with Tomo? I sighed, the relief washing over me—or was it total irritation? No wonder I was so conflicted. I was a total mess of emotions.

No one spoke in the car. Everything had to be secret these days, even from our taxi driver. He had silver hair and wrinkles worn into his face. What if he knew about the Kami?

No, now I was just being paranoid. I took a deep breath and watched the bay sparkle outside the window.

So Jun was amassing an army of followers. Wouldn't the police know who the Kami really were? But maybe those who knew couldn't say. And maybe they thought it was just a gang name. None of them had the power to kill like Jun, did they? I shuddered. He was becoming a prince, just like he'd wanted to. Who wouldn't be grateful to him for taking out criminals, for making the world safer? But he didn't have the right. No matter what the police weren't saying, they still saw Jun and the Kami as the enemy, so we still had some time.

We stopped at an ancient towering building that looked like something out of a samurai movie. "This place?"

Tomo nodded as he counted out yen for the driver. "It's a ryo-kan."

"That's a Japanese-style hotel," Ishikawa said, but really, looking at the place it was obvious that's what it was. The entrance had automatic glass doors, but inside, the hallways were lined with rice paper doors and vaulted wooden ceilings. It was like a giant version of the Three Palace Sanctuaries where we'd seen the Magatama.

Ishikawa leaned back, resting his hands behind his head as we wandered the lobby. "Relax," he said to me as he looked around. "I'll get my own room."

I flushed with heat. Should I tell him it was okay? The rooms here had to be expensive, and I was pretty sure Ishikawa didn't get much payment for the questionable work he did. He had a *baito*, a part-time job, at the karaoke place Tanaka liked, but he didn't strike me as someone who'd think ahead and save up for some kind of emergency trip like this. The train tickets alone must have cost him a lot. I was lucky, that way. Tomo hated using his dad's money, but this time it had come in handy for us.

"It's fine," I blurted. I wished I hadn't, but I had. "You can stay with us."

Ishikawa shook his head. "I'll get another room."

"It's fine," Tomo said. He didn't even look at us—he just kept staring at the window and rubbing the back of his neck. "We should stick together."

"You okay, man?" Ishikawa said, stepping toward him. "You look pale."

I realized then what the problem was. That look in his eyes—I'd seen it at the Imperial Palace.

"It's Amaterasu's mirror," I said. "It's calling to him."

Ishikawa looked at me like I'd grown another head. "It's what?"

I rested a hand on Tomo's arm. He tensed under my touch, a wild look in his eyes. "Let's go to the shrine, Tomo, okay?"

He nodded, and I led him outside into the cool morning air.

Ishikawa trailed behind us. "He's losing control again, right? *Oi*, Yuuto!" He smacked his hand against Tomo's back. "*Shikari shite zo!* Get ahold of yourself, okay?"

"I'm fine," Tomo breathed. "I just need to...to get closer."

"Wait here," I told Ishikawa, and he nodded, watching Tomo as I returned to the hotel to confirm our stay. We had everything we needed in our backpacks, so once he bowed and passed me the room key card, I nodded and returned to Tomo and Ishikawa outside.

We followed the signs for Ise Jingu, which were pretty straightforward. It was the major reason people came to Ise, after all. One of the imperial family members even lived here to watch over the shrine. *And over the mirror*, I thought. It's been kept carefully ever since Emperor Jimmu received it at the beginning of Japan's history. What truth could we see in it that we couldn't see in the one Tomo had sketched?

Tomo moved like a wounded animal on the hunt, lurching toward the shrine with hunger in his eyes. Ishikawa shot me a creeped-out look, but I just shook my head. He'd seen enough of Tomo's ability that he didn't need me to reassure him. He could suck it up and deal with it like we both had to.

Ise Jingu actually had two major shrine locations—you were supposed to visit Geku first, and then Naiku, but Tomo ignored the signs for Geku. It was Naiku that housed the mirror.

We walked through the streets of ancient-looking houses and shops, all of them worn wood and rice paper, like we'd stepped back in time. Vendors in aprons and head scarves sold souvenir crackers and plastic Magatama necklaces, steaming udon noodles and leather wallets and gleaming statues of zodiac animals. But to Tomo, it was like the city had vanished, like Ishikawa and I weren't even there. He advanced toward the mirror, drawn by the force of the ink inside him.

The lush mountains, carpeted in reddening autumn trees, nestled against the shrine like a barrier, a wall that rose up to the clouds dotting the sky. The wind blew and the trees rustled together in a great sound, like the breath of a *kami* blowing through their branches, all of them dancing in unison. I'd never seen anything like it. It was easy to believe the mirror could be in a place like this. It was like the landscape of one of my dreams. Nervously, I checked the nearby hedges for *inugami*. Who knew what was real anymore?

The leaves on the row of bushes shook with a loud rustle, and I tensed. Oh god. Were there wolves in Ise? There could be anything. Even just thinking about *inugami*...maybe that was enough for Tomo to create one, or for one to escape his notebook.

A creature burst from the bushes and I ducked, covering my head and screaming.

No pain, though. No sharp jaws of teeth. Only the sound of Ishikawa laughing.

I opened my eyes slowly, daring to peek at the bushes. A

chicken pecked at the gravel on the pathway, its head bobbing up and down.

"Beware the deadly chickens of Amaterasu," Ishikawa managed between laughs. The chicken circled around us, totally indifferent to our presence.

"Um," I said. "Why is there a chicken?"

We continued down the pathway, and I spotted another chicken near a group of trees.

Ishikawa shrugged. "Sacred chickens," he said.

"Sacred chickens?"

"Did you prefer *inugami*?" Tomo said, his tone way more serious than Ishikawa. He looked grim, haunted, pale.

I shook my head. "I'll take the chickens, thanks."

An unpainted, square-looking torii loomed above us. And behind it, the longest wooden bridge I'd ever seen, lifting over the shallow river that lapped against the shore of the shrine.

The bridge was made of fresh light cedar that smelled musty and sweet. It arced up so steeply that I couldn't see the end of it, only the top of the second torii that towered above the other side. The shore itself vanished into the thick forest of trees that shrouded Naiku in mystery.

"Uji Bridge," Ishikawa said. He took out his phone and passed it to me.

I stared at the *keitai* in my hand. "What?"

He rolled his eyes and leaned against the leg of the torii. "Take my picture, dumbass." He held his hand out in a peace sign.

"Are you serious?"

The posed smile dropped from his face as he gave me a mean look. "Yes. Now come on." He plastered the fake smile back on. I sighed, pushing the button to take the photo. Ishikawa snatched the phone from me to look at the picture.

Tomo spoke, but his voice sounded strange, like it wasn't quite his. "The bridge," he said. I knew that other voice, and turned to look at him. His eyes were pools of vacant black, beads of sweat slicking his bangs to the sides of his forehead.

"Tomo?" I asked quietly. "Should we leave?"

He didn't answer. "This bridge," he said. "This is the Ama no Uki Hashi, the bridge of the *kami.*"

I opened my mouth to answer him, but Ishikawa was at his side faster than I was. *"Chigau,"* he gently corrected. "This is Uji Bridge."

"The mirror is here," he said, stepping forward onto the planks of the bridge.

I stared at the giant torii. "Are you going to be okay?" He'd passed out walking under one before. He stopped thoughtfully, and then went around the torii instead, squeezing himself through the narrow gap between them.

Ishikawa and I stayed beside Tomo, one of us on each side. The look on Ishikawa's face told me he knew what I knew— that Tomo could lose control of the ink at any moment. I peeked over the side of the bridge into the river below.

Something dark was swirling in the water, the ripples spreading out in tendrils under the bridge.

I hesitated, curling both hands around the railing as I peered over.

Ink dripped from the bottom of the bridge into the water. I looked up at Tomo, and down at the water again. It dripped only where he stepped, following him across the bridge. It swirled into wriggling shapes before it lifted in a faint golden dust that clung to the boards of the bridge.

"Greene?" Ishikawa called. He and Tomo were halfway across the bridge already. "Little help?"

I ran toward them, wrapping my arms around Tomo's to help guide him across.

"I'm okay," Tomo said quietly. "I just need to…keep breathing…"

I could hear the water swirling below us. Was the ink forming into something?

We were near the other shore now. The fall weather meant not as many tourists around, but there were still enough to make things difficult. Tomo squeezed around the other side of the torii, to the other visitors' confusion. They turned and bowed underneath the gateway, giving us a look of disapproval, like we'd just eaten the last piece of the birthday girl's cake.

"Never mind them." Ishikawa laughed. "You're the heir of a god, Yuuto. Who cares what they think?" I knew he was just trying to take Tomo's mind off it, but it sounded eerily like the things Jun was always saying. *You're not human. You're a prince destined to rule.*

The path turned sharply to the right through a huge expanse of gardens that were probably impressive in season. As it was, everything looked half-dead and grim, like some sort of apocalypse had hit.

We were at the base of the mountains now, and they rose all around us, rolling hills blanketed entirely with trees. It felt like a different world. No wonder Tomo had said it was the Heavenly Bridge of the *kami* that we'd crossed. Something felt different here. I had so little ink in me, not even mine by right, and yet I could feel it pulling me forward, could feel it swirling as we neared the mirror.

Tons of small shrines dotted the area. At the end of the clearing, several stone stairs rose up to a shrine flanked by wooden fences that blocked off the area beyond. Above the fence loomed two thatched, angular roofs, the tops of the roof extending out like a bright white X. The other shrines were easy to access, and each of them had a little touristy kanji sign beside it. Not so helpful for me, but it didn't matter. I didn't need a sign to know what the barricaded area was.

The shrine of Amaterasu herself. The home of the mirror.

And completely off-limits.

Here we go again. Was Jun going to interfere again, all the way from Shizuoka? Was he even that powerful?

"All right," Ishikawa said. "Plans? There's a large temple there." He pointed to a building on our right, made of dark wood and white with golden scrollwork that wrapped around the rooftops. "The sign says it's dedicated to Amaterasu."

Tomo shook his head, his eyes staying on the thatched rooftop behind the wall. "It's in there," he said. "It's calling."

"You need to get your ears checked," Ishikawa said, looking along the perimeter of the fence. Would a sacred site like this have guards? He glanced at the myriad priests walking around in their long white and yellow robes. "We could probably outrun them in that getup," he added.

"Could you be serious for a minute?" I said. "Unlike you, I don't have a criminal record, and I want to keep it that way."

He narrowed his eyes at me. "Why'd you invite her along, anyway?"

I fumed. "You weren't even invited!"

"Sato," Tomo said, his voice trembling. "Katie."

"Tomo?"

He climbed the steps one at a time, his arm reaching toward the wall. "My whole life I've fought against this curse, never thinking that I could be free of the ink, never understanding why it was so destructive." He closed his eyes at the top, lowering his head as he gritted his teeth. "There's a war inside me, right now. I'm tired of the noise. I'm ready for the truth. And to see that, I need to get to that mirror. No matter the consequences."

"I get it," Ishikawa said softly. "The consequences are a lot bigger than jail time, huh?"

Tomo stepped toward the wall, running his hand along the wood panel. "Takahashi said I'd take out a whole sector of Japan."

"Stay here," Ishikawa said, pulling his dark news cap over his white hair. He shoved his hands into his pockets and strolled along the side of the wall, as if he was just another tourist. He blended right in—you could tell he'd had experience with this kind of thing.

"Couldn't you just draw a door again?" I asked, but Tomo shook his head.

"Too much of a crowd. Anyway, the sections of fence I could draw on are against steep cliffs. I don't think I could make the climb."

I glanced at Ishikawa out of the corner of my eye. He was standing by priest's booth at the left of the stairs, which was attached to the long wall. The cloth lightning bolts attached to the hut fluttered in the wind, floating up toward the tree branches. "Too bad we can't just fly," I said.

Tomo smirked. "I think ink wings would get just as much attention."

Ishikawa turned around and started walking toward the little building at the bottom of the stairs, where bamboo ladles were laid out to wash our hands before approaching the shrines. My heart was pounding, but I tried to walk down the stairs as casually as I could. I already looked out of place being the only blonde tourist at Ise Jingu this late in the year.

Three priests passed us on their way up the stairs. "There's so many of them," I whispered to Tomo.

"Yeah, more than five hundred."

I gaped. "Five hundred?"

"That's why we have to tread carefully. Believe me, Katie, every fiber in my soul wants me to break down that fence and get to the mirror. But I can't be so reckless. If I am, then Takahashi will win."

"Don't worry about him right now," I said. "Right now we need to fight Tsukiyomi."

Tomo grimaced as we walked toward Ishikawa. The copper spikes of his hair flopped against his head, slicked with sweat. How much energy was it taking for him not to lose control?

Ishikawa stepped toward us, hands still in his pockets. "Sorry, Yuuto."

"I figured," Tomo said.

"We'll come back at night," I said. "There's tons of forest all around the inner shrine. I'm sure there's got to be a way."

"I have an idea or two," Tomo said.

"Right," Ishikawa said. "Lunchtime."

We wandered through the complex, the gravel crunching underneath our feet. The trees towered above us, their trunks covered in green moss and ropes draped with Shinto cloth thunderbolts. Tomo reached for my hand and threaded his fingers through mine. The motion startled me—it wasn't like him to do that with so many people around. He was wincing with every step. I squeezed his hand. I could feel the power of Amaterasu here, too. It was like the dreams I'd had, but clearer, stronger. "Just a little longer," I whispered to him.

We found an udon place just outside Uji Bridge in the maze of ancient shops, and slurped the noodles down as quickly as they came out of the kitchen. Tomo ordered Ise Ebi with his, which I thought was a kind of shrimp, but it turned out to be a lobster with crazy antennae that could just about catch TV signals all the way from New York. They garnished his bowl with the head of the weird shellfish.

"That thing's creepy," I said, flicking the antenna with my chopsticks. It swung back and forth, waving like a flagpole over his udon.

"It's tasty," Tomo said, dropping a square of the meat into my noodle bowl. Seafood wasn't my favorite thing, but I'd had lobster a couple times with Mom when we'd visited her friends in Maine. I popped the cube of Ise Ebi into my mouth and chewed. A little rubbery, but soft, like it had been soaked in butter.

"Pretty good," I decided.

"So?" Ishikawa said. "How are we going to get to that mirror?"

I put my finger to my lips. "You want the whole city to know?"

Tomo didn't look up from his noodles, the broth glistening on his lips. "Katie came up with a plan."

"Er… I did?"

Tomo grinned, a dark look in his eyes. "We need to fly over that fence."

"Muri yo," Ishikawa warned, shaking his head. "You know how that went down last time."

"He's right," I said. "No dragons. They'll torch the place and probably eat you."

"I'm not planning on dragons," Tomo said, resting his chopsticks on top of the now-empty bowl. "I need something that can fly, but also something nimble and quiet on the gravel or through the trees. And something that's less likely to turn on me."

"Everything's going to turn on you," I said. "You know that, right?"

"The horse I drew didn't," he said. "Remember?"

I did. I could never forget riding the paper horse around Toro Iseki, my arms wrapped around Tomo as we galloped through the ancient village together.

"Horses can't jump that wall," Ishikawa said.

"A kirin can," Tomo said.

"A kirin?" I said.

Ishikawa scrunched up his face, swiveling on his bar stool at the restaurant counter. "You're going to draw a giraffe?"

Tomo reached across me to swat Ishikawa in the head.

"I-te!" Ishikawa cried out.

"Not a giraffe, you idiot. The other kirin. The horse with one horn."

"A unicorn?" My eyes bulged. "A unicorn is your master plan?"

He shrugged. "It's not exactly a unicorn. It's part goat, part ox, part dragon...actually, I don't really know what it is. But I know it'll get us over that wall, and probably without trying to maul us."

"*Probably* being the key word." Ishikawa smirked.

We counted out our yen and left the restaurant, nothing to do now but wait for nightfall.

A kirin, an Asian unicorn. It was scary to think about Tomo drawing anything right now, knowing how unstable he was. And in the heart of Ise Jingu, here in Amaterasu's shrine.

There was no way this could go well.

Tomo's hand moved in the darkness, the pen scratching across a page in his notebook. Ishikawa held his phone up to light the page, the ghostly LED light gleaming off of the nearby cedar and cypress trees. The air smelled sweet and cold, and of a fire lit somewhere nearby. Maybe by the priests, I thought; we'd spent some of our spare time waiting for night by researching the shrine, and had discovered all kinds of rituals the priests went through at different times of the day.

My legs pulsed with pins and needles as we crouched near the perimeter of the Naiku shrine. We'd managed to cross Uji Bridge without notice, but with the main shrine closed at night, we'd veered off into the forests to get as close to the wooden fence as possible.

"Keep the light down," Tomo whispered, and Ishikawa re-adjusted the phone. A beam of light could give us away easily to any priests that might be watching. Did shrines like this have security at night? I wasn't even sure, but I doubted we could just walk in and handle one of Japan's national treasures without someone asking what we were doing.

I wrapped my arms around myself, my coat buttoned all the way to the top. I'd slicked my hair back in a ponytail, tucking the end of it into my collar. If we were seen, I'd be the easiest one to spot. How many blonde girls were in Ise City at the time of the break and enter? I knew at least the train station would have video of me.

Tomo's fingers arced across the page, his face calm and focused. Drawing for him was dangerous, but it was also what he loved most in life. You could see it in his eyes, the joy his art brought him. I leaned over to see the drawing.

The sketch looked a lot like the horse he'd drawn that day in Toro Iseki, but the proportions were different. The legs of the animal were slender and curvy, each ending in a cloven deer hoof. He shaded the cleft in darkly, sketching jig-jagged flops of fur over the ankles. The face was broader than a horse's, more angular, more dragon-like. He drew sharp, pointed tufts of ears under a mop of floppy mane and then sketched in scales on the creature's face and along the stomach—scales, like a reptile. I'd never seen a unicorn that looked like this.

Tomo let out a breath, his hand trembling on the page.

"Tomo?"

His eyes were vacant pools of black, his drawing happening without his consciousness anymore.

Ishikawa saw it, too, and his eyes widened. "Shit, Greene," he said. "What now?"

I could hear the voices gathering on the wind as the world began to blur in muted rainbow colors. It was strange, seeing colors in the night, but I could see them whirling around us, ghostly on the wind. A negative rainbow, a darker, softly glowing version of the kind that might spread across the sky.

Murky lilacs and muted blues swirled on the wind, yellows that were like tarnished gold, and reds like blackened blood.

Somewhere in the distance, I heard Ishikawa's echoing voice. "Greene? Greene!"

The world was drifting in stars, sparks of light everywhere around us, lit like beacons in the forest.

I was between worlds, between the Kami and myself. I could feel it. I was drifting, like Tomo must be.

Something cold and strong grabbed my arm.

"Greene!"

I shook my head and the colors faded, the whispers quieted. Ishikawa stood over me, his face knit up in confusion. "What's going on?"

"Sorry," I said. My throat felt like I hadn't used it in a thousand years. "It's the ink. Tomo's stirring it up, and I must have lost control."

Tomo was still lost, briskly sketching in a lion's tail that splayed into feathered plumes. The tail flicked across the page as he filled in the details. One of the cloven hooves pawed the ground and the page ripped underneath the motion, curling up in a tiny spiral of torn paper.

The kirin looked like some kind of elegant but terrifying cross between a deer and a dragon. I didn't know how else to explain it—it was both primal and otherworldly at the same time. It looked like something that could exist, maybe, or could've existed, if only the boundaries of imagination were pushed just a little further.

Tomo shifted his pen toward the head of the kirin, and the scales he'd drawn sliced into the side of his hand. Trickles of blood beaded on his skin as he drew in the horn of the creature, but not the small golden spiral that I associated with unicorns. Instead, he drew a single antler, jagged and rough and ancient. It didn't point forward like a unicorn, but tipped back over the creature's ears and neck, jutting out in knobs of polished bone.

There was a rustle of leaves as the wind lifted around us, as it blew the scent of cedar and cypress around us. But there was another scent on the wind, something like the musty fur and hoofs of a wild animal.

The whispers were on the wind once more, the rainbow colors faintly visible.

The kirin stood among the trees, its head bobbing slowly as it took in the dark surroundings. Ink poured down from its withers like a constant waterfall, coating the creature with moving liquid fur, staining its hooves and the grass below them. The ink lifted from the ground around the animal in a shimmer of glistening, oily mauve.

Its eyes gleamed with an unnerving white light, and when it flicked its tail, ink splattered on the cypress trunks around it. An old string looped around its antler in a tangle, and from it hung small magatama-shaped jewels that shone with lights of dark turquoise and sapphire. They swung and clinked together as the animal shook its head. Cold air swirled in a cloud around the kirin's nostrils as it snorted.

Ishikawa stared, his face frozen between awe and fear. He raised his phone to take a photo, but the animal bayed and he dropped it to the forest floor, the LED light illuminating the curve of an unfurled fern.

"Put it away," I hissed. It didn't seem like a good idea to have photo evidence of Tomo's drawing come to life. Ishikawa stooped down and pocketed the phone, his eyes never leaving the kirin.

Tomo's pen dropped from his hand as he slumped forward over his notebook.

"Tomo," I said, resting a hand on his back. I kept the kirin in the corner of my eye, in case it decided to charge at us.

"I'm okay," he panted. I tried to see his eyes, but without Ishikawa's phone we were just silhouettes in the dark.

There was a crunching sound, and I looked up to see the kirin wading through the dried leaves to reach us. I tried to pull Tomo back with me, in case it wanted to maul him, but it moved slowly, its delicate hoofs somehow supporting its strong, powerful frame. The creature was taller and wider than a horse, but graceful on its hoofs, quiet. When Tomo didn't budge, I stepped away, pressing my back against a nearby cedar tree. The kirin reached its large muzzle out toward Tomo and snorted, the air ruffling Tomo's hair.

"Yuuto," Ishikawa said softly, his hands up in case things went wrong. "It has teeth, man. Get up."

Tomo lifted his hand slowly to the muzzle of the kirin. The tiny trails of blood had dried on the back of his hand. The creature shook its neck, black liquid spattering the trees, its scales shimmering in the moonlight before the ink flooded over them again. The jewels suspended from its antler glowed with their dark blue light.

It hadn't attacked us yet. Maybe it was a stable drawing, like the horse. But why were the drawings sometimes stable? I shook my head. There was always a flaw. Tomo was too powerful to ever stay in control for long.

He must have thought the same thing, because he rose to his feet, tucking his notebook and pen into his backpack and slinging it over his shoulder. "We don't have much time," he said, his eyes never leaving the creature.

Ishikawa stepped carefully toward the kirin and interlaced his fingers, palms up. Tomo pressed his hand against Ishikawa's shoulder and rested his knee into the locked hands. With a nod, Ishikawa pushed Tomo's knee upward just as Tomo leaped off the ground. He sailed through the air and onto the kirin's back.

The movement had looked way too practiced; I bet they'd snuck into a lot of places back in Shizuoka.

"Katie?" I looked up at Tomo. In the moonlight he looked so strange, a dark figure on a dark horse—well, deer-dragon-horse thing.

A demon on his unnatural steed.

I stepped forward, lightly touching the kirin's neck. The ink was warm to the touch, but it trickled down my fingers like water, without marking my hands. Below the ink, the scales of the kirin were as cold as polished metal. It pawed at the ground, the creak of its muscles like scrunching up a paper ball.

I reached for Tomo's hand, and Ishikawa gave my knee a push to help me up. The kirin felt tense and unstable underneath us—suddenly the plan didn't seem like such a great idea. "Sato?"

Ishikawa shook his head, the moonlight catching on his bleached hair. "I'll stay here and keep watch. I don't need to look into some rusty mirror to know the truth of who I am. Go on, Yuuto. Go admire your reflection, *ne?*"

Tomo nodded, and suddenly the kirin lurched to the side as we turned to face the fence. I wrapped my arms tightly around Tomo. The animal shifted from hoof to hoof on its spindly legs. "Are you sure it can support two of us?" I asked.

"The ink is part of me," Tomo said. "Would I let you fall?"

I didn't have time to answer before the kirin bolted forward. I pressed my lips together to keep from screaming. The kirin didn't run in a straight, smooth line like a horse, but leaped like a deer, swaying from side to side as its legs extended and collapsed like tent poles. I was sure my leg would be crushed against a tree trunk before we even made it to the fence, but somehow the creature dodged every obstacle. It let out a low noise, halfway between a whinny and some kind of tribal horn.

And then it pushed hard against the ground with its back

legs. We were flying for a moment, the world whirling past. The kirin collapsed on the other side of the wall, rolling as we tumbled off its back and onto the hard cold ground. The kirin lay there for a moment, its antler scraping against the dirt, the blue gems buried in the grasses. Then it rose slowly, its legs bending as it shook back and forth, as the ink flooded down its sides in tiny waterfalls of black.

Tomo spat out a mouthful of dirt, wiping his lips with the back of his hand. "You okay?"

"Yeah," I said, my shoulder throbbing like fire where it had hit the ground. "Although I'm pretty sure I'll have a huge bruise on my arm tomorrow. And I skinned my knee."

He grabbed my hand and pulled me up.

We'd made it—the inner shrine of Naiku. Dull orange floodlights lit up the two shrines inside the fence, the larger one just in front of us, the other next to a large empty square of dirt. "They rebuild the shrine every twenty years," Tomo murmured as we moved forward. "Right now it's on the left. Then they'll build on the right and destroy the left one."

"Why?"

He shrugged. "It's Amaterasu's shrine. They want to keep it new and clean. Or maybe the power builds up after a while."

Behind us, the kirin nuzzled at the grass. If you didn't know it was there, you could barely see it, black on black. Even the faint blue glow of the jewels swinging looked like tiny fireflies flitting around.

The shrines looked like tiny Yayoi huts, raised on stilts and built from unpainted wood. Tomo grabbed the railing of the shrine and hoisted himself up over the side. He reached down for me and pulled me up with more strength than I'd expected.

I knew what was happening. It was the power in him growing—the mirror was close.

Tomo gently slid the door of the shrine open. There wasn't

any security or locks to worry about here—the fence was meant to keep everyone out. No one could scale it, they thought. No one except a desperate Kami.

A large relic took up the center of the altar, the object covered by a dark cloth and surrounded by a variety of offerings. A bowl of rice, a silvery baked fish and a small black bowl of sand with two long wands of incense smoldering into the air. It smelled like the incense at Toshogu Shrine in Shizuoka, a mix of strong perfumes and bitter herbs.

"The mirror?" I asked. Tomo's fingers trembled as he ran them over the black cloth.

"The Yata no Kagami," he breathed, closing his hand around the softness of the fabric. He pulled it slowly and it slipped from the surface of the mirror, fluttering to the floor.

The back of the Kagami was like the one in my dream, like a large brass shield embossed with strange geometric designs.

Tomo's eyes widened, his face one of pained shock. I moved around the altar, to see what it was he saw.

I hesitated, unsure what to do.

The mirror's surface was cracked, a handful of glass shards reflecting a broken Tomo back to him.

"It's...it's shattered," he whispered.

The room flooded with heat and light, and I raised my arm to cover my eyes.

"You shattered it many eons ago," a voice said. Amaterasu stood at the shrine door, her kimono shining with gold and silver embroidery.

"Okami," Tomo said, but the figure shook her head.

"Amaterasu is long gone," she said. "I'm only what's left of the memory, trapped in the mirror."

"We came to...to learn the truth," I said. "The mirror shows the truth, right?"

She smiled sadly. "This is not the Yata no Kagami."

Tomo breathed in sharply, the air choking in his throat with a strange noise. "I don't understand."

"The mirror melted in a fire over a thousand years ago," she said. "But they reshaped it anew. It holds the same spirit."

"Is that why it's broken?" I asked.

Amaterasu raised her hand slowly, pointing toward Tomohiro. "Don't you remember?" she asked.

He looked pale, his breathing shallow. "I broke it."

She lowered her arm, her hand disappearing in the folds of her kimono sleeves.

I tilted my head—this was totally confusing. "What?"

"When I was Taira no Kiyomori," Tomo said. "In my dream. I must have shattered this mirror a hundred times."

I scrunched up my nose. "But...that was a dream."

"It was a memory," Amaterasu said. "The ink that slumbers in him is from Tsukiyomi and from me, the descendent of my son. The memory has descended with him."

Tomo fell to his knees, pressed down by the weight of the truth. "Then, the reason I dreamed of Taira and Tokugawa..."

"They, too, shared the blood of two *kami*." She nodded. "The kin of Tsukiyomi and Amaterasu are drawn to each other, generation after generation. The union brings only destruction, and the cycle continues."

"How do we stop it?" I said.

She looked at me, her gaze as cool as porcelain. "It cannot be stopped."

But it could. She'd told me in the last dream that it could, if Tomo faced the whole truth of himself.

"Is this everything?" I said. "Is this the complete truth of Tsukiyomi?"

"Isn't it enough?" she said.

Tomo was on the ground, trembling. All those nightmares he'd had...they were all rooted in truths he'd forgotten, the whispers of "murderer" and "demon" his heritage. Taira had killed countless soldiers in his siege against the imperial throne, as had Tokugawa. Tomo's history was one written in blood.

But it couldn't continue. That wasn't who Tomo was. I wouldn't let him follow that path.

I shook my head. "It's not enough," I said. "It's just a reflection of the past."

Amaterasu smiled, her eyes lighting up.

"You have noticed," she said. "The missing shards."

"Tell us," I said. "Please."

She looked from me to Tomo, and then rested her hand on the top of the mirror.

"You know of the jewel, forged by Tsukiyomi's tears and shattered by Susanou's cruelty," she said. "Made anew by bitter rage. Tsukiyomi saw the world through this warped lens. He thought the world a place of rot and corruption, of filth and putrid distortion. He festered in this belief until his heart became black and twisted."

"Amaterasu asked Ukemochi to prepare a banquet to change his mind," I said, remembering. "And instead he killed the host."

The memory nodded. "When Amaterasu heard what he had done, she knew she must stop him. She longed to protect what the August Ones had made. But she is a being of light—she hated the darkness it brought upon her soul to plot against him."

Tomo cried out, the sound jolting me out of the story.

I stumbled around the altar to his side. "Tomo?"

"The memory sears his heart," Amaterasu said.

Tomo hunched over on the floor as he gasped for breath.

Amaterasu clasped her hands in front of her. "The truth is so sharp it cuts. Is it better to stop?"

But we had to know the whole truth to save him. We had to know how to stop Jun.

"Tomo," I said, wrapping my arms around him. "You're still you, okay? You're not Tsukiyomi. You can still fight."

He nodded with effort, gritting his teeth. "Continue," he panted. "Please."

Amaterasu slid her hand along the side of the mirror. "From Tsukiyomi's tears the Magatama was forged. From his hatred... something else."

The light in the shrine dimmed, the incense flooding my nose with too strong a smell. The world felt oily; I didn't like this at all. I didn't want to know.

But we had to. We had to.

"What was it?" I whispered.

Amaterasu bowed her head. "Yamata no Orochi. The beast of never-ending hunger."

Once there was a demon so hungry he devoured the world.

"Orochi was Tsukiyomi's curse on mankind, a hatred so potent it became flesh and blood. No human could withstand it."

Orochi. It sounded familiar, but I couldn't think why. What was it even supposed to be?

"Susanou had nowhere to dwell but this land. Thrown from the Heavenly Bridge, exiled to the lands below, if Orochi destroyed the world, he would vanish with it. And so he fought the blight of man."

The ground began to rumble. An earthquake? No... something else. The oily feeling spread across me, like something was spilling outside the shrine. "Tomo?"

The memory of Amaterasu continued. "In the end, hatred gave way to survival. There is nothing more dangerous than a creature whose existence hangs in the balance."

The world was shaking, black and strange. We had to get out of here. Something was wrong.

"If you want to save yourself, Yuu Tomohiro, retrieve the Kusanagi, and cleave away the loathing of Tsukiyomi."

The cry of an eagle pierced the shrine, and Amaterasu vanished like a candle snuffed out, only the blackness of night surrounding us.

Tomo collapsed onto the floor, released from the suffering the mirror had put him through. "Tomo," I said, panic rising in my throat. "We need to go." I grabbed the black cloth and threw it over the mirror.

He sat up, rubbing his head. Outside, the kirin let out his strange mournful bay. I pulled Tomo toward the door of the shrine and we jumped down from the railing to the ground.

"What is it?" he asked.

The eagle cry shrieked through the air again. In the darkness, the kirin hopped nervously from hoof to hoof, the jewels on its antler gleaming brightly.

From outside the fence, we heard a loud shout.

I froze. "Ishikawa!"

There was no time. We stumbled toward the kirin, Tomo pushing me up first and then pressing his foot through the thin waterfall of ink until the toe of his shoe took hold in the metallic scales. He pulled himself up onto the creature and we were off, galloping in awkward bounds toward the fence. I was in front, but it was Tomo's drawing, and I hoped to god he was the one steering. The world blurred in front of me, dark and terrifying. The ground rumbled, and the air filled with the sound of rushing wings. What was that noise? I didn't want to find out.

With a strong push against the ground, the kirin was airborne, the cold night wind rushing past our faces. When it landed this time we were ready for it. I squeezed fistfuls of its mane, the hair sharp like straw between my fingers. The creature stayed upright this time and sprang between the trees, sprinting as it panted in long breaths that rattled its rib cage.

That's when I realized. The kirin was running for its life.

I looked behind us, the shape of an eagle blotting out the moon. Only it was larger than an eagle—way larger. Its wingspan was the length of two people, its feathers black as night and its eyes gleaming white as it searched the forest for us. It had three sets of sharp talons, and they reached out to try and snare us in the forest maze.

"The Yatagarasu," Tomo shouted into the wind. The raven of Amaterasu.

"The one you drew was a lot smaller!" I shouted back. I wished I was home with Diane, tucked into my bed.

The bird grasped at us and came away with claws full of tree branches.

"They must have a Kami at the shrine," Tomo yelled. "A powerful one."

I looked at the feathers as they oozed ink like blood, the soft golden dust rising from the raven's back. It was a sketch, no doubt about it.

That's when I remembered that Ise Jingu had been protected by a member of the imperial family for the entire course of its history. Not just to oversee rituals, I realized, but to keep the mirror safe from other Kami, from anyone who wanted to steal it.

"That's one hell of an alarm system," Tomo shouted as the kirin bounded through the trees.

Just as we burst from the cover of forest, the raven circled back toward the shrine. Relief surged through me as it disappeared from view. It was only a guardian, after all, designed to scare off intruding Kami.

The kirin slowed, run to exhaustion. We slid off its back as it knelt on all fours, the lights in the gems dimming. "That thing was huge," I panted.

Tomo hunched over, his hands on his knees. "If it's drawn by an Imperial Kami, then the artist would be a close descendant of Amaterasu," he said between breaths. "Makes sense she'd called a Yatagarasu, but we're just lucky that Kami has control over her powers."

Suddenly the kirin stood, its eyes glowing too bright.

My stomach twisted. Here was Tomo's loss of control, come at last.

The kirin darted into the forest, chasing after the raven.

Tomo's eyes widened. "No!"

We heard the baying of the kirin as it bounded through the woods, the outraged cries of raven as it turned back.

"Sato," Tomo said. "He's still in there!"

Lightning flashed in the sky, and the earth rumbled. Melting feathers of ink caught on the wind, blowing past us and into the city. The raven shrieked in the distance and lifted into the sky, its feathers dripping to the earth as it struggled to fly. Tomo pulled his sketchbook from his bag, his pen in hand, and flipped to the page with the kirin on it. The creature lay on its side, its belly sliced open, metal scales scattered like slippery fish on the ground.

Tomo looked away as he swiped the pen through the drawing. The kirin let out a horrible cry in the forest as the tears gathered in my eyes. The beating of the raven's wings got quieter as it returned to the shrine, as it, too, melted away, scratched out by its mystery Kami.

Death around every corner. I was so tired of it all.

It needed to end.

17

We sat in silence in the hotel room, a square paper lantern on the table flickering its light across our faces. We'd laid out the futons, but sat on top of them, thinking over what had happened. Ishikawa hadn't returned yet, but he'd sent a text to let us know he was okay. He'd seen a couple priests entering the Naiku Shrine, but we hadn't heard his warnings over the voice of Amaterasu's memory. The shout we'd heard had been to draw the priests off us, and he said he'd lost them somewhere in the mountains. He'd scaled a tree to look around, and was waiting until things calmed down to make his way back to town. I'd raised my eyebrows at Tomo, who'd run a hand through his hair and grinned.

"Sato's good at not being seen," he said. I guess a life of petty crime was paying off in a weird way. "By the way," he added. "Thank you."

I stared at him. "For what?"

He pressed his hands into the tatami and shuffled toward

me. "For reminding me in the shrine," he said. "That I'm not Tsukiyomi. That I'm me."

I tried to laugh. "Of course you're you. Don't be stupid."

"*Oi,*" he said, pretending to be annoyed. But we couldn't shake the fear of what we'd gone through, the truth of what had happened long ago. Tsukiyomi had unleashed a monster into the world, and Susanou and Amaterasu had had no choice but to stop him.

"I've heard of Orochi before," Tomo said.

I shuddered when he mentioned the name. "What is it, exactly? Is it real?"

"According to the mirror, it was. The Great Serpent. It had eight heads and eight tails, and it devoured humans."

Eight heads and eight tails... I blinked. "Like a hydra?" Now Tomo was confused. "It's a beast that had multiple heads. Every time one was cut off, two grew in its place."

"I don't think it's like that with Orochi. Anyway, eight heads are enough."

"So assuming it actually lived at some point, if it's long dead, why tell us about it?"

"The Kusanagi," Tomo said.

"What?"

"The last of the Imperial Treasures. The sword was cut from the tail of Orochi."

"Then we have to go to Nagoya to find the Kusanagi and get the last of the story," I said. "About what happened after Susanou killed the hydra."

"It's obvious," Tomo said, leaning forward to run his hand along the edge of the lantern. His fingers cast shadows on the walls as he moved them across the light. "Susanou used the sword to stop Tsukiyomi. We've known to do that, all along. This is the way to make a Kami go dormant."

"But it was Amaterasu who stopped Tsukiyomi, wasn't it? It doesn't make sense."

"Maybe they worked together?"

My stomach twisted. It didn't sound right. It was bad enough to hear Amaterasu say I'd betray Tomo. There was no way I'd go to Jun's side after all this. "How does this translate into stopping Takahashi?"

Tomo's hand hesitated on the lamp, the shadows still for a moment. "I've been thinking. Maybe Takahashi really can't take over the world without my help. That's why he's still pestering me, why he's helping us get the treasures. Maybe stopping him is as simple as stopping me. What if all he knows is that Tsukiyomi was killed with the Kusanagi? He said he couldn't kill me on paper like the others. Maybe he doesn't know the blade can cleave Kami from human, that we could stop him with it, too."

"Good point." A secret like the Kusanagi would definitely have been kept close to the imperial throne. With the threat of Samurai Kami trying to take over, the ability to erase the ink from an enemy would have been the best treasure for Amaterasu to give to Emperor Jimmu.

I wished the adrenaline surge in me would quiet. I was exhausted, but my heart wouldn't stop racing. I curled my arms around my knees, and then winced, startled by the sudden pain that spread from my right shoulder.

"Oi," Tomo said, his voice soft with concern. "You all right?"

"I hurt it when I fell from the kirin," I said, reaching back to try and touch the muscle. I cringed as the motion sent pain pulsing through me.

"Here," Tomo said, resting his hands gently on my hips to turn my back to him. I stared at the shadows the flickering lantern cast against the wall as he pressed gently on my shoulder. "The bone doesn't feel broken," he said, "but there's kind of a stain on your shirt. Can I...?" He cleared his throat. "Can I lift it up to check?"

My heart stumbled against my ribs. "Okay."

"You don't have to," he said, his breath a whisper against the back of my neck.

Our shadows moved against the wall. "I know."

His fingertips pressed against my skin, each of them like a tiny candle flame at the hem of my shirt. He hesitated, then gently pulled the T-shirt up toward my shoulders. His arm held mine out, his grip delicate, like he thought I might break. "You bled," he said as he tried to move the fabric over the wound. "Let me know if it hurts, okay?" I wanted to be brave, but it stung like crazy. He peeled it slowly, watching me for cues. I squeezed my eyes shut, but didn't stop him. The shirt lifted away, and he threaded my arm through the sleeve, and then lifted the shirt over my head.

I stared at the shadows on the wall, my knees pulled to my chest where my heart was pounding. I didn't know what to say, or whether to turn around.

"Wait," Tomo said, and I stayed still as he padded across the tatami to the bathroom behind us. I heard the water rush into the sink, and then he was back again, dabbing at my shoulder with his handkerchief, damp and lukewarm.

"Is it bad?" I asked.

"Not too bad," he said, like this didn't even faze him. Were we all going to pretend that my shirt wasn't off, that I wasn't sitting there in my bra? But I was grateful he was trying not to make it a big deal. This was a medical thing, after all. But then why did I want so badly to turn around and hold him?

"It's not a deep wound, but there are a lot of welts. It looks like you hit a bunch of gravel on the way down." I shivered as the damp cloth lifted from my shoulder. "It'll probably leave a huge bruise."

I groaned. "It feels like it."

"Just take it easy for a bit," he said. "I'd skip kendo practice for a couple weeks or you'll make it worse." He traced one of the scrapes with his fingertips, and I shivered. "Now we match," he said. "The marks of a Kami. Well, sort of."

We sat there for a minute, neither of us talking, his fingertips pressed lightly against my skin. I could hear his breathing, could feel the heat of it against my back.

The pressure built up in my heart like a storm. I couldn't breathe.

"Let me get you a shirt," he said then, kindness seeping from every word. "I have an extra packed in my bag." His fingertips trailed along my back and lifted, leaving emptiness behind.

I turned and grabbed his arm as he stood, pulling him back down toward me. I curled against his chest, wanting to hear his heart, wanting to be surrounded by the warmth of him.

His arms wrapped tightly around me, his fingers trailing carefully away from my aching shoulder. I breathed in the smell of him, the light of the lantern blotted out against his shirt. I wanted to forget the giant raven, the kirin, the Imperial Treasures. I wanted to forget the demon that slumbered inside his blood. I just wanted to be with Tomo, just him and me, to be human and normal, like he'd said to me that day when he'd showed up at school. *If my time is short, I want to spend it with you.*

He loosened his grip as I leaned back, looking up toward his face. His eyes gleamed in the lantern light, his bangs fanned across them like a copper veil. "You're beautiful," he said, and the words shivered through me like a dream. I reached up with my fingers to push his bangs aside, feathery as a paintbrush.

He closed his eyes as I grazed his skin, a response that made my heart well with confidence. I trailed my fingers down his cheek and then down his neck, his skin so warm and tan, so different from mine.

I pressed my lips against his and he stopped holding back, clutching me like he was drowning, desperate for air. His hands pushed me closer as we kissed, as we let go of the adrenaline and the tension and the unsurety that we'd locked inside ourselves.

I reached for the hem of his shirt and slid my hands under, the heat of his skin radiating in waves. He released his arms around me and helped me slide the shirt over his head, his arms stretched upward as I tossed his shirt onto the tatami floor. The lantern light danced off the multitude of scars up and down his arms, the crisscrossing of wounds from sketches gone wrong. I traced my fingers across them and he shuddered, pressing his mouth to mine again. He tasted of sweetness and fire, every touch a jolt that sent me reeling.

We fell against the futons laid out on the floor, the gap between them leaving my back and legs against the softness of the blankets, but my hip jutting against the hard texture of the tatami. It ground against my hip as we kissed each other, as we tried harder to get closer, to shut out everything that wasn't this moment.

The storm in me rose, but I felt like rain and thunder were crashing everywhere, unpredictable and wild. I didn't know what to do with this feeling, how far I wanted to go. My brain felt hazy, filled with touch and happiness and want. It told me to give in and let Tomo take over. He'd hold my heart gently in his hand. I trusted him with everything.

His hands twisted into the futon on either side of me as he pressed against me, as he trailed kisses down my neck. My skin flamed where it touched his, like we were one person, like we couldn't get close enough. Even so, he waited, wanting me to show him how far he could go. It stirred a realization in me that this was real. What I had with Tomo was something worth protecting, something that mattered. But I felt awkward, too. I'd never done this before, and he was asking me to lead.

The sliver of me that was still rational tried to consider what was happening. How much did I want to happen? How far did he want to go? What I wanted had always seemed such an obvious and comfortable boundary in the quiet of my mind. But now here, in the flickering lantern light, when the future was uncertain, when the time we had together could be short—and when the heat of his skin flooded my heart with such fulfillment, with such a feeling of right and truth—now I couldn't tell anymore. All the boundaries seemed fuzzy and optional, unimportant. Maybe you couldn't know what was right. Maybe you just fumbled through the dark and hoped for the best.

"Tomo," I said quietly, my lips on his ear. He made a gentle sound in his throat in response. "Are you sure?"

He lifted his head and looked at me, his eyes gleaming, his hair flopping over as it started to dampen with sweat from the heat of us. "I'm sure," he said, his voice velvet and breathy and certain. That he wanted to give me everything flooded my heart with craving. "Are you?"

"I'm... I'm not," I said, hating the sound of my own voice. "I mean, I want to." God, I wanted to. "But I... It's just that I had this plan for my life, you know? I know it's totally stupid, but... I don't think I'm ready. I want it to be you, but... not yet. Not like this."

I thought he might say something, like "Plans change," or "I don't have much time left," or something like that. But he didn't. He closed his eyes, trying to get ahold of his breathing. Had I hurt his feelings? Had I destroyed what could've been wonderful?

He opened his eyes, and playfully beeped the end of my nose with his finger. "Sorry," he said with a grin. "I don't put out on the first sleepover."

I stared at him with my mouth open.

"I know you're disappointed," he said.

I smacked him in the arm. "You're such an idiot."

He laughed, ruffling my hair as he pulled back the edge of the futon. He stumbled across the floor and reached into his bag, tossing me his extra shirt. I hadn't realized how cold it was in the room until the warmth of his skin wasn't pressed against mine.

I pulled the shirt on carefully, staring at the way the lantern light flickered across the contour of his chest. "Can we still make out?" I said, sliding in between the layers of futon. The comforter was already warm where we'd rolled against it.

Tomo grinned, sliding in beside me and pulling me into his arms.

The rain started to fall outside, pattering against the rooftops as the lantern on the table burned out. I lost myself in his invisible touches in the dark, in his warmth and soul and humanity.

18

The train ride back to Nagoya was quiet and awkward—not
for Tomo, but for Ishikawa and me. Tomo brushed his fingertips down the inside of my arm, and I quietly moved away
from the touch as Ishikawa tried to stare out the window at
the torrential rains.

He'd arrived back at the ryokan around two in the morning,
sliding the door open with a squeak that woke us from sleep.
The light from the hallway had beamed around his silhouette, had illuminated the tanned skin of Tomo's exposed back
as he lay beside me on his stomach, his arm draped over me.

The light from the hallway had lit the flush of pink that
rushed to Ishikawa's cheeks.

"Ishikawa," I'd said, panic rising in my throat. He'd looked
completely dejected and worn down, the rainwater flatten-
ing his white spikes into a tangled mound of twigs and mud.

Tomo hadn't even looked up at first, turning his head to
the side as he flexed his arms to push himself up. "Sato," he'd
mumbled, his voice deep and groggy from sleep.

At the sound of it, Ishikawa's whole face had flooded a deep crimson.

I'd panicked. Tomo didn't have a clue, but I knew how this would hurt Ishikawa. "It's not what it…"

"Spare me, Greene," Ishikawa had said, his eyes cast down as he bolted for the bathroom. "By the way, I'm fine, thanks. Managed to shake off the priests and get back here without being followed. Since you were worried and all."

"Jealous." Tomo had grinned as he flipped over, still half-asleep.

Yeah, I'd thought. *You're half-right.*

The memory loomed like a cloud of horrible awkwardness as I stared at Ishikawa on the train. He'd probably joked around with Tomo in the morning to cover it up. I'd seen them talking together when I'd stepped out of the bathroom, but when they'd turned to face me Tomo had grinned, totally oblivious, while Ishikawa had looked down at the floor.

Tomo curled his fingers around mine and I winced, pulling my hand away. Was he such an idiot he didn't notice his best friend's feelings? Not like I'd been careful, either, and I'd known the truth. It was my fault, too.

"So, Nagoya today," Tomo said, trying to lighten the atmosphere. He looked at me with concern, and it clicked in my thoughts—he thought I was embarrassed at the way Ishikawa had found us. *Not even close, Tomo. Think harder.*

"This is the last one, huh?" Ishikawa asked, staring out at the rain. "And then what?"

"Then we use the Kusanagi to cleave out Tsukiyomi," Tomo said. "And stop Takahashi."

Ishikawa frowned. "Isn't that dangerous? What if you stab the wrong soul and then *you're* gone? What if we make a slice and, I don't know, cut the chains that bind Tsukiyomi's spirit or something? And he takes over?"

Tomo frowned. "I don't think it works like that."

My throat felt dry, but I tried to move forward, too. "How do you cleave a *kami* from a human, anyway?"

"Probably we'll find out when we get the sword. Amaterasu's memory has explained everything so far."

I stared at the rain pouring into Ise Bay as the train swayed along the track toward Nagoya.

The end draws near, a voice whispered in my head. *There is only death ahead.*

Tsukiyomi's demise, I thought, and Susanou's. Not real death, but only sleep. I wouldn't let it be anything more.

A man in the next row was hunched over a newspaper, and the front cover had an article about the supposed new "Kami gang" at war with the Yakuza. I nudged Tomo, who could read the newspaper more easily than I could. But he merely narrowed his eyes and looked away, and I knew it wasn't good.

"I told you," Ishikawa said, glancing at the newspaper. "Things are bad. People are starting to hail the Kami as more than a gang. They're starting to see them as a movement, as a rebellion." He folded his arms across his chest, pressing his white hair against the seat as he stared at the ceiling. "They're calling the 'mystery leader' Susanou, and they're saying he's saving Japan the way Susanou once stopped the Mongols from invading. That jackass is becoming the adored champion he wanted to be."

The train system chimed, and a women's voice echoed in the speakers as the kanji 名古屋 scrolled in bright orange letters at the front of the train car.

"Nagoya is next," she said in a chirpy tone. "Nagoya Station."

"We don't have much time," Tomo said. "We have to take the sword and get the hell back to Shizuoka."

Take the sword? Even though it had been the plan, I hadn't

really thought about how we were going to *take* it. It had been hard enough to get to the first two treasures—wouldn't the priests notice that we were walking off with the most valuable sword in the country?

We transferred to the local train in Nagoya and got off at Jingu-Mae Station, where the sprawl of Atsuta Shrine spread out inside the depths of the modern city, fenced off only by dark green hedges sewn together with spiderwebs.

I stepped away from the station, but Ishikawa's hand reached out for my wrist. I turned to see him holding a clear umbrella. "Here."

"Thanks," I said, taking it from him. He nodded and opened another umbrella for himself. I looked over to see Tomo had one, too.

"I bought them inside," Ishikawa said.

Tomo clapped him on the shoulder. "Let's go." He walked forward, ready to face what awaited us, but I held back.

"Ishikawa," I said. "What happened in Ise. I'm…"

"Uruse," he said, his cheeks flushed pink. "Shut up, Greene."

I kept going. "I feel horrible. You were out there in the cold, and I… Well, we didn't mean for it to happen, and I'm sorry, and…"

"Katie." He'd used my first name, and the sound of it startled me into silence. He looked straight ahead, watching Tomo cross the street in the rain. "Like I've already said. If I can't be there for him, then you need to cover for me, okay?"

I swallowed. "Okay."

"It's just…it's just hard to accept sometimes. I'll be fine." Ishikawa grinned. "He's an idiot, so don't think that you're too lucky."

I couldn't help but break into a smile.

"And another thing," he said as he stepped forward, the rain pattering against his umbrella. "Call me Satoshi if you want. Doesn't bother me."

"Satoshi-kun," I tried out.

He gently smacked the back of my head. "Satoshi-senpai," he corrected. "Damn it, Greene, you're either stupid or you have no respect for your elder classmates." He ran ahead to catch up to Tomo. I watched them for a moment, the two of them walking together in the rain with matching umbrellas.

My heart ached, but I had to focus on why we were here. To give Tomo and Satoshi and me the normal life we all longed for. I stepped forward into the pounding rain.

Atsuta Shrine was like a smaller version of Ise Jingu, the wandering pathways through gardens and the gravel crunching underfoot, the thick cedar trees wrapped with rope and the white cloth lightning bolts. Tomo jumped the fence to avoid the huge wooden Shinto gateway, and we bypassed the main shrine as he headed toward a large square building on the right.

I ran to keep up with him. "You can feel the presence of the Imperial Treasure again?"

He shook his head, and I saw the worry in his eyes. "Actually, I don't feel anything." He'd been so desperate to reach the other two treasures, but he seemed normal now, his expression too calm.

"Let's check here first," Ishikawa said as we approached the square building. "It's the museum archive. They keep all kinds of antique swords and crap in here."

We stepped up the stairs into the darkness of the dimly lit exhibit. Ishikawa—Satoshi—was right. It was like a mini-museum, with gray-carpeted walls and artifacts mounted on clear plastic encased in glass. There were cases full of small magatama jewels and rusted swords, curved like katanas in sheaths of tarnished brass and silver. One case had a suit of samurai armor that looked like the one Jun had been wearing in my dream.

"Anything here, Yuuto?"

Tomo shook his head as he passed a display of demon masks. "I don't get it. It should be here, but... I don't feel it anywhere."

"We could try a different building," I said. "The main shrine, maybe."

"No," Tomo said. "I mean, I don't feel anything anywhere. The Magatama I could feel a mile away, and same with the mirror. It's like it had a heartbeat, a voice on the wind."

He was right. I'd heard the voice of them, too, a faint whisper, but still something calling me. But it was silent here. No voice, no whisper, no tingle on my skin of something more.

Tomo left the museum building and we followed him through the gardens. The rain rippled on the streams and stone channels that threaded through the shrine grounds. We passed two shrine maidens carrying boxes of charms, their bright red *hakama* skirts swaying as they hurried toward shelter from the rain. Dark slate clouds blanketed the sky, the morning sun barely lighting the paths through the trees.

I wanted to ask Tomo again if he felt anything, but the dark look of confusion on his face answered my fear. "Did they know we were coming somehow?" I asked quietly. "Did they hide the sword?"

"I'd still feel it," Tomo said, his eyes desperate.

"Guys." Satoshi was standing inside a nearby shrine building, his hands on his hips as he looked up at the ceiling. We stepped under the shelter of the porch roof, slipping our shoes off to join him. "I think I know what happened."

There was a broad painting near the rafters of the roof, an ancient-looking woodblock that was peeling at the edges. The artist had painted angry waters tossed with black inky waves, the surface foaming and swirling with some sort of storm. The ocean lashed against the rugged cliff of gray paint, where the colored dots of an army stood perched, pennants unfurled in the wind. In the swells of the surging waters, a small figure swam, his arms raised. Nearby, another larger figure flailed as a wave swept her toward the sharp rocks below the cliff. And at the bottom of the painting, a sword, sinking to the bottom of the sea.

Tomo stared, his eyes wide.

"It's not here," Ishikawa said. "The Kusanagi is gone."

"What do you mean it's gone?" I said, staring up at the rafters of the shrine. How could some hundreds-of-years-old painting have anything to do with finding the Kusanagi now? "The emperor uses the three treasures for ceremonies, right? He'd notice if it was gone."

"He means the real one is gone," Tomo said. "It's been gone for over six hundred years."

I stared at them like they'd grown new heads. "Explain?"

"This painting," Satoshi said, pointing to the inscription beside it. "It's Emperor Antoku. He was overthrown by the Minamoto clan, one of the most powerful samurai families in Japanese history."

"Kami?" I asked.

"Probably part of the ongoing Kami war, yes," Tomo said. His voice sounded so tired. Everything linked back to the *kami*, back to his own destiny.

I squinted at the painting. "So Emperor Antoku is that tiny figure in the water?"

"Antoku was a child when they attacked," Ishikawa said. "It says the larger figure is his grandmother. She pushed him off the cliff to help him commit suicide."

I nearly choked on my own spit. "Sorry?"

Tomo nodded. "What else could he do? The whole army had cornered him onto a cliff."

Like throwing yourself into the ocean was the only reasonable option. I couldn't even imagine. "How...how old was he?"

Ishikawa squinted at the inscription by the painting. "Seven. He was Taira no Kiyomori's grandson."

"Seven?" My stomach turned. He wouldn't even have understood what was going on at seven years old. I could picture him holding his grandmother's hand, trusting her as she shouted at him to jump into the water. I shivered at the thought.

Tomo frowned. "It says she threw the treasures into the ocean, too. The mirror was recovered by one of the Minamoto who jumped into the water after it, and the Magatama jewel washed up on the nearby beach. But the sword sank to the bottom of the sea."

"But...the sword the emperor uses..." I said.

"It's a copy," Ishikawa said. "Obviously they'd make another one over the next six hundred years. And it's probably kept in Tokyo."

"The mirror wasn't the original, either," I said. "We can just go back to Tokyo and get it."

Tomo tucked his bangs behind his ears. "Even if it's kept there, it doesn't matter. It's not the Kusanagi no Tsurugi. The mirror was different. A replica sword won't cleave a *kami* from a body." He clenched his fingers into a fist. "It means all of this was for nothing."

Satoshi clapped his hand onto Tomo's shoulder. "Yuuto, don't say that."

"I knew I shouldn't believe there was more for me," he said darkly. "I'm the same as I always was—just the bastard son of some world-hating demon."

Anger welled up in me. "Don't say that," I said. "We've come this far—there's got to be a way."

"There isn't," he snapped. "There is no way for me, Katie. There never was. This whole trip was a waste of time."

His words stung as I tried to hold back my tears. Without the Kusanagi, there was no way to stop Tsukiyomi. It was only a matter of time before he took over Tomo, and before Jun took over Japan.

Ishikawa saw the pain on my face. "Yuuto," he said, while he looked at me. "Pull it together, man."

But Tomo's face crumpled in disappointment. "That's the point, Sato," he said. "I can't. I'm going to... I'm going to..." He crouched on the balls of his feet, his hands pressed against the dark wooden floor of the shrine. "I'm going to lose my-self," he whispered.

I sat on the floor beside him, wrapping my arms around his arm, pressing my ear against his shoulder. "I won't let you," I said. "We'll find another way."

"Without the Kusanagi, there is no other way," he said. He looked up, and I could see the tears glistening in his eyes as he held them back, as he fought to stay in control. "You need to get the hell away from me, Katie. For real, this time. Forever."

I closed my eyes, screaming at myself to think. All the dreams wouldn't have led us here if it was a dead end. Did the ink in us just not realize that it would be impossible? How else could we get the sword? It hadn't been found in six hundred years. If it was still at the bottom of the ocean, wouldn't it be useless? Rusting away, maybe covered in seaweed or coral or something, completely absorbed by ocean life. How could we use a dulled sword like that to cut away a *kami* soul?

"Wait," I said. "Couldn't you draw it? A replica wouldn't work, but if you drew it, it would have the power of the *kami* in it, right? It would be alive, like all your sketches."

"She has a point, Yuuto," Ishikawa said. He reached a hand out of the shrine, to see if it was still raining, and then closed up his umbrella. "Couldn't you draw your own Kusanagi?"

"I don't exactly have a good track record of drawing weapons, Sato."

Ishikawa touched the front of his shoulder, where the bullet had gone through. "You think I need reminding?"

Tomo stared at the floor as he thought. "Katie...do you remember the first thing that happened to me, the first time the ink in me woke up?"

Tanaka had told me the story when I'd first started at Suntaba School. I nodded. "You'd drawn the kanji for sword for Calligraphy Club," I said. "The stroke that flicks across the bottom cut your wrist open."

"I think that was the Kusanagi," he said. "This is what the ink's always been trying to achieve, since that first drawing. It's always tried to attack Tsukiyomi's blood in me. It's why the nightmares always whispered to me that I was a murderer, that I was a demon. They weren't speaking to me, Katie. They were speaking to Tsukiyomi. But if I can't draw the sword without dying myself..." He shook his head and rested his chin against his knees.

"Then draw Orochi." It slipped out, before I could stop it.

Ishikawa smacked his umbrella lightly against my arm. "Idiot."

"Orochi?"

Ishikawa rolled his eyes. "You think an eight-headed serpent won't kill him just as easily?"

"But the sword is in one of its eight tails," I said. "If you can get the sword that way, it won't cut you while you draw it."

"Again, you somehow forget the eight-headed dragon. With eight heads. And the number of heads is eight."

"Sato, enough," Tomo said. "It kind of makes sense. The

way Amaterasu spoke about Orochi back there... I kept thinking, Why do I feel so afraid? What is this terror gripping my heart? Orochi is long dead. I must have known, somehow... I must have known what was coming."

"Oi, matte yo," Ishikawa protested, putting his hands up in the air, his umbrella hooked over his wrist. "Wait, wait. You're actually considering drawing this eight-headed beast of horrible legend?" Tomo answered with silence, and Ishikawa widened his eyes. "No, no, no. There's no way this could go well. Did you forget the giant dragon you drew in Shizuoka? The gun that shot me in front of Hanchi? The freaky demon face and wings that sprouted from you before you collapsed on the street? Your powers are totally unstable, Yuuto. There's no way in hell you can survive drawing Orochi."

Tomo rose to his feet slowly, stepping out of the shrine's shelter and onto the muddy gravel pathway out of the shrine. "You're right, Sato," he said quietly. "I'm not stable enough to draw Orochi."

"Tomo?" I stepped toward him, my umbrella folded under my arm.

His face was stone. "That's why I'm going to ask Takahashi."

19

I couldn't form the syllables he'd said into meaningful words. "I'm sorry, what?"

"Are you a complete idiot?" Ishikawa said. "Takahashi isn't going to help you draw Orochi to get a sword that will stop *him*."

But Tomo was already walking toward the entrance of the shrine, toward Jingu-Mae Station and the way home.

"He's lost his mind," Ishikawa said to me.

"Agreed." I ran ahead to catch up to him.

Tomo didn't even wait for me to ask. "Takahashi is the only Kami I know who's powerful enough to draw it," he said. "He's stable, and his drawings come off the page. It's no good if it won't come off the paper."

"Yeah, but last time we saw him he threatened your life," I said. "He's not going to help you unless it means helping him. And the point of the Kusanagi is to save you and stop him."

"Then I'll have to give him something he wants," he said, like it was as simple as that.

"Like?"

He stopped to put his return ticket to Nagoya Station through the slot in the metal gate. The doors burst open with a chime. "Look, I don't know yet. I'll figure it out on the way, okay?"

"Couldn't he just draw the sword?" I asked.

"I don't trust him to give it to us," Tomo said. "He'd just use it against us, wouldn't he? But Orochi fought against Susanou. I don't think the drawing will be on Takahashi's side. My only hope is to get to the blade before he does."

"Drawing that monster is suicide," Ishikawa chimed in. "You know that, right?"

We boarded the waiting train, leaning against the opposite doors as we talked.

Tomo shrugged. "So maybe I can get Takahashi to draw him bound in chains, or deep asleep or something."

"How about a drunken stupor?" Ishikawa suggested, and I raised an eyebrow. "What? That's how Susanou defeated the original Orochi. Got him drunk and cut his heads off."

"Nice," I said. "Could you do something like that?"

Tomo nodded. "But there's only one person who can draw Orochi, and it's Takahashi, no matter how badly I don't want that to be true." The train doors closed and we lurched forward as we rattled down the track. "It's always been Amaterasu, Tsukiyomi and Susanou. Even now, we can't complete this without Susanou's descendant."

"It's a huge risk," Satoshi said.

"Yeah," Tomo said. "But it's the only one we have the choice to take."

I was silent as the train raced toward Nagoya Station, as we slipped through the crowd and boarded the bullet train for Shizuoka City.

My phone buzzed then with a text from Diane. I swallowed my panic, hoping she'd believed my message that I was at Yuki's for a sleepover. Yuki had known to cover for me if she checked in.

Out shopping with Kanako, the text said, her teacher friend. Yuki can come over to the house if she wants. A pang of guilt shadowed my heart, but it's not like I could help what I had to do. I dialed Yuki and put the phone to my ear. It rang and rang, and went to voice mail. I hung up.

"Calling your aunt?" Tomo asked.

I shook my head. "Yuki."

Ishikawa grinned a little too widely, trying too hard. "Checking in with the cover story, huh?"

Tomo's cheeks turned pink, but he smiled. "Shut up."

Ugh. Opting out of the conversation, I dialed Yuki again. *Please pick up and save me from this awkwardness.*

The phone clicked, but it was a guy's voice who answered. *"Moshi mosh?"*

I waited for my voice to catch up with my brain. "Tanaka?"

He sounded sheepish. "Uh…hi, Katie-chan. What's up?"

"I…why do you have Yuki's phone?"

"Oh, um." There was a rustling sound, like he'd stumbled or something. A raven called in the distance. "Yuki's in the bathroom right now. When you called back, I thought maybe it was urgent. You okay?"

I bit my lip to keep from laughing. "Fine," I said. "I can call later."

"Sure, okay," he said. "Yeah, um. Yeah."

"Tanaka, wait," I said. I hesitated, unsure what to say. "Can…can you keep Yuki safe today?"

"Doushita?" he asked, his voice quiet with concern. "What's going on?"

"I'm not sure," I said. "But I'd feel a lot better if you stay close to Yuki."

He paused, like he was going to pry for more answers, but he didn't. "No problem," he said. "You can count on me."

"Thanks." I hung up, not sure exactly what I'd walked into. There could be a totally innocent explanation. Maybe. But it wasn't time to worry about that. We had more serious things ahead. Knowing Yuki and Diane would be out of the way today made me feel better about the danger ahead.

"Do you still have Takahashi's *keitai* number?" Tomo asked.

I fumbled with my phone. "Yeah, here."

"Text him to meet us at the Minami Alps."

"The what?"

Tomo took my phone and punched in the kanji for me before passing it back. "He'll know where they are."

"I'm coming, too," Ishikawa said.

Tomo shook his head. "It's too dangerous."

"I'm not scared of that dipshit, Yuuto. I'm coming with you. You can't stop me."

I sent the text, my hands trembling.

Jun had been my friend once. I prayed silently that he would remember that, before the end.

We rode yet another train out of Shizuoka City, the houses thinning around us, the busy world shrinking away. The mountains rose up before us, nearly as tall as Fuji itself, all of them lush with trees that would be green again in the coming spring. The chill of mountain air permeated through the train windows.

"The Minami Alps," Tomo said. It was a popular hiking spot, he'd explained, but not when the weather was this freezing. I knew what he was thinking, of course. Meet somewhere others couldn't get hurt. I pulled my scarf tighter around myself as we stepped out of the train and into the wilderness.

We must have walked for half an hour, until we couldn't

even see the train station, until there was nothing but trees and fading sunlight filtered among them. The path through the woods curved into a clearing, and we stepped away from everything we knew, to face the fields of the Minami Alps.

The autumn forests pressed against the borders of the clearing, the mountains loomed like shadows—a painting of a dying world. In the summer, it must have been lush and green, with wildflowers swaying in the breeze. Now the winter had almost overtaken it, as the bitter cold of fate had overtaken me. Everything was on the edge of death, holding on to that last hopeless hope of one more breath. Just one.

Fuji loomed in the distance, along with other jagged peaks that blotted out the late-afternoon sun. It was hard to imagine we'd been in Ise this morning and Nagoya at lunchtime, where we'd slurped down kishimen noodles and failed to find the last of the Imperial Treasures. The sun would set in an hour, and then it would be bitterly cold in this exposed field.

"Do you think he'll actually come?" I asked as Tomo leaned against a nearby cedar tree.

"He wouldn't come for me," Tomo said, his head tilted back against the rough bark. "But he'll come for you."

I felt a flush of heat down my neck. "That's not true. We found out he was only using me because of the ink inside me, right? I was nothing to him."

Ishikawa sighed, patting my shoulder. I winced, the bruise still fresh. "Greene," he said, shaking his head. "When are you going to learn?"

"Learn?"

"That you weren't nothing to him," Tomo said, closing his eyes.

"That's not... You don't know that." But there had always been a tenderness in Jun, a kindness, that despite all the horrible things he'd said and done, they couldn't erase from him. There was still something in him warm and familiar, that even until now I couldn't bring myself to call him something as distant and unsurmountable as Takahashi.

高橋潤. Takahashi Jun. Literally, his name meant a bridge that was too tall, that was strong and impassable and undefeatable. And his first name meant *benefit*, a drop of sorely needed rain on the desert. The drop that would quench the thirst of the world. Or the tear that would stain its cheek.

I shuddered. A lofty name for a lofty dream, one that had borne him too high. It was time to fall.

We waited in silence, the mountain breeze whispering through the trees around the clearing. Ishikawa had his phone out, scrolling through the internet for more info on the Kusanagi and Orochi, but there wasn't much to be found.

"Susanou fought Orochi to rescue this guy's daughter," Ishikawa said. "The monster had already eaten the first seven girls, and the parents begged him to save the last. He turned her into a comb to ornament his hair."

"Dreamy," I said. "Every girl wishes she'd be turned into a comb."

"Why would they want that?"

I rolled my eyes. "Never mind."

Ishikawa clicked his phone off and slid it into his pocket. "You're weird, Greene."

That's when Tomo cried out and collapsed into the grass. We both shot over to him, grabbing his arms.

There was a rustle in the forest near us, and we looked up.

"Not now," I whispered. I could hear the groans of voices as the ink in Tomo awakened.

The voice in me stirred, too. It said quietly, patiently, *Jikan de gozaimasu.*

It is time.

★ ★ ★

Tomo heaved in each breath like he was drowning. He coughed and ink spattered in black drops on the ground.

A figure stepped forward from the forest, dressed in an elaborate kimono of plum and lavender, tied with a golden obi. She'd done her hair up in a bun, with a string of tiny purple flowers dangling back and forth as she walked.

It was Ikeda, I realized after a moment. I'd only ever seen her in her school uniform or her motorcycle jacket. She wore a fluffy white stole around her shoulders to keep out the cold of the coming winter, the kind girls wore in January for Coming of Age Day. She looked so elegant.

She stumbled when she saw Tomo on his hands and knees, the two of us desperate to help him. "What happened?"

"It's the ink," I said. Tendrils of black trailed down his arms and dripped onto the ground below. "He's losing control of himself."

Jun stepped out from behind her, clad in a black men's kimono that I'd seen him wear once before, the day he'd learned the truth about his link to Susanou. He looked regal and princely, his blond highlights and silver earring the only trace of his modern identity. When he lifted his arm to tuck his highlights behind his ear, the kimono sleeve slid back and revealed his familiar black bracelet with silver spikes.

He and Ikeda looked like they were from a different era, a different world. They looked like gods. Like *kami*.

"Katie," Jun said gently, his voice lacking any of the wrath it had had that day in the train station. "Are you all right?"

Tomo clutched at his heart, letting out another cry.

"I see," Jun said. "Deep breaths, Yuu. Calm down."

"Stay out of it," Ishikawa snapped.

I shook my head. "Help us, Jun," I said. I ignored the glare that Ishikawa shot at me. Who cared who helped Tomo, as long as someone did?

Jun knelt at his side. "Yuu, can you hear me? Don't get lost now. Find your way back." He turned his icy eyes to me. "What set him off?"

"I don't know," I said. "We've been waiting here for you for a while. Ishikawa was reading about the *kami* on his phone, and suddenly Tomo just fell over."

"Reading what about the *kami*?"

"Susanou and his comb chick," Ishikawa offered.

Jun frowned as he thought. "Wait...the story of Orochi?" I nodded. "Orochi was born from Tsukiyomi's hatred for Susanou. It must have stirred the memory in his blood."

Ishikawa let out a single laugh as he folded his arms. "That or he felt you approaching. I don't get it, Takahashi, you go around threatening Yuuto, yet you try to help him whenever Katie's around. Which is it?"

"Like I said from the beginning," Jun answered, his voice calm. "Yuu is something that never should have existed, and a danger to all of us. He's come to the end, now. If he doesn't get this under control, I don't think any of us will be walking off this field."

"Tomo," I said, pressing my hand on his back. "Please." My palm felt hot, like I was touching the steaming surface of a bath. I pulled away and discovered the ink pooling on his back, spreading out into feathered wings as he cried out.

"Is this why you called Jun here?" Ikeda shouted. "Do you know the danger you've put us all in?"

"He wasn't like this a minute ago," I wailed. I could feel a heat welling up in my chest, one that made the trees sway and the field ripple in front of me.

"Don't you start, too," Ishikawa said, and I felt the grip of his fingers on my arms. I tried to shake the feeling, to bleed out the power that was surging in me.

"Wait, that's it," I said. "Give him his notebook. The power is building up. His notebook, Satoshi!"

Ishikawa scrambled to Tomo's bag and produced the black notebook and pen. I grabbed it from him and flipped to a clean page, where I drew a quick butterfly. Its wings barely fluttered on the page, but my mind cleared, and the world became still again. I put the book in front of Tomo, forcing the pen into his hand. I didn't know what to make him draw, so I just helped him sketch out another simple butterfly on the page. The pen slipped and the ink from Tomo's arms dripped everywhere. A cloud of a hundred butterflies sprang up from the spilled ink, flapping their paper wings with the haunting sound of ripping pages. Jun ducked as they swarmed into the sky, one of the wings slicing a long cut into his skin, just under his left eye.

He gasped inward, clutching at the cut as blood welled up to the surface of the wound.

Tomo panted, his eyes and pulse returning to normal, but his face as pale as the paper butterflies.

Ikeda dabbed at Jun's cut with a lilac handkerchief she fished out of her bag.

"I'm... I'm fine," Tomo said, but I could see the tinge of red on his cheeks, the mortification at meeting Jun on the ground and out of control. He didn't have much left to bargain with now. Jun could see how desperate he was.

"What's with the getup, anyway?" Ishikawa said, motioning at the kimonos Ikeda and Jun wore. "Funeral or something?"

"School concert," Jun said. I tried to picture him playing his cello with Ikeda accompanying on the piano. And all the while, he was the leader of the Kami gang, building an army, taking over the world—destroying the Yakuza because he couldn't face his guilt over killing his own father. His world was so messed up, and yet I still felt sorry for him.

Tomo stood slowly, his hair slicked down with sweat. "Takahashi," he said. "You're here."

Jun's eyes hardened as he looked at him. "I am. And by the state you're in, I see you've found the Imperial Treasures. I'm sorry I couldn't assist you at Ise Jingu. I was busy with other things."

"Things like brainwashing?" Ishikawa snapped.

Jun smiled, his eyes dark. "Oh, believe me, they come to me willingly. All the Kami who've been struggling. All the Kami who've been put on meds for hallucinating about their drawings, who've been outcast for their godly ancestry. You'd be amazed how many were crying out for a leader." He reached a hand out, motioning to Tomo. "And now Yuu is finally here at my feet."

"Did you know?" I asked. "The story of the treasures?"

Jun nodded. "The jewel bears the marks of love turned to hatred. The mirror shows the truth of the depth of despair. And the sword cleaves the past from the future."

My thoughts raced. That wasn't what Amaterasu had said to me. *The jewel bears the marks. The mirror shows the truth. The sword saves all.* Why had Jun been told something different? But there was a seed of truth in everything she'd told me.

"If you know all this," Tomo said, "then you'll know that the sword is lost, and has been for a long time."

Jun raised an eyebrow. "Lost? No, I didn't know."

"Then how did you know the meanings of the treasures?" I asked.

"It was passed down in my family, like all the Kami training I had to endure. It was echoed in my nightmares, as it has been yours."

244 • AMANDA SUN

"Takahashi." Tomo looked at him with eyes of stone, his chin jutting out as he readied himself to ask.

My heartbeat drummed in my ears. Please let him help us. Please.

"Yuu?"

"Long ago, you wanted me to join you. But now I know you want to stop me."

Jun smiled, the coldness of it unnerving. "I saw potential in you, if only you could learn to temper your power. But the truth is, Yuu, that as a descendent of Tsukiyomi, as heir to the wrath that nearly destroyed the world, you are nothing but an abomination that threatens our existence. Your power cannot be tempered or controlled. It is a fire raging out of control."

Tomo's voice was steady, determined. "Then you know as well as I do that only the Kusanagi can stop me."

Jun nodded slowly. "Three choices lie before you. You can let the darkness surging in you take control, and destroy those you love." He glanced at me, but I looked away. "You can die, and your power and threat die with you, while the world is spared. Or you can use the Kusanagi to render you frail and powerless, to silence the ink in your veins for a time."

"For a time?" Ishikawa said. "It isn't forever?"

Jun shook his head. "There is only one way to silence a Kami forever," he said. I shivered. "And so you've found your way out, Yuu. The Kusanagi. Except it is lost to time."

Tomo tucked his bangs behind his ear and tilted his head back. "There's another way to obtain it."

"Drawing it would kill you," Jun said. "You're lucky you didn't get shot by the gun you drew for Hanchi, or the dragon that rose over Toro Iseki. I'm surprised you haven't died from your nightmares by now, to be honest." He reached up to rub the silver earring in his ear. "I have to admit, you do have a strong will."

"Takahashi." Tomo took a deep breath, his hands curled into fists. He bowed forward slightly. "Draw Orochi for me."

Ikeda's eyes widened, and she looked to Jun for his reaction. I held my breath, pleading, praying, that he would say yes.

Jun laughed, the sound so dissonant against the dying sunlight, so harsh against this strange and barren landscape. "You don't dare ask me to draw the Kusanagi, which you fear I'd wield against you, but ask me to draw a demon beast? What does it matter if I have the sword? You plan to use it on yourself, anyway. Who cares who wields the blade? Or do you think I won't stop with you?"

Tomo's eyes flashed. "Would you?"

Jun paused. "Probably not. You aren't the only descendant who suffers bastard demon blood. None would challenge me with the Kusanagi at my side."

Tomo unzipped his jacket and threw it to the ground, baring his arms to Jun. "Without the sword, there's no way you can stop me. And you know there's no time left." Ink dripped like blood from the scars down his arms. "This is my demand, then. Draw the Kusanagi and yield to me. Or I'll destroy everything, right now."

Jun stared. "You wouldn't do that. Not with Katie here."

"He wouldn't have a choice, moron," Ishikawa said.

"Let's end this," Tomo said. "Once and for all."

Jun's voice was quiet. "I can't."

I let out my breath. "Jun, please."

Ikeda winced at the familiarity of my tone, but it didn't faze Jun. "Katie, I'm sorry. I can't do what he asks."

"What the hell?" Ishikawa burst out, but Jun raised a hand to quiet him.

"I can't draw it," he said again, "because I'm not a descendant of Tsukiyomi."

I hesitated. "I don't follow."

"The Kusanagi was found in the tail of Orochi," Jun said. "Orochi was birthed by Tsukiyomi's hatred for the world. The power in that sword, the power to destroy even the ink itself, is from Tsukiyomi. I don't share his blood. If I draw the Kusanagi, it will be an empty shell of a forgotten blade. A useless copy."

Tomo took a deep breath. "Then help me fight Orochi. I can draw him, but it was Susanou who defeated him. If I draw something that dangerous, I... I won't..."

Jun smiled. "Don't let your pride get in the way," he said. "You won't be able to control such a drawing. I know that. You are a more powerful *kendouka* than me, Yuu. Did you know that? But I always win our sparring matches. Do you know why?" He lifted his hand and the ink lifted into the sky in sparks of gold, spiraling in ribbons through the air. "Because I have control. Because I've spent my life training my ability, embracing my power. I do not fear my lineage, not any longer. I do not fear death or your retribution. I am a prince, Yuu, a god. I am superior to you in every way."

"You're no different," I said. "You're descended only from Susanou. He was thrown from the Heavenly Bridge down to Earth. He was rejected." I waited for my words to strike Jun, but his expression remained the same. "Tomo has ancestry in the sun and the moon *kami*. If you're a prince, then he's rightfully emperor over you."

Ikeda's eyes flashed. "And what's he doing to serve his empire? The streets are filled with the hungry and the crying. What's Yuu doing but hiding in his room, trying to deny the ink in his veins? I'm a Kami, too. I know the nightmares, the fears that chain your heart when you try to live your life. But I'm not running. I've never run away."

"Ikeda," Jun said. "Yuu had to run away. He was doomed

from the beginning. A demon can't do good for the world. He can only shrivel up and die."

My throat was parched; I could feel my pulse drumming through me. "Jun, please. Help us fight Orochi."

"You know you're asking us to unleash hell?"

"We don't have a choice."

Jun pursed his lips as he thought. "When you have the Kusanagi," he said after a moment, "you'll use it against me, too. You'll try to cut me down."

None of us answered. It was true.

"I will help you, Yuu." *What?* I couldn't have heard him right. "But I have conditions."

Tomo's said nothing, the ink streaming down his arms.

"The Kusanagi belonged to Susanou. I will keep the sword, when you are done bleeding the ink out of yourself. You will not challenge me with it, or attempt to stop me any longer."

My heart froze. If we didn't stop Jun, the world would be ripped in half. Already the gangs were fighting—soon it would spread to civil war, an entirely new world where life and death were at Jun's whim. Sure, he said he worried about justice and protecting the weak and all that, but I could already see how the power of leading the Kami had overtaken him. He'd killed Yakuza—no, other people. Humans. He'd killed to get what he wanted. How could the world trust someone like that?

Jun wanted to help us because then his only rival, his only equal, would be gone, and nothing would stand in his way. But if we didn't get the Kusanagi, Tomo's life would be doomed, and maybe worse. What would Tsukiyomi do when he fully awoke? Would he destroy the world? He and Jun would fight until the end, and what would be left? A cold, shredded world.

Tomo let out a short laugh, and the sound of it startled me.

"Are you afraid of me, even without the ink? How could I stop you after I can't make my drawings come to life?"

Jun looked irritated, a faint flush of pink on his cheeks. "I'm not scared of you. You're annoying. Even now I should be rising to power, but instead I'm in a field in the mountains drawing snakes and little sticks. It's like swatting a fly, Yuu. Stop buzzing in my face."

Tomo's eyes flamed with the bait.

"And with the Kusanagi, any rival Kami could be easily silenced. So yes, I will fight Orochi with you, but when it's over, the sword is mine, and you leave me alone."

Tomo's voice was deep, determined. *"Wakatta."*

Ishikawa and I stared at each other, just as I saw Ikeda look at Tomo with surprise. He agreed to the terms?

Jun laughed. "I know you're bluffing, but I'll help you, anyway. I'll show you that you don't have the strength to oppose me." He reached down for Tomo's fallen notebook and pen, and tossed them to him. Tomo hunched over as he caught them, and it was then I realized his hands were still shaking.

The butterflies hadn't been enough to settle him. He was in no state to draw.

"Oh, and one more condition," Jun said.

The panic seized in my throat. What would it be?

"Atama wo sagete."

Tomo narrowed his eyes.

"Oh, please," Ishikawa mumbled. "That's petty and lame."

"No," Jun said. "It's fitting. Show me respect for the abomination you are, the bastard of Tsukiyomi. Lower your head."

He wanted to break Tomo's pride, to humiliate him. My hands tightened into fists. "What the hell's wrong with you?" I shouted. "What do you want? Tomo's life has been just as hard as yours. Why do you have to punish everybody for your own mistakes?"

But Tomo was bending his knees, lowering himself to the ground.

I shook my head. It was too much. The tears blurred in the corners of my eyes as my veins lit with anger. "Tomo, don't."

Tomo pressed his hands against the cold soil, and touched his forehead to the grass. I blinked my tears back.

Ishikawa smirked. "It's easy to bow when it doesn't mean anything," he said. But I saw the resentment burning on Tomo's face, the humiliation and the bitterness. I saw it as he sat back with the notebook on his knees, as he clicked open his pen and held it to the empty page.

Anger is something Tsukiyomi knows well, said a whisper in my thoughts. *If his wrath bursts forward, the world will flood beneath it.*

Jun took a step back, the fabric of his *hakama* skirt rustling as he clasped his hands in front of him. Ikeda stood beside him, a ghost of the Amaterasu who'd visited me in my dreams.

In the distance, the sky glowed orange and purple as the sun set behind the mountains.

"Now draw," Jun said.

20

The moment Tomo's arm arced across the page, I knew I'd lost him. His eyes grew vast and alien, like pools of ink. The whispers of *kami* gathered on the wind. He drew the arch of the monster's back first, and the long tails of a dragon or a snake. He outlined the first of the heads in a pale gray scribble, adding long horns and spines and stretched sinew around the mouth. But the sketch didn't look vicious until he drew in the eye, a sharp lizard eye that darted back and forth to watch as Tomo drew the rest of it.

The slender, draconic necks slithered around the page like tethered snakes. I wondered why he didn't draw it to look a little friendlier. I mean, did he have to draw teeth so sharp they tore the edges of the paper? And what happened to the chains he was supposed to draw in, or the tubs of sake to drown the heads in? But Tomo had lost himself in the sketching, and wasn't thinking straight. How could he? He'd never drawn anything this primal, this close to the truth. It was like all those other drawings had been leading up to this one sketch, like all this time, he just hadn't been able to put a shape to his nightmares.

Look at him, the whisper inside me said. *This is who he really is. This is the full truth of him.*

I saw the smile on his face, the dark pride at creating something so terrifying. Maybe this what Amaterasu had been talking about. To truly know himself...to know that part of Tomo relished the darkness. He'd told me before how he loved the feeling of the current of the ink sweeping him away, that he didn't care if it drowned him.

I hadn't believed it then. But seeing him now, as he jumped into the black ocean willingly, I knew it was true.

You see now the threat that Takahashi Jun saw? This is who Tomo is. He's fought it all along, but if it wasn't true that he was darkness at his core, he wouldn't have needed to fight.

I do see, I thought to myself. He was kindness and human, but he was just as much darkness and demon. I could see the threat. I could see it now so clearly.

Feathered raven wings oozed their way down Tomo's back as he drew. Horns pushed through his hair, spiraling around the copper spikes.

He will consume the world, the voice warned. And I finally believed it. After all this time, he truly frightened me.

A low moan echoed through the clearing. It was sunset, but dark clouds gathered to block out what remained of light. The world began to shake, and I could feel the vibration in my heart.

Ikeda pulled her white stole tighter around her shoulders. "Jun," she shouted over the rumbling. "He needs to stop drawing."

"It's not the drawing that's causing this," Jun yelled back. "He's finally acknowledging the truth to himself. Tsukiyomi is taking over. I only hope he can finish the drawing before it's too late."

"Too late for what?" I shouted, the gathering moan of cries on the wind drowning out every sound. Ishikawa bent over Tomo's shoulders, his palms black as he tried to shake him out of his trance.

"If Tsukiyomi takes him over before we get the Kusanagi, we won't be able to stop him," Jun yelled back. "He'll destroy the world."

Ishikawa's eyes bulged. "Are you serious? I know you guys talk big, but...for real?"

"He must finish the drawing," Jun said, wrapping an arm around Ikeda as she stumbled on her geta sandals in the trembling earthquake.

The low moan grew into a horrible hissing sound. Eight behemoth snakes hissing at once. I could see the shadow of Orochi in the distance.

God, I didn't want to look. A nightmare come to life.

It was at least three stories high, slithering toward us in a mound of papery coils that dripped ink all over the clearing. Its sixteen eyes glowed with a strange white light as it neared, each of its eight mouths open and snapping with fangs the size of people. I couldn't stop myself—I let out a horrible scream. The sight of the monster sent every thought I'd had reeling. I wanted Tomo to cross it out before it got too close.

Ishikawa and Ikeda screamed, too. Even Jun looked startled. He's underestimated Tomo's power again, that the creature he'd draw would be this monstrous.

And then Tomo cried out, but it wasn't in horror like us. He cried out because the ink was flowing through his veins, because Tsukiyomi was taking over.

"This is it, Yuu," Jun snapped. "If you give in to the ink, it's over." He held out both hands, his palms open. Ink trailed down Jun's arms and collected on his outstretched fingers, the blackness dripping in a slow waterfall, carving itself into glossy weapons. "We are *kendouka*," he said, "trained in the shinai used by samurai for practice. But practice has to end sometime." Instead of flat bamboo swords, the liquid dripped into the shape of sharpened blades, two katanas made of ink.

Armed with one in each hand, Jun turned to face the towering monster. "I know you!" he shouted. "I banished you from the earth once. Today I will destroy you again!" He looked over his shoulder at Tomo, still on the ground. "Get up and fight!"

Tomo gritted his teeth, his body shaking. "I... I can't..."

"Get up!" Jun shouted.

The tangle of snake heads snapped at the air as they approached us. I had to fight every instinct in my body to run.

Ink dripped down the sleeve of Ikeda's purple kimono as it formed into the shape of a *yumi*, a Japanese longbow that stood even taller than she was. An arrow formed in her other hand, which she notched into the bow as she bent down beside Jun. She wasn't a *kendouka*, I knew, but the sight of the *yumi* surprised me. I didn't know anything about her, I realized. She played piano, she owned a motorbike and now I knew she did Japanese archery. But I'd only labeled her one of Jun's dumb goth followers, never as her own person. The remorse flashed through my mind as she pulled back the bowstring, ready to follow Jun into battle.

I grabbed Tomo's arm and pulled him to his feet. His body shook with the effort to stand, even as the ink dripped down his arms. "Come on, Tomo," I said. "Let's get the Kusanagi."

He nodded, sweat rolling down the sides of his face. The ink pooled in the palm of his hand, the liquid twisting and shaping into the blade of a katana, the hilt shimmering with golden dust. The wings on his back molted feathers everywhere, new ones constantly growing in as the old melted away. One wing was featherless, angular and leathery like a demon's. It was like his body couldn't decide which direction it was going, which way to manifest the ink. He gripped the sword, his hand shaking.

Orochi's hissing slithered through my thoughts and I turned

to see it towering above Jun, its heads weaving between one another as they eyed him hungrily. The center one lunged at him, its long neck flexing, its fangs dripping with black ink. Jun rolled out of the way and its teeth sunk into the earth like two daggers, shaking the whole valley. I stumbled backward into Ishikawa, who had seized up in terror.

"What have you drawn, Yuuto?" he said quietly to himself, his voice near my ear.

I wanted to tell him this was the Orochi of legend, that Tomo had only sketched what had existed once before. But long ago, Tomo had told me his drawings were an extension of him, that his own spirit lived, however briefly, in those drawings. *They aren't alive*, he'd said. *They're part of me.*

Which meant this monster, this rage and desire for destruction, lived inside him. It always had, or he wouldn't have been able to call it forward.

Oh, Tomo.

Ikeda loosed an arrow and the beast roared as the shaft lodged in one of its jaws. The struck head swayed back and forth before hurdling toward her. It snapped its jaws shut as she ran out of the way, another arrow forming from the ink in her hands.

Tomo shouted out the same loud *kiai* he used in his kendo matches and raced toward the monster. He sliced into one of Orochi's necks, ink gushing from the wound as it oozed down the creature's scales. The heads turned their attention to him, and Jun raced to the other side, whirling his two katana into the creature's side one after the other. The beast cried out, knocking Jun into the air with its powerful neck. He flew through the air and crashed into a cypress tree before crumpling beneath it.

"Jun!" Ikeda shouted. She loosed another arrow, this time into one of its eyes. I nearly retched as I heard the squelch, the beast shaking the head violently, the arrow lodged deep inside its eye socket.

"What can we do?" Ishikawa said. He reached to the nearby cedar tree and yanked off a branch as thick as he could manage, brandishing it toward the creature.

A tree branch wasn't going to cut it. "You'll get killed, Satoshi."

He flung the stick at the ground so hard it flipped over when it hit. "Well, what am I supposed to do? Yuuto's going to get killed out there! I don't have any Kami powers. All I have is a pocket knife."

"I don't know! Get behind it and cut the sword out of its tails?"

"Are you an idiot? You think this knife is going to cut through that hide?"

Ikeda ran toward us as she notched her bow, pulling the long string back. How could she use a bow that huge? But the arrow flew, and bounced off Orochi's chest to the ground. Ikeda swore. "Do something!" she snapped at me.

"Like what?" I shouted back. "Can't Tomo just scratch through the Orochi drawing? That would kill it."

She shook her head. "It would dissolve before we could get the sword. Your presence makes Yuu and Jun stronger. So get moving already!"

She was right. Ishikawa couldn't do anything, but I could.

Yes, the voice whispered inside of me. *It's time now.*

I raced toward Tomo's notebook, lying open and ripped in the grass. The small sketch of Orochi snapped at my fingertips, the wounds on its neck oozing ink that dripped over the sides of the page. My fingers were drenched in it as I tried to flip the oily pages to a clean one. I grabbed Tomo's pen and wiped the dirt off it before pressing the nib against the page.

My mind blanked.

Orochi lunged at Tomo and I heard him cry out, saw him grabbing at his shoulder as blood dripped down the back of his black wings. "Tomo!" I cried. Tomo dodged the next of its heads, racing around the back of the creature toward its tails. Another of the heads darted out and grabbed at his back, throwing him straight up into the air. Panic choked me—Tomo couldn't survive a fall from a distance like that. He'd die. But halfway down his wings started flapping, enough to slow him down so that he only landed with a thud. He'd feel it, but he'd live.

I thought of the giant raven that had protected Ise Jingu. Couldn't that fight a monster like this?

I quickly sketched an awkward, angular raven. That was the messenger of Amaterasu, wasn't it? But my bird didn't move on the page or appear in the sky above. The cold wind swirled around me, and the raven's feathers lifted slightly on the page. And that was it.

I screamed at the page, scribbling the lines of the raven darker. Tears began to pour down my cheeks. What was the point of being a man-made Kami if I was so useless?

I tried to calm down, to think about what Ikeda had said. Don't try to do it on my own. Lend my ability to Tomo and to Jun. But how?

When I'd called down the power of Amaterasu to stop Tomo and Jun from fighting, I'd needed Ikeda to trace over my drawing. Maybe I could trace over Tomo's. I flipped the pages, looking for something I could use.

There. A Yatagarasu, the one that had tapped on my window and attacked us on the train. I traced its lines darker through the scribbles Tomo had crossed through it. Maybe if I colored the raven darker, it would be strong enough to break through the bars of the cage he'd sketched around it.

On the page, the raven's eyes lit with a deep blue light, like the jewel I'd seen on the kirin's antler. It was working.

Thunder rumbled in the sky, and the piercing caw of a raven echoed through the air.

Ishikawa swore as the giant bird swooped above him, its shining blue eye gleaming like a flame.

Orochi cried out as Tomo struck another blow to its severed neck. The final cut lopped the head off and it hit the ground with a thud, its eyes dull as it rested in a pool of ink. Seven left.

The raven reached out with its talons, all three sets of claws digging deeply into another of Orochi's necks. The beast shrieked and its remaining heads honed in on the bird, lunging at it in a flurry of fangs and feathers. It shook the bird off, but the central head flopped unsteadily, barely attached to its neck anymore.

The bird was enough distraction—Jun managed to cut through another neck. Two of the heads now lay on the ground, forked tongues lolling out between the huge, sharp fangs. Ikeda loosed another arrow, and it struck in the narrow gap between the tottering neck and the head, enough to dislodge it from the body. The remaining five heads shrieked and hissed. Behind me, Ishikawa retched into the grass. I barely held back as I darkened the bird, hoping to give it whatever power I could.

The raven curved in the air, lifting its wings high in the sky as it swooped down again. Jun sliced his two blades into the side of the monster and it shrieked into the air so loudly I covered my ears. The katanas stuck in the monster's flesh, and Jun pressed his foot against its scaly hide to pull them free. They wouldn't budge. His arms strained with the effort as he pulled, the blades inching forward, the ink pouring down the creature's side.

The five heads wove among themselves as they lunged for him.

"Jun!" Ikeda cried out. She shot an arrow as she ran, but

it flew too high, right over the targeted head. Her bow clattered to the ground as she cast it aside, stumbling in her kimono toward him. The ink pooled into a spear in her hand as she ran.

"Ikeda!" I called out. I pressed my pen against the wing of the bird, and the raven in the sky veered toward the heads plunging toward Jun. It dug its claws into one, but the other four kept moving.

Jun tumbled backward as the blades slid out of Orochi's skin. I screamed as I saw the fangs of one mouth bare, as the ink dripped from them into Jun's hair.

It happened in an instant. Jun raised his katana and thrust it toward the open palate of Orochi's mouth. But Ikeda lunged in front of him, her spear plunging through the beast's cheek, and before Jun could stop himself his blade pierced through her.

I screamed as the thunder cracked around us.

Ikeda's eyes widened as she collapsed on Jun. The snake head drew back, shaking the ink spear from its cheek. The Yatagarasu clawed at the eyes of the multiple heads with its three legs as Tomo leaped onto the beast's back and started carving through its hide, searching for the Kusanagi.

I dropped Tomo's notebook as the cold wind swirled the scent of blood and ink through the field. Orochi moaned and roared as Jun cried out, Ikeda collapsed in his lap.

"Naoki!" he shrieked, his hands tangled in her hair.

Another of Orochi's heads slithered toward him.

"No!" Ishikawa grabbed his tree branch and lunged at the head. "Over here, you big ugly!" He swung the branch and the head snapped toward him. Ishikawa rolled through the packed dirt out of its reach, stumbling to his feet and swinging again.

I raced toward Jun and Ikeda. "Get her out of here!" I shouted, pulling on her limp arm. Her startled eyes stared up at the sky, her white stole stained with ink and blood and dirt.

"She's gone," Jun moaned, clutching at Ikeda as he pulled her close to his chest.

The hot breath of Orochi wafted against my back, and I turned to see its sharp fangs looming in front of me.

I was helpless. I had nothing to fight it with. The anger and powerlessness surged through me as I stared at it.

The head dropped to the ground beside me, rolling sideways as the fangs tipped over. Tomo straddled what was left of the neck, the stump of it wriggling with nerves.

"Naoki," Jun sobbed as the ink spread out in wings on his back. He brushed his fingers over her face, leaving trails of ink like tears on her cheeks.

"Takahashi!" Tomo yelled as Orochi thrashed underneath him. "I need you!"

"Go," I shouted at him. "I'll take care of Ikeda." Jun looked dazed, like he couldn't control his own arms and legs. I grabbed his wrist, the spikes of the bracelet sharp against my palm. "Get the Kusanagi," I said, and Jun stumbled forward, his wings flapping.

The raven let out a twisted cry, and I looked up to a waterfall of feathers spiraling around me, black ink pouring from a jagged bite mark in its side. Its lifeless body slumped to the ground and began to dissolve, lifting like golden fireflies on the bitter wind.

I looked down at Ikeda's lifeless body, her elegant purple kimono stained with darkness. The Orochi was destroying everything. This couldn't be happening. It wasn't supposed to go like this.

Tomo, what have you done? What have you drawn? Did this hatred always live inside you, wriggling to get out?

I heard a whisper in my heart. It spoke, as it had before. *Once there was a demon so hungry he devoured the world.*

I looked at Tomo, the way his eyes shone as he fought against Orochi. His wings flared out, his horns dripping down his hair as they formed and reformed. Now Jun lifted into the air, his kimono robes fluttering as he flapped higher, his two katana aimed at the back of the creature's rib cage.

Susanou killed Orochi, the voice whispered. *He slayed the beast of never-ending hunger, the monster born of Tsukiyomi's hatred for the world.*

Jun let out a horrible strangled cry and dove toward the creature's back. I looked away, but the earth rumbled with Orochi's cry. When I looked again the beast was flailing backward, trying to strain its necks back to reach Jun.

Tomo cut into the base of the beast's tails, and the heads lunged toward him. Jun fell to the ground and rolled onto his back, directly under Orochi's now-exposed heart.

I clapped my hands over my ears at the sound of the flesh giving way, the horrible screech the beast made as it gave up the life Tomo had sketched into it.

Tomo and Jun raced for the lifeless tails of the monster, carving through each of them, searching for the sword. Jun pierced the skin at the base of the tails, and the sound of metal clanging against metal echoed through the clearing.

Susanou killed Orochi, and claimed the Kusanagi no Tsurugi, the voice whispered loudly as it snaked through my thoughts.

And then Susanou killed Tsukiyomi, right? I knew what came next. I remembered my dreams, Jun soaked in ink—no, blood—telling me he was sorry. And Tomo, motionless on the ground, the way Ikeda was now in my arms.

I shook my head.

Jun pulled the Kusanagi from the base of Orochi's tails as

the beast melted into a pool of ink, as the blackness lifted like clouds of golden fireflies around us.

Though Orochi was dead, it wasn't over. It was just beginning.

21

"Naoki," Jun said, stumbling toward us. He fell to his knees, the Kusanagi at his side as he pulled Ikeda toward him. Tears slicked down his ink-streaked face.

My voice shook. "I'm so sorry."

"It's not your fault," he said, his blond highlights clinging to his face as he rocked back and forth. "She was my best friend, Katie. She always stood by me. Always."

Tomo's quiet voice sounded from behind us. "She loved you."

Jun shook as he tried to stop his tears. "I didn't deserve it. When the nightmares threatened me with death, I always thought they meant my own. I had nothing left to live for, so they didn't scare me. But I was wrong. I had Naoki to live for. I had everything and I didn't even see it." He choked on the words, his shoulders shaking as he tried to muffle the sob. I rested a hand on his shoulder, unsure what to say.

Beside him, Kusanagi glinted in the grass. It looked less

elaborate than I'd imagined, an old boring and common sword, not at all worth the price Ikeda had paid.

The dark clouds had cleared and lifted away, and the golden dust of Orochi's blood glimmered on the sword's edge. The hilt was without ornament, simple and inscribed with Classical Japanese that I couldn't read. But I'd never seen a blade that looked so sharp. Looking at its strange edge, the way it glinted with a faint rainbow along its edge, I believed it could cleave Tsukiyomi from Tomo. It could cleave Susanou from Jun.

Jun's fingers wrapped tightly around the sword as he lowered Ikeda off his lap to the ground. His eyes had frozen over again, his emotions held tightly to himself.

"Let's finish this, Takahashi," Tomo said, but as he spoke, a hundred others spoke with him, like a strange echo in many different voices. He hovered above the ground, his ink katana in his hand, and a glowing jewel around his neck. The Magatama, recreated from his own ink.

"You want me to break you, little boy?" Jun said. He gripped the Kusanagi so tightly the blade shook in his hand. "The rules have changed. I've decided not to spare your human life."

No. God, no. "Jun," I said, my voice wavering. The dream flashed back in my head—Jun covered in dark ink, Tomo not moving. "Don't do this!"

"Naoki is dead, Katie," Jun said, the blade shaking. "It's too dangerous to leave Tsukiyomi inside, even if he's sleeping. Yuu Tomohiro has to die."

"Then come for me," Tomo said darkly, the ink rolling off his wings like a waterfall. "And we'll see who survives."

Ishikawa cupped his hands around his mouth. "Yuuto. Don't be an idiot! Come down."

"Tomo," I said, reaching my hand up for him. He was too high to reach, his clothes rippling in the wind as he hung in the air. "Don't forget who you are. You're not Tsukiyomi, remember? This isn't what you want."

He hesitated, his eyes searching mine as he tried to remember.

In that moment Jun leaped at him, tackling him out of the sky. The two hit the ground hard, rolling across the grass as Jun held the Kusanagi over Tomo's neck. Tomo pressed back with his katana of ink, the two blades locked against each other as they struggled.

Tomo kicked Jun off him with so much strength that he sent him hurdling backward. Before I could reach him, he was on top of Jun, punching him so hard that Jun's face twisted to the left.

"Easy, man," Ishikawa said, grabbing Tomo from behind and pulling him off. Tomo snarled like a beast, and the sound of it horrified me. He didn't even sound human.

Jun got to his feet, gingerly tossing the blade in his hand to feel its weight. He swung it in a slow circle and then sliced at Tomo with it. The air around the Kusanagi sang, and the smell of metal and warmth drifted on the air, like the wind itself had been severed.

Tomo and Ishikawa stepped backward as Jun advanced. He swung again, the blade slashing the skin under Tomo's eye. The blood dripped from the gash down his cheek. "Now we match," Jun said, reaching his fingers to the cut on his own cheek from the butterfly's razor wing. He swung again, and Tomo's katana connected with the blade in a metal hum that echoed.

The tears blurred in my eyes, my fingers caked with dirt and dried ink. "Stop it! Stop!" I grabbed Jun from behind and pulled with everything I could muster. Tomo lunged toward him, katana outstretched, but Ishikawa wrenched him backward.

"I'll kill you!" Jun shrieked. "I'll kill you for what your drawing did to her!"

"It's not worth it," I shouted as Jun squirmed against me. He was stronger, but I dropped my whole body weight toward the ground, throwing him off balance. "Ikeda is gone, Jun!" I screamed. He went limp in my grip. He stopped struggling. We stood there, panting, the warmth of his body rising and falling as he gasped for air. "She's gone."

Ishikawa was restraining Tomo, but barely. He was beating his wings against him, scratching him up with the quills of his feathers and the spikes on his leathery wing as he tried to lunge at Jun. He let out an angry, frustrated shout as he tried to shove Satoshi off. The shout echoed with a hundred voices on the cold wind.

Jun dropped the sword into the grass below, falling to his knees. "Let him kill me," he sobbed, the tears running freely down his face. "Let him do it."

"Of course not," I said, reaching for the sword. They were both idiots. Thank god Ishikawa was here to help me.

I wrapped my hand around the hilt of the Kusanagi, warm from Jun's steady grip.

A wave of fire lit through my veins as I touched the sword, and a shock of white lightning blinded me as I collapsed to the ground. The electricity jolted through me, like every nerve in my body sparking at once. I held on to the sword, barely, as the ink in me exploded with life and memory.

I couldn't see anything in the white light except the faint outline of a woman in a golden kimono. Amaterasu, from my dreams. The whisper inside me, awakened by the sword.

I reached my left hand out for her as she watched me on the ground.

"Get up," she said. "Now is the time."

I sat up, but I wasn't in the Minami clearing anymore. I

268 • AMANDA SUN

was in that small island in the sky, the ink waterfalls roaring around me and the pagoda in the distance. "Time for what?"

"Time for the cycle to complete."

"I don't understand."

"Tsukiyomi has awakened," she said. "You have seen the true nature of Yuu Tomohiro, the depths of the blackness in his heart that he has hidden for so long. It is time for you to betray him, as I once betrayed Tsukiyomi."

The words chilled me to the bone. "I told you I would never betray him."

She tilted her head sadly. "You don't have a choice. If you do not, he will destroy the world. You must save the world, as I did."

My throat was dry, my face pale. "You're asking me to cleave Tsukiyomi's spirit from Tomo, right? But he'll survive."

She lowered her head. "Susanou's heir spoke the truth. He is too dangerous alive. Tsukiyomi's hatred is too great. If you do not kill him, Diane, Yuki, Tanaka, your father...all the world will perish."

This couldn't be happening. "But...you said there was another way. That if he knew the truth of himself, he could be saved."

Her face was stone as she folded her hands against her stomach. "You would never have searched for the Imperial Treasures otherwise."

The betrayal stung like a knife. "You...you lied to me. You lied to get me to this point!"

"To save this world, I would do anything," she said. "Even betray the only being I ever loved. Now, show me the extent of *your* love."

The sunlit island faded, and I was back in the clearing again. Ishikawa was on the ground, his face and arms covered with blood and ink and welts.

Jun watched the skies, the horror mirrored on his face.

I looked up and saw Tomo. His mouth was open as he cried out in agony, the ink ravaging his entire being. It poured from the corners of his mouth and trailed down his arms. It dripped from his wings and horns, and draped over him in robe-like waterfalls. It was choking the life out of him—he was drowning.

I raised my hand to my mouth, horrified. The weight of the Kusanagi pulled against my wrist.

He suffers, the voice of Amaterasu whispered to me. *End his suffering.*

Tomo's wings gave out and he lowered to the ground, the ribbons of ink swirling around him like a tornado. His hands and legs stretched out into the storm as he writhed in agony. The ink—it was tearing him apart.

"He won't survive Tsukiyomi's awakening," Jun shouted into the wind. "You have to stop him!"

Me? But…it was Jun soaked in ink in the nightmares. It was Susanou who destroyed Tsukiyomi, wasn't it?

No, Amaterasu whispered. *I was the only one. It has to be an act of love to end his suffering. You have no other choice, child. Takahashi cannot wield the blade.*

"No," I said, pressing the sword into Jun's hands. "You can do it, can't you? Cleave the *kami* from the human?"

"I can't," Jun yelled. He grabbed the sword from me and approached Tomo. A blinding wave of light shot him backward, the Kusanagi clattering along the ground. The force of the hit left Jun groaning on his back. "Only a descendant of Amaterasu can complete the cycle of betrayal," he panted. "You're the closest thing we have right now."

I picked up the sword, looking at the faint rainbows that danced along the honed edge of the blade. It was all a lie to get me here, to hand me this horrible task. Is this all that was left for us?

Tomo's voice cried out for me. "Katie," he whimpered, pain shooting through his voice. I'd never heard him sound like that before. The suffering in it shook me to tears that blurred my vision. "Katie," he wailed, louder, reaching his hand out for me. The ink swirled around him like a hurricane, golden dust and flashing blue and plum whirling around the field. The tree branches and grasses whipped wildly around from the bitterly cold gusts of wind.

Ishikawa pulled at his hair. "Greene, do something!" he pleaded. "Make it stop!"

"You have to do it," Jun said, rising to his feet. "He can't withstand the power of Tsukiyomi. It'll rip him to pieces! He'll die if you don't."

"He'll die if I do!" I wailed. What was I supposed to do? There had to be another way.

Tomo's voice was racked with pain. "Katie!"

"I have to save him," I said. "Tomo!"

"He's not Tomo anymore!" Jun snapped as the ink whirled around us. The words stung me out of numbness.

I gripped the sword tightly in my hand, taking a step toward Tomo.

In the end, there is always death. That's what Amaterasu had said from the very beginning. The only choice I had was how, and who. The whole world, or Tsukiyomi. Tomo had been doomed from the beginning.

Tomo reached for me, his spirit completely broken. "Please," he begged, the ink swirling around him as he strained for his hand to touch mine. "Betray me, Katie. I'll forgive you. I love you. Do what you have to do!"

"Urusai!" I shrieked at him. "Shut up! How can I do this when you tell me you love me? Why does it have to be like

this? It's not fair!" The tears blurred the world as they stumbled down my cheeks.

"Please," he panted. "Stop me. Amaterasu gave you the power you need to stop me. Do it!"

Jun was wrong, I thought as I stared down at the sharp blade of the Kusanagi no Tsurugi. It was still Tomo, deep in his heart. Even now he was fighting; even now he refused to let the wrath overtake him.

Until his last breath, he was Yuu Tomohiro. Until his last breath, I loved him and he loved me.

I was standing right in front of him now, the ink swirling around him in a storm of agony. He shouted as Tsukiyomi tried to take hold, his cries like the wails of *inugami* or *oni*, Japanese demons. I wanted to clamp my hands over my ears. I wanted it to stop.

I tightened my grip on the hilt of the Kusanagi.

He reached out his hands to the sides, opening his chest so I could direct my hit.

"I love you," I said quietly, lifting the sword out to my side.

He waited for the sword to cut through him, to cleave life from him, to take away hope. "I know," he panted through the agony.

My hand shook, the blade heavy with memory. It knew its mark; it knew where to strike.

I raised the blade into the air as the tears curved down my cheeks, as the sobs racked my lungs.

He squeezed his eyes shut, his teeth gritted against the pain.

The wind and ink swirled around us.

Now, Amaterasu said. *Take courage and save him.*

I took a deep breath. "I'm sorry," I sobbed.

The ink whipped against my face, dripping from my hair, from my cheeks.

And then I dropped the sword to the ground. It clanged as it hit the earth, as it settled against the dirt.

"What the hell are you doing?" Jun yelled.

"Greene!" Ishikawa shouted.

Pick up the sword, Amaterasu whispered sharply. *The world will tear in two.*

"Katie, no!" Tomo shouted. The ink storm raged around him as he tried to reach for me. "Pick up the Kusanagi. Please!"

I shook my head as I wept. I couldn't accept this. There had to be another way.

"Katie!" Tomo shrieked. The ink lit with bright gold, and the Magatama around his neck shattered into white-hot pieces, catching on the windstorm and swirling around him. He shrieked like I'd never heard before.

Tsukiyomi was tearing his body apart. Horror welled up as I watched him scream. I'd made the wrong choice. I hunched over to search the brush for the sword. Why had I been so selfish, so weak? I couldn't bear to lose him, to betray him. I'd sacrificed the world for a selfish desire.

As my hand touched the cross of the sword, Ishikawa's hand wrapped firmly around the hilt. He pulled the sword from me and screamed his loudest *kiai*, running toward Tomo. His face was racked with tears, his spirit broken as he screamed into the night. The cold realization froze me like ice.

Ishikawa cried out in agony, his heart breaking as he plunged the Kusanagi through Tomo's heart.

"Tomo!" I shrieked as the ink plummeted like a waterfall. Tomo arched backward as ink dripped from his mouth. I shoved Ishikawa away, wrapping my arms around Tomo's chest as he lowered to the ground. I cradled him to me, his body limp and heavy, just like in the nightmare. Shards of the Magatama stuck to my palms, flowers of blood springing up from their cuts. I wiped them against my jeans and ran my fingers down Tomo's face. He was peaceful, his eyes closed, the pain finally gone. "No," I whispered. "Don't leave me. It's not fair."

I heard the Kusanagi clang against the ground and I turned to see its blade, coated with dark blood and ink. Tomo's blood. I lunged at Ishikawa, beating my fists against his chest. "You bastard," I raged. "You total idiot bastard!" He didn't fight back, nearly choked by his sobs as I attacked him. "What the hell kind of best friend are you?" I shrieked. My heart was shattered like the Magatama. The world moved slowly, dreamlike, as if none of this was real.

Ishikawa fell to his knees, leaning over Tomo. He smoothed the copper bangs out of his eyes and leaned over him, pressing his lips to his forehead.

I shoved him back. "Get away from him!" I shouted between sobs. "You killed him!"

"I had to," he sobbed. "He was dying, Greene. I couldn't let him suffer like that."

I crumpled in on myself, letting the tears overtake me. Ishikawa's warm arms wrapped around me and I let him hold me as we cried together.

In the end, there is always death, whispered the voice in my heart.

In the end, there is always life.

My body warmed with a buzzing heat like every nerve was on fire. The earth began to tremble in time with my pulse.

Ishikawa leaned back, his eyes wide. "What's happening?"

The world felt like fluid gold, like I could see behind what was real to the strings that tied the world together. The ink was malleable here. I could shape it into anything I wanted.

I reached my hand to Tomo's chest, and the ink in me lit like a flare as it spread to him with its warmth.

Amaterasu had betrayed Tsukiyomi because she loved him,

and the betrayal had festered in his heart until now, the cycle happening over and over, in Taira, in Tokugawa and where it had seeded into Tomo's heart. But as I felt the heat spread to Tomo, I realized something. Ishikawa had stopped Tsukiyomi. Amaterasu hadn't betrayed him this time.

The cycle is broken, Amaterasu whispered. *Tsukiyomi can be free from his wrath.*

Tomo gasped for breath, sputtering ink as he coughed.

Ishikawa faltered, his eyes wide. "Yuuto," he whispered.

"Tomo," I said, squeezing his hand. He squeezed back faintly, and I knew he was regaining strength. The wound in his chest flared with golden light.

He closed his eyes, gritting his teeth as what little power I had went into him. As the ink filled him with life, I felt the emptiness in my heart, the little chair in the corner empty, the whispering voice of Amaterasu lost on the wind.

I'd never been meant to possess the ink, and in the beginning, it had nearly killed me. But in the end, it had given me the power I needed to save everything precious to me.

The light dulled, and then it was just the five of us in the clearing, the clouds gathered above us as the sun dipped below the horizon.

The snow drifted down like cherry petals, gently, softly, covering the world of ink with a layer of pure white. The snow caught on Tomo's eyelashes and in the spikes of his hair as it fell, as he blinked into the sky.

I heard Jun whimper, and looked over. He had his hands curled around Ikeda's cold fingers, and the glow of luminescent plum passed between them. Hope fluttered in my heart. Ikeda...was she... Was she alive?

She blinked away the snow on her eyelashes, and Jun burst into relieved tears, leaning over her as the plum light dimmed.

He'd been able to share the power of his ink, too, in that golden world, to bring her back from the brink of death.

Ishikawa ran a hand through his white hair, shaking off the snowflakes. The snow was falling heavily now, covering Tomo in a blanket of pure white.

He coughed, turning his head as he held tightly to my hand. "Katie," he mumbled.

I let out a garbled laugh or cry, my heart bursting. "I'm here."

"Sato."

Ishikawa's eyes lit, and he smoothed the snowflakes out of Tomo's copper hair. "I'm here, man. I'm always here."

"You..." Tomo coughed.

Ishikawa leaned in. "Yeah?"

"You...stabbed me in the heart, jackass."

Ishikawa laughed until the tears fell from his eyes. "I'm your best friend, idiot," he said between strangled laughs. "Of course I did."

"I'm sorry," I said. "I'm sorry I couldn't do it."

Tomo shook his head. "If you had, I'd be dead right now," he said. "You refused to accept our fate. You fought this until my last breath. *Arigatou*."

I leaned over and kissed him, the snow on his lips melting between us.

Around us, the snow drifted slowly down, a whirl of white, a world made new.

22

The snow crunched under my boots as I walked through Sunpu Park. The castle loomed over me, its angled tiles dusted with white. I wove through the courtyard on the way to the station, running my fingers along the giant wooden doors pulled to the sides to let pedestrians through.

It was hard to imagine back to the day Tomo and Jun had fought for the first time, the day everything had started to unravel. The courtyard was silent now, my footsteps echoing on the tiny bridge that arched over the moat.

"Katie!" I looked across the street to see Yuki with Tanaka, a soft pink scarf wrapped around Yuki's neck, and a hand-made red scarf around Tanaka's. "Did you just get out of kendo practice?"

I nodded.

"*Zannen na,*" Tanaka whined, pushing his glasses up his nose. "It's too bad about Tomo-kun. It would've been Suntaba's first time at such a high-ranking tournament."

Yuki smacked him gently in the arm, her lacy mittens

matching perfectly with her scarf. *"Shou ga nai yo,"* she said. "It can't be helped. Think about who you're talking to, *ne?"*

His cheeks flushed pink. "Sorry, Katie-chan."

"It's fine," I said. "There's always next year." Except Tomo and Ishikawa wouldn't be at Suntaba next year. "Kamenashi's probably going to be the next team captain, but I'll do my best, too."

"We're heading to the coffee place in Oguro," Yuki said. "Want to come?"

I smiled. "Thanks, but I'm taking Tomo his homework. He's still recovering from his...kendo accident." The lame excuse that we'd had to rely on.

Tanaka nodded. "Wish him our best, okay? And tell him Sensei told me my calligraphy's improved thanks to his help."

"I will." I grinned, waving at them.

Yuki waved, a smile on her face, and they turned to walk, Yuki's hand slipping into Tanaka's.

I headed down the steps into the tunnels that connected to Shizuoka Station. It would be December next week, almost a full year since I'd been in Japan. Everything had changed since that time, since Mom and I had lived by ourselves in that tiny house in Albany. I hoped she'd be proud of me, of what I'd accomplished. I know she'd be glad about the bond I had with Diane, that we somehow completed the puzzle of each other, even without our missing pieces.

I walked past the metal train gates just as Jun stepped up to them. His eyes caught mine as he slid his ticket into the slot. It zipped into the machine and the gates opened. He leaned forward, his blond highlights slipping in front of his ears.

"Katie," he said quietly as the travelers milled around us in a cloud.

"Jun."

It felt like the whole world was moving but us, like time had stopped.

He shifted the bag on his shoulder, his bangs tilting to one side, nearly cover his eye. *"Genki?"*

I nodded. "Things are good," I said. "You?"

"I just got back from visiting Ikeda in Kenritsu Hospital," he said. "She's awake now, starting to eat on her own."

Relief flooded through me. "That's great. That's wonderful."

"Yeah."

"So...you're done, then?" I meant the Kami taking over, the attack on the Yakuza.

"The price was too high," he said, rubbing his silver earring between his fingers. "When I almost lost Ikeda...what you said was right. It's not worth it, not now. How many others would die in a Kami war?" He shifted his weight, looking around to make sure no one was listening to us. "Maybe it's better if the ink is kept a secret for a while longer. Power is something others will kill for, and I don't want people like Ikeda to get hurt." He sighed. "Times haven't changed that much since the Samurai and Imperial Kami fought each other. I know how Tsukiyomi felt. I still don't like the state of the world, but...there are other ways for now."

For now. "Then..."

Jun smiled. "I gave up some of Susanou's power to save her," he said. "It's going to take a while to be quite as powerful as I once was."

I bit my lip. "Do you want to be that powerful?"

"Everyone wants the power to change the world." He grinned, kicking at the marble floor with his shoe. "But it takes time to learn how to use it."

"So...what now?"

He tilted his head. "It'd be better if we don't talk too much.

After the suspicion around Yuu and me, and now with Ikeda in the hospital... I don't want the police to focus in on any of us much."

"You know, there's no justice for the people you killed," I said.

He paused. "I know. But I can't exactly turn myself in. I'm just going to do what I can to make things right. And that starts with Ikeda. She's put up with so much."

I nodded.

"I've got to go," he said. I looked at him, his once-cold eyes melted. He'd never looked so human.

"Want to go for that coffee?" I asked, confident of his answer, wanting to end things completely.

He bowed his head. *"Gomen,"* he apologized. He stepped into the crowd of passengers and I lost sight of him. I wondered if I'd ever speak to him again. I started to turn, but then his hand shot up in the middle of the crowd, a farewell as he kept walking, putting distance between us.

I wondered if it was true, that his power could return. I didn't think you could get Kami ink back that you'd relinquished. I certainly couldn't feel the ink in my veins anymore. None of my sketches even fluttered a tiny bit. It was like I'd dreamed it all.

I grabbed Diane's bike from where she'd left it for me in the parking shelter, and then turned northeast for Otamachi Ward. I sailed along the streets in the snow, the tires slippery through the slush. I turned the corner and nearly collided with a girl.

I slammed on the brakes, skidding in the snow, and bowed my head. *"Sumimasen,"* I excused myself.

The girl looked at me, her eyes wide and her hair slicked back into a ponytail. "Katie?"

Oh god. "Shiori?" I felt itchy and awkward. I wasn't sure what to say.

But she smiled warmly, and then I saw the bundled-up baby in her arms, the tiny little face that was so new to this world. She wore a soft pink coat with teddy bear ears sewn onto it.

"She's okay," I said, and Shiori nodded.

"We were out of the hospital by the end of the week. She's doing great."

"What's her name?"

Shiori jiggled the squirming girl up and down. "Aya," she said.

I reached my mittened hand toward her, stroking the girl's tiny cheek. "Aya-chan," I said as she wriggled in Shiori's grip.

"We're on our way home from the store," she said, lifting a crinkling white bag in her hand.

"Oh," I said. "I thought…" I shut up, but knew it was too late as the heat rose up my neck.

"You thought we were coming back from Tomo's place?" she said. I couldn't do anything but nod. A thoughtful look came on her face as she stared down the street, but then Aya twisted in her arms and she pulled her up to her shoulder. *"Maa,"* Shiori said quietly, patting the little girl's back. "The truth is, these days I have someone else I love even more." She smiled at me, little dimples forming on her cheeks. I smiled back. Shiori wasn't alone, not anymore.

I curled my mitts around the handlebars and nodded to her as I cycled down the street. The tires skidded in the snow, but I loved the feeling of the fresh wind pressing against my face.

I leaned the bike against the silver nameplate on the wall that said The Yuu Family and pressed the buzzer. The gate unlocked and I walked up to the door just as Tomo pulled it open. His arm hung in a cast strapped around his neck, his torso covered in bruises and cuts. His blue pajama bottoms hung at an angle off his lean hips, and his copper hair was pressed in awkward angles, like it had just been slept on. He still had a sleepy expression on his face. He must have been napping.

He lowered his head to scratch the back of his neck, and I saw that the black roots of his hair were growing in. He caught my eye, and smirked. "What are you looking at?"

"What, no hello?"

"Hello. What are you looking at?"

I grinned. "Your hair," I said. "You look nice with black hair."

He looked horrified, like I'd caught him tap-dancing or something. He grabbed the top of his head with his palm while I giggled. "It's cute," I said, stepping into the *genkan* and resting my bag on the raised floor, reaching down to pull my boots off.

His chest pressed against my back suddenly as he held me tightly, his good arm wrapped around my shoulders. The smell of vanilla and miso flooded my thoughts as I breathed him in, the tickle of his hair against my neck and cheek.

"Tomo," I said quietly. I curled my fingers around his arm, closing my eyes as I lived in his embrace, as he encompassed my world.

"I didn't think I'd get to do this again," he said. "I thought it was over."

Me, too. But I didn't want to give it a voice. It was past now. We'd fought, and we'd won.

Tomo released me and held the back of my coat with one hand as I slid my arms out of the sleeves. We went up to his room, where he smoothed out his comforter, his cheeks flushed pink.

"Were you sleeping?" I grinned.

"No," he said, straightening the edges of the blanket. "I was, um, I was studying."

"Mmm-hmm." I looked at his desk, a mound of entrance exam books on one side, a stack of application forms on the other. "Tokyo University of the Arts," the top paper said. My heart swelled. "Tomo."

"Hmm?"

"You're applying to Geidai?"

He tried to keep a straight face, but I could hear the delight in his voice. "*Maa*. I thought I might as well write the exam, and then we'll see."

Two weeks ago, he couldn't write *sword* without getting killed. Now he could study art freely. "And your dad?"

Tomo let out a laugh. "Some things never change," he said. "But he'll come around eventually. Maybe."

I opened my bag and placed the homework in between the piles of papers and textbooks.

"Oh, *sankyu*," he said.

"You're welcome. It gives me an excuse to see you every day."

He laughed. "You don't need a reason."

"How's your arm?" It had been dislocated and broken when Tsukiyomi's power had nearly ripped him apart. When you watched him climb the stairs, you could easily notice he'd pulled a muscle in his leg, too. Between the injuries and the bruises, he'd had to drop out of the national kendo tournament.

"Doctor said I should be able to write the entrance exams in February if I follow his rules carefully."

"And are you?"

Tomo grinned slyly.

"Tomo."

"I don't take orders well."

I sighed, lying back on his bed. "Entrance exams are important, you know."

"Katie." His voice was deep and lovely, and I wanted to kiss him over and over, now that we were free. But instead I sat up as he sat beside me, as he passed me a cute cartoon notebook. It had little pandas and brown bears picnicking on a background of soft blue, complete with sakura trees and smiling *onigiri* rice balls.

"What's this?" I said.

His cheeks reddened. "Open it."

I turned the cover slowly, and my mouth opened in surprise. "Oh."

It was a new notebook of drawings, sketches more beautiful than I'd ever seen. Flowers sketched with shadows of gray and careful lines of black, so real I swore I could smell them. Drawings of wagtails and deer, of horses galloping and dragons lifting into the sky. I turned the pages quickly, hungry for more. The beauty overwhelmed me, overtook me, until I'd forgotten everything but the softness of the pencil lines, the special voice of Tomohiro that had no words.

This was how he saw the world. This was what was in his heart. He drew other things, but what he was really drawing was himself—bare, raw, beautiful.

I turned the next page and hesitated.

He'd drawn me. My face, turned to the side as I looked out a train window, my hair slipping out of a ponytail in messy strands. I turned the page and it was me again, the curve of my back and my leg as I sat on the edge of a pool, my head turned up toward the sky. And another, where I sat at a desk, my head propped up on my hand, my pencil on my notebook, wisps of hair catching on the wind from the open window.

I turned the page. A half-finished sketch of me reaching for a book on his bookshelf, a sheet clutched to my body like one of those marble statues. It clung to my body in a pretty intimate way, and I found my cheeks getting hot as I looked at it.

Tomo laughed nervously, pulling the book out of my hands. "You weren't supposed to see that one." He closed the cover of the book, putting it gently on his bed. "I couldn't really fill in the details yet, anyway."

I flushed darker. But the drawing hadn't been crude or pervy. It had been in a delicate fine-art style, like something you'd see in a museum. I felt a rush of gratitude, that he could see such beauty in me the way I saw it in him. "They're beautiful," I said. "You're so talented."

His face was as red as an *umeboshi* plum. "Not really."

I bumped my shoulder into his, a faint wave of pain emanating from the kirin bruise that was now fading. "Don't be so modest. But stay off your wrist now, okay? You need to write your entrance exams to get into art school."

"I know." We sat for a minute. I couldn't stop thinking about the drawing. I wanted to kiss him all over. "How was kendo practice?" he asked, and the question jolted me out of it.

"Fine," I said.

"Did you beat Satoshi to a pulp?" He grinned.

"Satoshi wasn't there."

Tomo leaned his head back. "Huh. So he is, after all."

"Is what?"

"He told me he was enrolling in a cram school," Tomo said. "He wants to take entrance exams."

I gaped. "Seriously?"

Tomo nodded. "It's probably too late for this year. But some schools have retakes in the summer. He might be able to get it together by then."

What happened had really changed all of our lives, sent us spinning off in directions we hadn't known we could go.

"And you?" he said.

"Me? What about me?"

"Are you... Are you going back to America?"

Dad had called again over the weekend to invite me back. He hadn't mentioned the Kami to Diane—would she even believe him? But he kept sending me emails, photos of the lake, insisting I would have fun.

The lake was beautiful, even if it came with a lot of family drama to work through. I missed my life on the western side of the world, where I never culturally goofed or said the wrong thing without realizing. With everything that had happened, I had to pull a miracle by February or international school was probably in my future.

But so what? Tomo wouldn't be at Suntaba next year, anyway. And I could still see Yuki and Tanaka outside of school. Maybe international school wouldn't be so bad.

"I don't know what'll happen," I said. "But right now, my home is here in Shizuoka. With you."

He looked up, a shy smile spreading across his face. His fingers trailed over my arm and linked with mine. I could see the scars that trailed up his other arm, crisscrossing with one another in a history map that was uniquely his.

"None of them have come off the page, you know," he said.

"Hmm?"

"The drawings." He'd seen me looking at his scars. "They haven't attacked, not even one. They still move, but the darkness in them is sleeping. I can feel it."

"And the nightmares?"

"I still get them sometimes," he said. "But I also get new dreams. Amaterasu and Tsukiyomi walking along the Heavenly Bridge together, flocks of ravens circling them, things like that."

"Nice." I smiled.

"Katie," he said, his eyes filled with worry. "He's still in there, you know. The darkness is still there."

Of course. Because as long as Tomo lived, the threat of Tsukiyomi resurfacing existed. "You can't help it," I said. "You're descended from Tsukiyomi, and from Amaterasu. You have light and darkness both in you."

He lay back on his bed, staring at his ceiling. "Yeah. But I was thinking. So does everyone." I lay back beside him, and he pressed his warm shoulder against mine, our fingers still twisted together. He held up our entwined fingers, turning them gently in the beam of light from his window. "There's a darkness in my heart. And I'll fight it for the rest of my life." He squeezed my fingers. "I'm glad we're fighting together."

"Yeah," I said. "Me, too."

I didn't know if the darkness would ever waken in him, if it would slumber forever now the cycle had been broken. But I knew Tomo would fight it as he always had, that we would carve out the fate we wanted, that we would cleave the past from the future.

I knew that it was worth everything to fight.

And I knew that nothing could stop us.

★ ★ ★ ★ ★

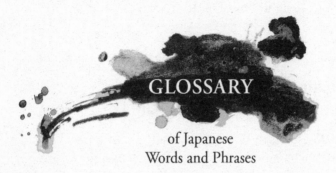

GLOSSARY

of Japanese
Words and Phrases

Abunai:
"It's dangerous" or "Watch out!"

Arigatou:
"Thank you"

(Aru)baito:
A part-time job

Atama wo Sagete:
"Lower your head"

Chan:
Suffix used for girlfriends or those younger than the speaker

Chawan:
The special teacup used in a tea ceremony

Chigau:
Literally "It's different," or "It's not like that," but it's used as a more polite way to say "No"

Conbini:
A convenience store

Daijoubu:
"Are you all right?" or "I'm/It's all right"

Dame:
"It's bad." Used to tell someone not to do or say something

Dekiru zo:
"You can do it." Slang used by male speakers

Depaato:
A department store

Doushita:
"What happened?"

Ee?:
Can be used when one is surprised, impressed or simply listening and processing what someone is saying. Roughly translates to "Is that so?"

Ee to:
"Um," means the speaker is thinking of what to say

Gaijin:
A person from a foreign country

Genkan:
The foyer or entrance of a Japanese building. Usually the floor of the *genkan* is lower than the rest of the building, to keep shoes and outside things separate from the clean raised floor inside.

Genki:
In good health or spirits

Genmai:
Roasted brown rice tea

Gomen:

"I'm sorry." Also used to refuse a date request

Hai, kochira desu:

"Yes, this person/this place"

Hakama:

The pleated skirt-like clothing worn by *kendouka*

Hidoi:

Mean or harsh

Ikuze:

"Let's go," said in a tough slang

Inugami:

A dog demon from Shinto tradition. Known for their un-controllable wrath and murderous instincts.

Irrashaimase:

A welcome greeting by store clerks

Isami:

Courage

Itadakimasu:

"I'm going to receive." Said before a meal like *"bon appétit"*

I-te/Itai:

"Ouch" or "It hurts"

Jikan de gozaimasu:

"It's time." Very polite Japanese

Kamaboko:

Fish cake

Kapparu:
"Couple," a dating couple

Kashikomarimashita:
"I understand," said by waiters taking orders

Keitai:
Cell phone

Kendouka:
A kendo participant

Kirin:
A traditional Asian unicorn. "Kirin" is also a homophone for "giraffe."

Kotatsu:
A heated table used in Japanese homes in the winter

Kouchou:
A school headmaster or principal

Kouhai:
A fellow student younger than the speaker

Kun:
Suffix generally used for guy friends

Kuromoji:
A bamboo stick used to eat traditional Japanese sweets

Kusanagi no Tsurugi:
The sword of legend, one of the Imperial Treasures of Japan

Maa:
"Well," but it can be used as a subtle way of affirming something ("Well, yes")

Machinasai:
"Wait," said as an order

Maji de:
"That's impossible"

Momiji:
Maple

Moshi mosh(i):
"Hello?" Said when answering the phone

Moushi wake gozaimasen:
Literally "There is no excuse." A very formal apology.

Muri:
Something impossible, or unreasonable; a bad idea

Ne:
"Isn't it?" It can also be used as "Hey," to get someone's attention.

O temae choudai itashimasu:
"Thank you for making the tea," said during tea ceremonies

Obasan:
"Aunt," or said to an older stranger to be polite

Ofuda:
A Shinto scroll traditionally said to exorcise demons

Ohayo:
"Good morning"

Okaeri:
"Welcome back," said when someone returns home

Oi:
 "Hey"

Oni:
 A Japanese demon

Matte:
 "Wait"

Ryokan:
 A traditional Japanese inn

Sama:
 A suffix used to raise the person to an honorific status

San:
 A polite suffix used for people you don't know well, or those older than you

Sankyu:
 "Thank you"

Sanshu no Jingi:
 The Imperial Treasures of Japan: the sword, the jewel and the mirror

Senpai:
 A fellow student older than the speaker

Shikari shite:
 "Get ahold of yourself," or "Calm down"

Shou ga nai:
 "It can't be helped"

Sore dake:
 "That's all"

Sou ka:

"Is that right?"

Sumimasen:

"Sorry" or "Excuse me." Can also mean "Thank you" in certain contexts.

Takoyaki:

Breaded balls of octopus, often served at festivals

Temaki:

A cone-shaped, hand-rolled sushi

Torii:

Shinto entrance monument to a shrine. The O-Torii is the famous orange gate in front of Itsukushima Shrine.

Tsugi:

"Next"

Umeboshi:

A Japanese pickled plum

Urusai/Uruse:

"Shut up," or "It's noisy"

Uso:

An expression of disbelief, literally "That's a lie"

Wakatta:

"I get it," or "I understand"

Washi:

A special paper placed under traditional Japanese *wagashi*, or sweets

Yamata no Kagami:
Amaterasu's mirror, one of the Imperial Treasures of Japan

Yamenasai:
"Stop," said as an order

Yasakani no Magatama:
A crescent-shaped jewel of legend, one of the Imperial Treasures of Japan

Yatagarasu:
A three-legged raven, the traditional messenger of Amaterasu

Yumi:
A Japanese longbow

Yurusenai yo:
"I won't forgive you"

Yuuki:
Bravery or courage

Zannen:
"What a shame"

ACKNOWLEDGMENTS

I have been writing the Paper Gods series for six years, and dreaming of it much longer. It's a surreal feeling to stand on top of this mountain, to look down over the view of Shizuoka captured on the page and to know that I have shared a story with you all that I've longed to share. It's with deep gratitude that I thank everyone who climbed this mountain with me, who made this dream possible.

Thank you, T. S. Ferguson, for your unwavering confidence and enthusiasm for *Storm*. With your help, I was able to shape this book into everything I hoped it could be. I so appreciate the faith you put in me, and the insight you pour into the edits that enrich my books.

Melissa Jeglinski, you are the best agent a girl could hope for. You're always there and I feel truly blessed to work with you. Thank you so much for seeing potential in the Paper Gods and being there for me every step of the way.

Thank you to everyone at Harlequin TEEN for making *Storm* look absolutely beautiful. Thank you to Mary Sheldon, Amy Jones and the Marketing and Production teams. A huge thank-you to Gigi Lau, Kathleen Oudit and the Art team for creating a gorgeous cover that left me speechless. I'm so incredibly fortunate to work with such an amazing team.

Warm hugs and gratitude to my friends and family for their support, word wars and encouragement. Julie Czerneda, for your friendship, mentorship and inspiration. Thank you Yumiko Okajima for checking over Japanese phrases in *Storm* to get them just right. To Mara Delgado and Kate Larking, Elsie Chapman and the Lucky 13s, and the MSFVers—thank you all so much for your friendship and support! Thank you to the readers and bloggers, and all who take the time for that meaningful connection between author and book lover.

I couldn't have written *Storm* without support from the Canada Council for the Arts. They made it possible for me to live in Japan while revising the book so that I could get the details just right. Thank you for allowing me to live my books while I completed the series, so that I could look out over the drowsy lights of Shizuoka by night, and sit in Sunpu Park by day.

Thank you to the station lady who waited outside the Nihondaira bus stop to give me a coupon for the ropeway lift, to the Ojiisan who presented me with a brown sugar candy after I climbed the sheer steps up the mountainside beside Sengen Shrine. The label read *Otsukaresama deshita*, meaning gratitude to others for a job well done. This is the feeling I want to extend to everyone who worked on *Storm*. Thank you for helping me share the Paper Gods with readers around the world. *Otsukaresama deshita.*

A Dark Power Is About to Rise in Japan...

"The work of a master storyteller."

—Julie Kagawa, *New York Times* bestselling author
of ***The Iron Fey*** series

Coming
July
2015

Own the full ***Paper Gods*** series!
Available wherever books are sold.

 **HARLEQUIN**®TEEN
™ www.HarlequinTEEN.com

HTASPGTR

New York Times Bestselling Author

JULIE KAGAWA

THE IRON FEY

"Julie Kagawa is one killer storyteller." —MTV's *Hollywood Crush* blog

Book 1   Book 2   Book 3   Book 4

Coming November 2015

Book 5   Book 6   Book 7   Anthology   The Iron Fey Boxed Set

Available wherever books are sold.

juliekagawa.com

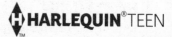

HARLEQUIN® TEEN

HTIRONFEYTR7

A reckoning is brewing...
Should they retreat to fight another day,
or start an all-out war?

Coming
May 2015

Read books 1 & 2 of the epic *Talon Saga*
by *New York Times* bestselling author
Julie Kagawa!

www.HarlequinTEEN.com

juliekagawa.com

HTJKTALONR2

Alexander the Great meets *Games of Thrones*
for teens in Book 1 of the epic new
Blood of Gods and Royals series
by *New York Times* bestselling author

ELEANOR HERMAN

IMAGINE A TIME
WHEN CITIES BURN...
AND IN THEIR ASHES
EMPIRES RISE.

Coming September 2015.

www.HarlequinTEEN.com

HTEHLOKRI

Is Amanda being haunted by an evil presence…or has she simply lost her mind?

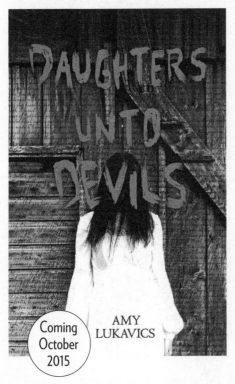

Coming October 2015

AMY LUKAVICS

Secretly pregnant, 16-year-old Amanda wonders at first if her family's move to the prairie will provide the chance for a fresh start, but it soon becomes clear that there is either something very wrong with the prairie, or something very wrong with Amanda.

GOD BLESS THE LITTLE CHILDREN

H HARLEQUIN®TEEN
™ www.HarlequinTEEN.com

HTALDUDTR1

THE GODDESS TEST NOVELS

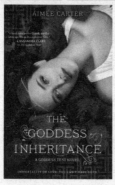

Available wherever books are sold!

A modern saga inspired by the Persephone myth.

Kate Winters's life hasn't been easy. She's battling with the upcoming death of her mother, and only a mysterious stranger called Henry is giving her hope. But he must be crazy, right? Because there is no way the god of the Underworld—Hades himself—is going to choose Kate to take the seven tests that might make her an immortal...and his wife. And even if she passes the tests, is there any hope for happiness with a war brewing between the gods?

Also available:
THE GODDESS HUNT, a digital-only novella.

 HARLEQUIN®TEEN
www.HarlequinTEEN.com

HTGSTR4